ROGUE

SHIP

HEATHER HANSEN

Book Design By Zoe Mellors.

ISBN 978-1-7355637-6-3

THE ROGUE WAVE SERIES: BOOK 2

ROGUE SHIP

enjoy

—Heather Hansen

HEATHER HANSEN

enjoy

Alaric strode through the tall gates and onto the path that led up to the large plantation house. His boots grinding the small pebbles under his feet as he made his way to the steps. The warm breeze blew in from the edge of the ocean, bringing in the sweet scent of the salty water. He was not halfway up the stairs when the front door opened. Catherine came out, spotting him mid stride.

"Alaric, I am glad you are here." She exclaimed, gently touching her hand to his arm. "I was just off to get a few things for the wedding and to meet with Doc." She spoke excitedly, "He is going to help me make a list of different herbs, ointments, and medicines I will need to help me better tend to the workers."

"You will do a mighty fine job doctoring them. They will be in good hands. And I am sure the wedding is going to be lovely." He glanced over to the sugar cane fields that began at the edge of the house on the far side. "Do you know where I might find Lucas?" I wanted to see how he is getting along with the crops." Alaric asked, shifting his weight slightly.

"Yes, last I saw him, he was in the back, would you like me to take you to him?" She offered, taking a few steps down the stairs.

"No, thank you. I will not keep you; you have a busy day ahead of you from the sound of it, I am sure I can find my way." He assured her, allowing her to continue down the steps as she waved her goodbyes to him.

He found his way around the grand house. He breathed in deeply as he passed the roses and other flowers that bloomed in an array of various colors. He paused, glancing up at the house that stood next to him. The bricks piling onto one another, parting in spots where a window was placed. He could see the stables further down the path. They owned many fine horses, he had gone with Lucas to look at them, a few days ago. It had been sometime since he had been around such magnificent beasts. The horses they had owned in Ireland, to work the farms had been wonderful work horses and were strong enough to carry heavy loads to the other, larger towns, but they had not been nearly as grand as the ones that stood in the stables at the plantation. Lucas and he had saddled up and took a ride through the fields to get a better idea of just how grand the plantation grounds were and to see which areas might suit better for different crops. Small buildings laid along a dirt path at the far end of the grounds. The huts were well maintained, and a few pits had been dug for cooking. Children ran around, kicking a coconut back and forth. They stopped immediately when Alaric and Lucas had ridden by. Some of the smaller children running and hiding behind the older ones. Lucas and Alaric did their best to reassure them that they meant no harm. They introduced themselves and continued on so the children could get back to their game. It was not an entirely common situation. Many plantations did not permit the children to play, often times they were told to be in the fields with the parents. If they or the children stopped tending to the crops when they had not been permitted, they could be beaten or worse. Alaric had suspected by the fear on the children's faces that the previous foremen had not been as understanding or as compassionate as Lucas. Many, if not all of the children seen at the small houses had been born on the plantation grounds. Lucas had told Alaric that most of the slaves were healthy and well fed, the problem that plagued them the most was injuries and the occasional illness, which Catherine had tried to help with in the past by calling for the local surgeon who had done truly little for them. Now though, the children and the adults alike would be well taken care of. Catherine would be able to treat them affectively and quickly. They had ridden out to the boiler house; it was far hotter inside the building than he had expected. Lord Benedict had told them that the boiler house was the most dangerous part of the running of the plantation. If even a drop of the burning liquid met flesh, it would stick to it, burning deep and leaving a nasty scar. Lucas had shown Alaric what he had learned about the running of the planta-tion, of the process of cultivating the sugar cane, pressing it through heavy rollers before boiling it down. One of the men that worked in the boiler house explained how the accidents would happen and that even the most careful of workers was still at risk of being burned. His own arm was badly scarred. He informed them how the wound had not healed properly and still pained him after the long hours of using the arm. He had been careful to transfer the scalding liquid, but the machine was not working the way it should that day. When he had tried to stir the liquid down, as it was not boiling all the way through like it should, it had popped. Blowing the liquid sugar cane towards him. There had been nothing he could do, it stuck solidly to his flesh burning deeper with each moment it remained glued to his arm. Finally, it had cooled enough where it no longer burned him and over several days, he had slowly been able to wash the cracking sugar cane from his arm, scorched flesh and muscle being reveled below. Lucas had assured him he would speak with Doc and Catherine to see what could be done to help with the pain though, he did not believe there was much that could be done for such an old and deeply scarred wound.

Voices broke through his thoughts, bringing him back and reminding him of why he was there. The path curved through the lavish gardens, the sugar cane plants and fields becoming more visible.

"When was the last time the fields were burned?" Alaric heard Lucas ask. He came round the corner of a large hedge and caught sight of his friend standing next to a man he guessed to be one of the plantation workers. He walked up to the two men, curious to find out the reason behind the failing crop. With the other plantations doing so well and this one being in one of the best areas, there was no reason it should simply be producing a poor crop for so many years.

"I don't rightly know, Sir. I have been here longer than most but cannot recall a time the fields were ever burned." The tall man spoke, adjusting the old hat he wore to help shade him from the blistering sun. An old piece of fabric was tied about his neck, many sailors had the same, it aided in keeping their necks cool and prevented them from burning.

"Mate," Alaric said, greeting Lucas who had noticed him

approaching.

"I'm glad you could make it over. I'd like you to meet Bongani." Lucas gestured to the man who stood beside him. "Bongani, this is my friend, Alaric Stein. We grew up together and he was my first mate for many years aboard *The Trinity.*

Bongani bowed slightly, "Tis good to meet you, Mr. Stein."

"The pleasure is mine," he said, glancing from the men to the rows of crops that filled the landscape in front of him. "I heard you say the fields have not been burned in sometime. It can help the soil and fields greatly when they are. Of course, it has to be done correctly but it is not too difficult." Alaric pointed to the crops and looked back at Bongani.

"Aye, that is what I was going to say. It also seems that they have not been harvested or planted routinely, or on time, even." Lucas squinted into the sun. "Apparently the previous foreman's have either known very little about crops or have not stayed long enough to make things right."

"And what of the Baron? What does he have to say about the poor management in the past?" Alaric asked, brows furrowing.

"He knows the previous foremen knew nothing of the fields they were to manage but they were apparently the only men he could find to take the job. He told me that himself, back in France." His gaze switching between the two men.

"Seems a bit odd. We have seen men sign onto our ship,

even though they were shaking with fear. They did it only because they could not find work elsewhere." Alaric paused, looking back out over the poorly looking sugar cane. "I'd think many men would have jumped at the chance to be foreman for the plantation and I'll wager several of them know a thing or two about the plants." He said, gesturing towards the fields once more.

"Aye, I'm betting you are right on that as well. I will have a talk with the Baron and see what more I can find out. As for the crops. I say we burn the entire field. Give it a bit for the soil to be turned and well fertilized. I will see what the Baron can do about getting us new shoots of sugar cane." Lucas walked over to one of the plants, breaking off a leaf. "I would also like your opinion, Bongani, on tobacco and cotton. It may be a good idea to add those plants to our crop. Sugar cane, you see has been rising and falling in price and profit for some time now, whether the plantation yields a goodly amount or no. Tobacco and Cotton though have been staying at a steadily high price." Lucas Concluded.

"I have heard tell that other plantations on the islands do much the same as that. They do not stay with one crop alone. I see no harm in trying. It could be what turns this plantation around." He nodded his approval. "I best get back to it. Do you want me to tell the others to begin the burning of the fields?" He asked hesitantly, turning back to Lucas.

"Not just yet. I would like to speak with the Baron and get the new seed cane in time. I would also like you to meet with the Baron with me. It might be good for him to hear what you have to say as well since you know the others that work the fields and know more of what the management has been like over the last few years."

Bongani looked taken aback but simply expressed his understanding and thanks, before turning and heading down a narrow path that led between the plants.

"Looks like you are settling into your new role just fine." Alaric said, following Lucas into the foreman's house.

"I will admit, I do miss *The Trinity* but this," he said, waving an arm wide. "It is proving to be an intriguing and interesting challenge. It has been a nice change and I am enjoying myself. Did you see Catherine before you found me? I know she would love to speak with you."

"Aye, I did. I happened upon her as I was coming up the steps. I am glad her father is letting her continue her surgeon's practices. She has a gentle and steady hand and has learned a great deal. I take it the mess with Lord Anderson has finally been resolved then? Catherine mentioned getting preparations for the wedding." Alaric took a drink from a cup that Lucas had handed him.

"I believe it is all over, yes. Lord Anderson was not at all pleased when the Baron called their engagement off. Apparently, he had many plans for his and the Baron's plantations. The marriage between him and Catherine would have been a fine opportunity for him." Lucas scoffed. "He made quite the scene the other day. The Baron had summoned him to speak with him in his study about the engagement. The shouting began not five minutes after they had shut the door," Lucas chuckled, "the bastard stormed from the study, knocking over a vase that sat along the wall. He continued his muttering

11

and rambling as he marched himself through the front door. Catherine and I were coming in from the gardens. We had heard the crash and wanted to make sure her father had not been hurt. Lord Anderson caught sight of us on the steps. If the man had kept his mouth shut, I would have let him leave without another word."

Alaric watched his friend, cocking an eyebrow at him. "As Catherine was standing right there, I take it the man will make a quick and full recovery?"

"Aye, a broken nose was about the extent of it. I am sure in a few days' time there will be little evidence of the incident." Lucas said, letting out a laugh.

They fell silent for a bit, enjoying each other's company. It had been several days since they had returned to Barbados, and they had scarcely seen each other since.

"Have you planned out where you will go first?" Lucas asked, looking into the cup in his hand.

"Nassau." He let out a breath, "It seems a good enough place to start. Even if we do not find him there, and I doubt our luck will be that grand, I am sure we will be able to find a man or two that knows him and where we might find him."

"I agree." Lucas stared out the small window that sat on the opposite wall, looking out at the front entrance of the estate, unsure of what else to say.

"I wanted to thank you again for letting me take *The Trinity*. I am sorry you cannot be with me on this voyage, but

I am happy to know you will be plenty busy with the plantation and tending to your family." Alaric said, knowing the emotion was clear in his voice. He gave a reassuring smile. He was happy for his friend and knew he had made the right decision. As much as he wanted Lucas on the voyage with him, it was not that aspect that was making things difficult. Being back in Barbados had been even harder than he had thought it would be. Every time he walked past the stalls and shops, he thought of Benjamin and how excited the boy had been when he would give him a few coins to spend. Even the sounds of the seagulls and the waves lapping against the beach reminded him of the times he would return to the island and go see Benjamin. Each time, the boy's eyes would light up with excitement. Anne, the woman who cared for him and several other children on the island had told him that Benjamin would sit and look at books of the sea for hours and beg her to take him down to touch the water.

"I will be staying for the wedding of course but plan on leaving the following day." Alaric said.

"I thought as much. The sooner you are on your way, the sooner you can find Thomas and rid the seas of him. I am sure you will find men that have sailed with him or have at least heard of him. Just be cautious, it is likely he knows you will come after him. He is far more vicious and cannier than we had thought originally. He may try and set a trap if he gets wind that you are getting close to finding him." Lucas warned.

"I have thought of that. We will be careful who we ask, we do not want a friend of his to hear us asking about the ports for him. We will have to take it slow." Alaric stood, "I will see you in a couple days for the wedding, unless you need me to help you get the fields burned. As dead as they are, the flames could spread quickly."

"I would not mind your help with the fields at all if you do not mind. I would also like you to meet with the Baron with me and Bongani. You and I have harvested our fair share of fields and another opinion on getting these going would be appreciated. We can meet with him this evening."

"Alright, I'll be here. I am going to head to the ship and see that everything will be in order to sail in a few days then I will meet you back here." Alaric set the cup on the small table they had been sitting at.

Alaric paused, his foot resting on the board that led up to *The Trinity* from the dock. He looked up at the towering mast, the sails properly tucked up, waiting for the chance to be unfurled and released.

"Ol' Shorty," Alaric greeted the older man who was busy working on a whipping knot. A few of the lines had frayed and were threatening to snap, the knots and new line would help to hold them strong. He strode over to where the man stood.

"Ah good to see you, Lad. I've been working on this line most the morning," he said, pointing a stubby finger at the perfectly tied knot. "I finally got them lines joined proper and strong." He added, yanking on both ends, demonstrating his handy work.

"A fine job you did. How are the rest of the lines? I know the sails are as good as new, even the extras, Miss Catherine mended those before we made port." Alaric asked, running a hand along the mast.

"Aye, that she did. The sails are ship shape and that was the last o' the lines that needed fixin'. I will be mending the stove with Cook later, he says it not be cookin' proper." He shrugged, "Now tell me, how are Miss Catherine and the Capt'n gettin' on?"

Alaric chuckled, "as well as expected. Lucas has hardly wiped the grin from his face since the Lass said yes." Alaric glanced at the island then back to Shorty. "That is actually what I wanted to speak to you about. I know I told you that I'll be taking the ship to find Thomas. I am hoping to set out the morning after the wedding. I suspect the ship will be ready by then?"

"Aye, aye, we expected you'd say that. Where is it we will be heading to first? Thomas is not entirely a fool of a man and will no likely be out in the ports havin' a grand time, not after what he did." Shorty had moved over to a hatch that had gotten jammed when a heavy crate had been dropped on it while they were unloading. He was bent over and whittling away at a shard of wood that was preventing the hatch from opening.

"No, I don't expect he will be. I plan to head to Nassau and any other pirate filled ports to start. We will see what we can find out about him and go from there. I rather imagine it will take some time to find the man." Frustration and anger evident in his voice.

"Ah, but find him we will," Shorty let out a grunt as the small blade he was using finally broke the wood free, "There we have it, good as new," he chuckled.

"I am to head back to the plantation, but I will talk with you more about the plans once we leave port." He said to Shorty who waved a hand in the air and headed towards the galley. Alaric walked to where he kept his chest of clothes. It was stowed near his hammock that lay amongst the crews'. *I suppose I should move my things to the captain's cabin,* he thought, lifting the chest. He rather looked forward to having the cabin to himself. He was used to the smell of the sleeping quarters and the endless snoring of the men, but he would definitely not pass up the opportunity to have the large cabin.

Alaric maneuvered himself and the chest through the swaying hammocks and up the steps towards the captain's cabin. Setting it down and opening the hatch, he looked about the room. He smiled, he looked forward to being aboard the ship again, he had not cared too much for the battles but now he craved one. He knew what Ol' Shorty and Lucas had said was all true. He would need to be cautious, but he could not wait to sail out and find the bastard he was after.

"Good afternoon, Captain." A voice said behind him, bringing Alaric back to the present.

"Ethan, good to see you." He said, lifting the trunk back up and setting it inside the cabin at the foot of the bed.

"When are you setting out?" He asked, stepping inside.

"The morning after the wedding." He stood up, watching Ethan. "Will you be joining me?" He liked Ethan and knew he could use him as part of the crew. Lucas had said Ethan would likely request to continue on with him.

"That is why I am here; I was hoping you would allow me to. I am aware of what Thomas did and I know you wish him dead, rightfully so." He took a step closer, "I ask though, for a chance to question him about the bracelet he wears. It was my sister's and in order to find the man that attacked her, I need to know how he came across it." Ethan worked his jaw.

"Aye, Lucas told me what happened. I am sorry to hear about your sister. I will do what I can. If all goes well, you will get your opportunity to speak with him. I can't make any promises though, I will kill him before he gets a chance to slip away again." Alaric spoke firmly.

"Fair enough. I thank you." He replied, turning, and stepping from the cabin.

Alaric rummaged through the chest, he needed to change before meeting with the Baron. He smelt of the tavern and ale. He threw off the shirt he wore and strode over to the small cabinet that held the water jug and basin on it. He poured the cool liquid over his head and grabbed for the rough bar of soap. Running his hands over his face he felt a bit more refreshed. He reached for the shirt he had pulled out and slipped it on, heading for the hatch.

Molly let out a sigh, groaning as she dragged herself off of the thin, worn mattress of her bed. "I'm up," she said through gritted teeth to the knock that sounded on the door to her chamber. Her room was the last one in the long corridor that stretched across the plantation house on the servants landing. Throwing on her plain gown and quickly tying the apron on over it, she gathered her long hair into the best loop she could, shoving the tendrils under the maid's cap. She scrunched her face, looking into the rounded mirror that was no bigger than her hand, being sure not even one stray piece hung below the cap. She rushed from the door, not wanting to get an earful from the butler at her tardiness.

"Eat your porridge quickly, Miss Maclean. You won't want to be seen doing the fires when the Master wakes." The butler said, giving her a hard look, his beady eyes challenging her.

Simply nodding, she did as she was told. She did not mind being rushed from the servants' hall, she did not get on much with any of them and they kept their distance from her, afraid she would bring bad luck as well as the Master down on them. Taking a bit of the sticky, warm, meal in front of her, she quickly ate it, not bothering to stop and try and taste the mundane fair.

The bucket clanked loudly, causing her to flinch for fear someone would hear her. Despite the house being so large, sound travelled remarkably well through the thin walls, echoing up the winding staircase that let out into various landings of the house. The butler had been right, she needed to get the fires cleaned and lit in all the rooms before the plantation owner woke. He had a houseful of guests the previous evening but with no one else around to see his treatment of her, she had to keep out of sight as much as possible. He often entertained and had large dinner parties, those were the easy days, he would never allow heads to be turned his way, in any manner other than admiration. It was when the guests left, he would seek her out, finding any reason he could to punish her, in any way he saw fit.

The long brush smacked loudly against the door as she opened it, pausing, she waited, listening for any sign of movement. Molly cautiously entered the second dining room, it was the first room the Master would be in, it was the room he broke his fast in and read the many letters he would already have received. Molly quickly sat the bucket on the bricks, near the fireplace. She really did not understand why he insisted on having the fires lit every morning, it was not as if it was cold, certainly not as cold as Ireland had been. She shuttered, remembering tucking her legs under herself, pulling as much hay and straw as she could over her small, trembling body to try and stay warm.

She laid the sheet down, being sure to cover every spot of

the rugs up, not wanting to leave any trace of soot on them. She had lost count of how many times she had cleaned and lit the fires. She knew the exact way to strike the flint, lighting the fire in mere seconds, though when she was a wee lass in Ireland, her mother was very poor and could never purchase flint. She had learned then how to start a fire quickly and efficiently with just a couple small sticks she would find laying around.

The sparks flew from the flint, bright flames clinging to the thin strips of wood. They quickly grew, engulfing the fireplace in warmth and light. Molly stood, gathering the cleaning supplies, and placing them all back in the bucket.

"Not so fast," Molly felt her body grow cold, despite standing so near the fire. "Looks like we two are the only ones up here."

"Not for long, the butler and footmen will be coming in to serve your morning meal." She replied, shifting her feet, standing a bit taller. Not that it made a great deal of difference, Lord Willington was a large man, with no mercy. "I best get to the other fires," she said, swallowing the lump that had formed in her throat.

"I don't think so. See, when they see you in here with me, you know they will close the door again. No one will help you; no one will come, they never have." He stepped closer to her, closing the gap between them.

Molly stumbled back into the bricks beside the fire, she felt her hand brush against the handle of the bucket. Her fingers wrapping around it and gripping it firmly, just as firmly as Lord Willington's grip on her waist. She closed her eyes, trying desperately to block out the feeling of his hands on her. She squirmed when his mouth touched against her neck. She knew the movement was a mistake, it would only anger him.

A snarl emanated from his throat, his hand rising up. Molly could not think, she braced herself for the hit that she knew would come. She fisted her hands, suddenly remembering the bucket she still held. Without another thought, she swung it at Lord Willington. The impact causing her hand to ache. Dropping the bucket, she rushed to the door that led to the main hall, briefly looking down at the master's fallen form. A long cut stretched across his forehead. A steady stream of blood flowing from it, dripping to the rug.

Molly rushed from the door and down the plantation steps. Someone was sure to have heard the commotion. She did not wish to be anywhere near the property when they found Lord Willington. If she had killed him, she would hang for sure. If he were still alive, her fate would be far worse. She was not willing to stay on the island and find out. Lifting her skirts she ran towards the port, not wanting to look back for fear she would see Lord Willington baring down on her.

Slowing a bit as she neared the docks, not wanting to draw attention to herself, she looked around, she needed to find a ship to board. She heard men's voices coming from the tree line, ducking behind one of the nearby shacks that held nets, hooks, and lines. She watched the men emerge, curious as to why they had come from that direction. She had heard tell of the hidden trails and paths around the island. It was said, pirates, privateers and enemy vessels used the hidden paths to remain unnoticed by the inhabitants. The men appeared better dressed and kept than many of the pirates were on the island and they did not sound as if they came from Portugal or Spain. Molly took a step forward, wanting to get a closer look. If they had a ship on the other side of the island, she might be able to board it. If Lord Willington lived or if the soldiers came for her, they would never suspect her boarding any other ship than the ones currently in the dock. She followed the men, listening more carefully, she still needed to be sure she would not be landing herself in any more danger than she already was.

She watched the small group of men curiously, quickly ducking behind the building again when the taller of the men, the one who seemed to be giving the others orders, looked her way. Stepping out onto the dirt path that led through the stalls, shacks, and taverns, she crept closer, hoping to get a chance to approach them and find out more. She watched them enter a tavern, she daren't go in and follow. She looked about, spotting the large tree that stood near the tavern they had entered. She would have to wait there as long as she could. She prayed they were quick; she did not fancy the idea of staying on the island any longer than necessary.

To her delight and surprise, they did not stay long in the tavern. They were heading for the docks. Stepping from out behind the tree, she began to follow. She paused, a man separate from their group called out to the leader, she could not make out the exact words but did not miss the fact that the man she had been watching was just called, Stein and that, said man had a thick Irish accent. Her mouth fell open, she had not encountered anyone from Ireland in her time on the island. The men looked to be having a disagreement of some sort. The occasional word from their heated conversation drifting her way. From what little she could make out, the stranger was accusing the Irish man and his captain brother of robbing him of his ship. Molly listened harder, it appeared the Irish man was indeed a captain. She could not take her eyes from him or from the scene that had begun to unfold in front of her. The captain seemed completely at ease and unperturbed by the man challenging him to a fight. Molly marveled at how quick and fluid his movements were, the fight seemed over quicker than it had begun, leaving the captain and his men to move along on their way, nearing the crowds of the port. Molly rushed forward, afraid of losing sight of the tall captain and missing her chance to board his ship and be rid of and safe from the island and Lord Willington.

3

"With all due respect, Lord Benedict, I believe starting the field all over will be the best way. The fields need to be burned, they should have been in the past, that is one of the many reasons the crop is failing, that and lack of maintenance. The soil needs to be well fertilized if there is any hope for a future crop. The plants out there are simply too old, it will never produce enough." Alaric heard Lucas say as he approached the Baron's study. He knocked on the wall just inside the door.

"Mr. Stein, it is good to see you again. Please come in. Your friend and I were just discussing the fields." The Baron beckoned him in.

"So, I heard, and I would have to agree with Lucas. It may seem daunting, but burning the fields, fertilizing them, and replanting is your only option. It should have been done more regularly, a section at a time." Alaric stood next to Lucas; his arms crossed over his chest.

"That is what I was afraid you would say," The Baron's face showing his frustration. "I knew fields were burned on other plantations, but I had always believed it to be because of an infestation of some sort. If you believe it must be done though, I trust your judgement, Lucas. I hired you on as foreman and given your past farming experience, you know a fair share more than myself." The Baron replied, giving into the request.

"I will need new cane shoots and I would like to give tobacco and cotton a try as well, Lord Benedict. They will be more profitable and having more than one type of crop will be good for business." Lucas added, watching the Baron's expression.

"Alright, I will get as much as I can." The Baron looked about the room at the three men standing in front of him.

"I do have something else I would like to ask you. You have told me that the men you have hired before me knew little to nothing about farming, you have also told me the ones that did, never stayed long. Why is that? Seems to me, many men would have jumped for this job." Lucas asked, glancing at Alaric.

The Baron shrugged, "I do not rightly know the answer myself. The men that left, they each told me that they had been hired on by someone else who paid more." Lord Benedict looked down at his desk, looking over the ledgers that sat on them.

"Someone hired each of the men that were knowledgeable about the plantation and the running's of it, right out from under you? Do you believe it to be a simple coincidence? Do you believe it is the same man or different men hiring them?"

Alaric asked. He had a feeling he knew who was behind all of it and judging by the look on his friend's face, he suspected the same man.

"I could not say. I do not believe I have very many enemies, but it happened too many times to be a mere coincidence." Lord Benedict looked distraught.

"I can tell you right now. Our old friend the Governor. I would not put it past him. When he tasked me with the delivery of the deed, he certainly seemed to have had a plan in mind for some time. I'd wager he has been trying to rid you of this plantation for quite some time by hiring or at least paying off your knowledgeable men." Alaric nodded in agreement as the Baron took in this new bit of information. "Rest assured Baron, the Governor will not pay me off and there is not much he could do to me now. No, I do not think he will trouble you any longer, he will have guessed that we are aware of his schemes and will not want it publicly known." Lucas reasoned, reassuring Lord Benedict.

"Very well. We will just have to continue on. You may burn the fields and I will get you the seed cane as well as the cotton and tobacco. It will be a setback to be sure but there is no moving forward without it being done, like you have said." The Baron sank deep in his chair behind his desk, "if I had not been so blind these past years, none of this would have happened."

"No, the Governor might have found a way of ridding you of the plantation at a faster and at a more serious rate. You have been able to keep it and now have the chance to bring the fields back. Let us focus on restoring them." Lucas looked to Bongani who had said no more than a word or two.

"I will have the others ready to burn and fertilize the fields as soon as you say so, Sir." He said, his heavy accent rumbling over his words.

The thick smoke filled Alaric's senses. Pulling a bit of cloth over his nose, now thankful that he had remembered to tie it about his neck. He wore it on occasion while on the ship to keep the beating sun from his neck.

"The wind is on our side," Alaric choked out to Lucas who stood beside him.

"Aye, and good thing too. I want the fields to burn slowly." He replied, nodding to the flame engulfed field. Women and men lined the fields, ready to take action if the winds shifted. Lucas had ordered trenches to be dug, a steady stream of water flowed through them, surrounding the fields.

As the fire burned its way along the old sugar cane fields, the smoke filled the air, the sound of the plants crackling and popping as the flames consumed them. It would not take long for the first field to be burned. Once done, they'd begin on the next while some of the workers flattened and tilled up the freshly scorched soil. The ash would in turn liven the dirt and get it ready for new sugar cane shoots to be planted. After the wedding, Lord Benedict had assured Lucas he would fetch the new shoots and seeds himself. It would be several weeks before Lord Benedict returned, but it did not make much of a difference. The fields would still need a bit of work and time before planting began. It was a big undertaking, restarting the fields from the beginning, but there was little choice.

Alaric looked around, walking the boundary, making sure no sparks flew to unwanted areas.

"Have you been harmed?" He asked, an older man had backed away from the others, holding the upper part of his leg.

The man nodded, lifting his hands from the injury. "I stepped too close to the flames. The burnin' plant caught my leg."

Alaric nodded, guiding the man towards the huts. "The flames can be misleading, they often appear further away than they really are and even once the flame has left the plant black and charred, it will still remain hot for many more minutes." Catherine had set up a table to tend to workers if there were any injuries. "Miss Catherine," he called out, alerting her to her next patient.

Carefully lifting a small child from the table, she nodded, ushering the two men forward. Alaric helped the man onto the table, careful not to bump his injured leg.

"It will be alright," Catherine murmured soothingly. She gently pulled the burnt and frayed material away from the injury. Carefully grabbing bits of cloth that clung to the scorched skin. Grabbing a pair of scissors, she cut away at the pants to better see the wound and be able to clean it.

"I will see to it that more material is brought down so new pants can be made. I am afraid these are passed mending." She spoke, keeping the man's attention from the stinging pain that radiated in his leg. She poured a strong scented liquid over the burn, cleansing the area. The man scrunched his face but remained focused on what Catherine said.

"What happened to the child you were tending before we walked up?" Alaric asked, knowing the child was likely more than fine but wanted to help as best he could. He had noticed the man's face grow pale when Catherine began to dab at the burn, making sure all the bits of fabric no longer clung to the injury.

"She will be just fine. She had tripped and scraped her knee, just enough to draw a small bit of blood, but it was enough to make the tears flow and we can't be having that, now, can we?" Catherine smiled, finishing up with applying a salve and loose-fitting bandage. "I expect to see you each day for the next few days to be sure the burn is healing proper, and that fever has not set in. I will provide some more willow bark and have it steeping. It should help with the pain, but if it gets too much to handle, please have someone fetch me."

The man thanked her, heading back towards the fields just as another child came forward, showing Catherine a splinter that poked deeply into his finger. Without a second thought, she grabbed a small tool, pulling the small shard quickly from the child's finger before he even had time to explain what had happened.

Alaric returned to his post; the fire nearly having finished its job on the first portion of the fields. He watched Catherine assist another that had been injured from the fire as Lucas talked to a group of men. Instructing them on how to begin clearing the burned area. They would need to wait a day or two to be sure the fire was no longer smoldering.

Alaric stood next to his friend, who grinned with anticipation. The music had begun, and everyone was seated. Catherine had insisted the wedding take place at the plantation, in the gardens. She had said that it made her feel as if her mother was there. He was pleased for Lucas and Catherine and had been looking forward to the wedding. He was also very eager to sail first thing the next morning.

The day before had seen him busy helping Lucas burn the far fields and showing the rest of the men and women who worked the crops how to control and contain the fires. It had gone well, only a couple minor burns had occurred, which Catherine had easily been able to treat.

Catherine rounded the corner. Her cream and golden yellow gown swayed as she walked steadily down the path. Her eyes shown and remained fixed on Lucas.

"You look gorgeous, Lass," Lucas whispered as he reached for her hand. Catherine blushed, her nerves and excitement only allowing her to smile up at him.

Alaric stood, watching the ceremony in front of him. He had not been to very many weddings like this one, occasionally one of the men from *The Trinity* would find a lass and get married on one of the islands but they were never as large or as grand as this one. Typically, only the men from the ship were present, as well as one or two people from the bride's side. They would then head over to a local tavern or back to the ship to celebrate.

The crowd clapped and cheered as the couple kissed and walked back down the path. Lucas shot Alaric a grin, who returned the gesture. Lord Benedict announced that the celebration was to begin. Drinks and food of all kinds were brought out by the footmen and placed on the tables. Some footmen carried trays about, winding through the guests and offering refreshments.

"It's the grandest of celebrations, to be sure. I don't believe I have ever been to a finer one." Ol' Shorty said, coming over to Alaric. They reached for a drink, each grabbing one off a tray that was brought past them.

"It is indeed," replying, as he looked on the crowd of guests that had shuffled about, gathering into small groups around the garden. Ladies waved fans delicately as they spoke about the ceremony. Alaric could hear a group of men discussing the new shipment of goods that they had just received.

The music began again. Folks turned to one another, hoping for a dance. Alaric looked around the crowd, seeing if there were any Ladies worth risking a dance with. Several of them had glanced his way more than once already. He was determined to enjoy himself on his last night in port and thought of no better way to begin than with a dance with a lovely woman or two. Through the bustle of excitement, chatter, and fabrics of a every variety, he spotted a young woman standing near Catherine. She seemed to be introducing the woman to Lucas. *Perfect,* he thought. He walked over to the group and gave a small bow. "My Lady, Lucas, would you do me the honor of introducing me to your friend?"

Lucas shot him a knowing look, "Lady Adeline, allow me to introduce to you my friend and brother, Captain Alaric Stein." He said.

"A pleasure to meet you, Captain. I take it you are a Privateer like Captain Harding?" She asked, boldly looking Alaric over.

"Aye, that is true. Lucas and I grew up together and have sailed alongside each other for many years." He replied, returning the look. "Lady Adeline, the music sounds wonderful, would you mind sharing a dance with me?" He asked, holding his arm out slightly for her to take.

"I would love to," Lady Adeline glanced over to Catherine who stood there, hardly able to contain her laughter at the audacious exchange. "If you will excuse me," she said politely.

"Of course, enjoy yourself," Catherine managed. "Come, let us join in as well," she said eagerly, looking up at Lucas briefly, before pulling him towards the dancing.

4

"Eddie, man the helm, prepare to weigh anchor. Ready the sails, lads." Alaric bellowed to the crew. He gestured for Gray and Henry to pull in the plank. The men were in their positions, they had all been eager to be back on the ship and ready to sail out once more. The wedding the night before had lasted several hours with the music and dancing hardly lessening for more than a moment. He had enjoyed himself greatly and had woken early that morning with the same exuberance that he had fallen asleep with.

"Aye, Capt'n," Several of the crew responded. Alaric looked back at the island; the sails unfurled with a loud snap. He felt the ship sway as it headed from the port.

"To Nassau, men." He shouted, causing a chorus of cheers to ripple through the crew. He turned slightly, his boots scraping against the planking of the ship. *The Trinity* was nearing the outskirts of the port, Nassau was not far from Barbados, and it would not take long for them to get there. He knew of a couple of taverns that many of the sailors frequented. He did not expect to find Thomas merely sitting there waiting for him, but he had a feeling that the man had just as many friends as he did enemies. He reckoned that someone would be willing let them know where the man might be hiding out.

Alaric made his way to his cabin, he needed to go over the maps and plan on where to head to after Nassau in case they did not get any leads. There were several islands that men like Thomas frequented, Alaric himself had been to them on many occasions. It was a matter of narrowing down which ones Thomas was more likely to be well known at or not. Alaric kicked open the chest that sat against the far wall. It contained several rolled-up maps, some of which he did not even need to look at, he could sail the routes with his eyes closed. They did help though, even knowing all the routes, it was easier to map out his plans when studying them. He pulled an old worn one out, the islands around them dotting the old parchment, the waters weaving its way between and around the various ports. Being a Privateer for the West Indies, they rarely left these parts of the sea and knew many of the owners of the establishments on the islands, as well as many of the inhabitants and sailors.

There was a knock at the hatch, "Come in," Alaric responded, only glancing up from the map briefly, to see who was entering.

"Captain," Ethan ducked into the cabin. "I am assuming you have been to Nassau on a few occasions." He looked down at the map of the islands.

"Aye, several times. Have you ever been?"

"Once, yes, a couple years ago for the Royal Navy. One of our Brigs was set upon by pirates. The Brig did not stand a chance against the number of ships that attacked it. As you can imagine, the Navy was not pleased and believed that if those pirates got away with it then many more attacks against the Navy ships would occur." He paused, "they were right too, several more attacks have happened, that is why so many of the pirates are trying to get their Letters of Marque or hiding away in other parts of the seas."

"I did hear about some of those attacks. Did you find the pirates that did it? Were you able to capture them?"

"Yes and no, a few of them we were able to capture. They were then tried and hanged, but a few got away. I remember Nassau being quite the den of excitement for pirates and other sailors. We went there to find out more information on the ships we were after. We got fortunate, we met with some good men, merchants, I believe that had past dealings with the very ships we were after. They told us about a hideout that was often used by the pirates when they were waiting on special deliveries or were making trades that they rather no one else know about. It was there that a battle ensued and many of the pirates were killed or captured."

"Aye, many such hideouts exist. We have used a few ourselves to find pirates and even Spanish ships that have managed to sneak past us. I wouldn't doubt that Thomas uses such hideouts. I am hoping that we can find out which ones he frequents or better yet if anyone knows where he was headed to next."

"I am not sure if this will help much but I wanted you to have a look at it," Ethan placed the logbook on the desk in front of Alaric. "I took this from Thomas's cabin during the battle. I had hoped it would prove his guilt but instead it proved his innocence in my sister's attack. It seems he has gone to Africa on more than one occasion. He seems to stay around these waters but has also gone to the Colonies."

Alaric let out a laugh, "Not bad, Mate," he flipped through the pages in the ledger, scanning the documents. He noted the same that Ethan had. Thomas typically stayed near the West Indies. It gave Alaric more assurance that likely there were several other sailors that knew of him in the area. "We will be in Nassau soon. We will go ashore, just a few of us, I do not want to draw too much attention to our crew or ship. There is a tavern or two that we can ask around at."

"I will await your orders," Ethan said, turning and leaving the cabin.

Alaric looked at the logbook once more, shaking his head. Ethan had been right to take the book, it could prove Thomas's guilt in more than one instance, Alaric did not doubt that. It would also help him to better understand which routes Thomas traveled the most. All the islands were relatively close to each other, and it did not take long to get from one to the other. Many sailors went back and forth between them, looking for work or avoiding being caught by the Navy, if they were suspected pirates. Thomas might very well be at one of the islands, with luck, he would be, though it was more probable that he was staying clear of The West Indies for a while.

"Captain," there was a knock at the hatch. "Captain we are nearing Nassau and are readying to anchor."

"Thank you, Joseph," Alaric replied, belting his sword onto the leather strap that hung low on his waist, and tucking his flintlock into the other side. He opened the hatch and made his way on deck.

"Eddie," he approached the helm, where the man stood. "I want you to stay aboard, I will need you to man the ship. Be prepared to sail, we will be back before sunrise." Alaric clapped him on the shoulder. He knew he could trust Eddie and knew the crew respected him. Alaric signaled for a boat to be lowered. They had anchored just off the coast of the island. Alaric had not wanted to anchor in port and draw any unwanted attention or alert Thomas and his men if they were on the island. He knew of a path that led through the trees, it was difficult to find but he and Lucas had used the path many times, it led straight to the heart of the taverns and other establishments.

Alaric climbed his way down the hull of the ship and into the small awaiting boat. Ol' Shorty and Ethan followed suit. It was a short distance to row to the hidden inlet of the island. Trees and bushes were thickly pressed together, making the path they were about to use, perfectly hidden. He glanced back at The Trinity, his men had done what he had asked and already dowsed the lights on the ship and in the cabin to help conceal it from any curious eyes that might pass by. The sun had just set, the dark night giving them the secrecy they wanted. The water lapped against the small boat as it slid onto the soft sand that spread below the vegetation. Alaric stepped from the boat and led the other two men onto the path that winded through the trees. Insects could be heard, as well as the occasional call from a night bird. In the distance the ruckus of the port and taverns threaded its way through the jungle and to the men.

They paused at the end of the trail, peering through the trees. Alaric took a step forward, breaking onto the path that ran alongside the taverns and other buildings. Ol' Shorty and Ethan following close behind. "We can start at the tavern up there. I know the owner, he or one of the women who works for him might have some information for us." He said, pointing to a gray building, a sign hanging above it, reading *The White Whale Tavern*. "Let's circle around the back of the building, we can get a look at who is inside." Alaric instructed quietly to the group. They kept hidden amongst the trees, careful not to be seen as they made their way around the establishments. They came to the old wooden door on the opposite side of the building. Alaric lifted his fist, knocking three times and taking a step back. The door slowly swung open, exposing a large man with a beard that stretched nearly all the way barrel his barrel like chest.

"Ah, if it isn't Alaric Stein," the man looked about the other two men, "are my eyes playing tricks on me? I do not see Captain Harding?" He cheerfully ushered the group through the back entrance and into a small room that led into the kitchen.

"He went and got himself married to a lovely and rather stubborn young lady. She is a Baron's daughter. They own a sizable plantation in Barbados now." He gestured to the other two men. "I believe you know Ol' Shorty and this is our friend Ethan."

They exchanged greetings, moving closer to the kitchen to be able to better see who was in the tavern. "Who is it you be looking for this time?" Abe asked, taking the dirty apron off from around his neck.

"Have you heard of a man named Thomas Banning? He is a pirate in these waters, rarely leaves them though, he has been known to voyage to Africa for goods for the plantation owners, on occasion. I believe his ship is *The Amity.*

"Aye, I know the lad. He ain't much liked round here though. He comes in and e'eryone tries ta stay clean away from him. 'Cept those that are looking to gain a high price at whate'er the cost." Abe shook his head, scoffing. "Aye he has come here a time or two and caused more than a little trouble for me. See, no one'll stand up against him. Them is all scared of what he'll do. He hasn't been in here in several months though. Last I heard, he was headed to France or someplace round there."

"Aye, we ran into him along the way. That is why we are asking after him. Do you know of any other places he goes or if there are any men in the tavern that might know?" Alaric asked, glancing past the large man and into the tavern once more. Laughter and shouts spilled through the opening, a single worn curtain hung in the doorway, separating the sitting area from the kitchen.

"See that man sitting just there," Abe pointed a round finger towards a man that sat at the far end of the tavern. He lifted a cup to his lips as he watched the men around him gamble and hold tight to the women that walked around the tables, serving food, drinks and offering up any other entertainment the men might pay for. "That there is Gael, he is here most nights, that is, when he is not on a merchant ship. He has had dealings with Banning and does not think too kindly of the man. He might know where you can find him."

"My thanks, Mate," Alaric said, leading the way to where the man sat. "Mind if we join you?" he asked, looking over at the man and sitting before he could reply.

"Do I have a choice?" Gael questioned, raising an eyebrow at the men that now sat around him. He twisted the cup around on the wooden table, eyeing the newcomers.

"We do not want any trouble, be assured of that. We come only to ask about a man that we were told you have had unpleasant dealings with." Alaric said, leaning back in the chair and glancing around the room, making sure no one was listening too closely to their conversation.

"Oh? And who might that be? I have run into many men that have been *unpleasant*." He said, still gauging whether or not the men in front of him were just that.

Alaric chuckled, the noise rumbling in his chest, "Aye, so have we. We are searching for a sailor that goes by the name of Thomas Banning." Alaric watched the man's eyes go dark, his hand moving to his side.

"What business is it that you have with him?" He asked, sitting forward, "whatever it is, I do not want any part of it."

"What is it he did to you? We are not his allies, by any means." Alaric assured the man.

"I was coming back from Africa, a large shipment of goods onboard. I was bringing them back to the islands. He came upon us, firing suddenly, no warning shots. We stood no chance. He destroyed my ship, most of my crew was left dead or dying, my goods hardly touched. He took my ship, my crew, for no other reason than to sink us and leave us for dead. The few of us that survived were lucky, a ship came upon us and took us aboard." Gael stopped, looking into his cup before draining the last of the drink.

Alaric and Ethan exchanged glances, "do you have any idea where Banning may be headed to now or where any of his hideouts might be?" Ethan asked, thanking the barmaid that had walked over, setting fresh cups on the table.

"Perhaps, though I do not know how often he is there. I have heard that he frequents St. Kitts and Tortuga. I warn you; you do not want to be meddling in his affairs, he is no decent man and has men all over the islands that will gain a fair price from him if they report that he is being followed."

"We have little choice in the matter, he took something from me that can never be replaced, and I will not rest until he pays for what he has done. Not to mention he has questions for the man, that need answering," Alaric replied, thrusting his thumb in Ethan's direction. "We thank you for the information." The men stood in unison and headed for the door. The sun would be rising in a couple hours and Alaric wanted to be on his way.

They were sailing close to St. Kitts. Alaric hoped that they would find more valuable information out about Thomas's current location, he did not particularly fancy going to Tortuga. Trouble seemed to break out anytime they had to go to that particular island. He looked up at the tall masts that stood steadily in front of him, the sails were spread wide, pulling the ship through the nearly clear blue waves. His eyes caught movement high up, just above the yardarm. He squinted in the sun, trying to make out what the shape was. A loud screech met his ears, *just a seabird*, he thought. His breathing paused; something did not quite fit. Shouts began below the Foremast, "Eddie, take the helm," he commanded, not waiting for the man to grab hold of the wheel before leaping to the deck. "What is it?" He shouted at one of the sailors that was quickly making his way down the mast.

"It's Henry, Captain. He slipped, the rope, it's caught round his wrist." The sailor replied frantically.

Alaric reached for a hatchet that was strapped to a nearby sailor's waist. He shoved it in his own belt, grabbing for a rope that lay coiled up on top of a barrel and began climbing.

He looked down briefly, catching Ethan's gaze. He nodded for him to follow. Alaric made his way up the ratlines, praying the boy could hold on long enough for him to reach him. A fall from that height would kill a sailor. He heard a grown, desperation and panic in the boy's voice. Alaric carefully neared Henry, the line was caught around the boy's wrist causing his hand to twist slightly in an unnatural way. Alaric sat, his legs dangling on either side of the yardarm. He worked quickly, tying a loop into the line he had brought up with him, he flung it over Henry's head and shoulder. "Put your other arm through the loop and hold tight, lad. I am going to cut the line to free your wrist."

"Aye Capt'n, I am ready," he struggled, gripping the line around him tightly. Alaric glanced back at Ethan who had tied the other end of the line to the mast in order to hold the boy securely and not bring all three of them tumbling down to the decks below when his wrist was freed. Alaric pulled the hatchet out, bringing it down hard against the line, it snapped suddenly causing Henry to swing, nearly crashing into the mast as his wrist broke away from the tangled line.

"I'll get him down and to Doc, you finish tying off that line that came loose from the sail, I reckon that is what Henry was doing when he slipped." Alaric spoke quickly, making his way back towards the ratlines in order to help Henry down.

"I am sorry, Capt'n. The bird, it came out of nowhere and knocked me from the yardarm. If the line hadn't tangled around my arm, I would have met the decks."

"You held fast; you've done well." Alaric said, steading

Henry as he stumbled down the lines.

"Come now, lad. Let's get you fixed up." Doc said, motioning for Henry to follow him to the surgery.

Alaric rubbed his hands over his face and headed to his cabin. He opened the hatch, the smell of freshly cooked fish, potatoes and a variety of vegetables filled his senses. His stomach replied with a loud grumble. He did not hesitate, moving around the table, kicking off his boots and picking a bite of the steaming fish. He sat back in the chair and let out a breath. In all his years sailing, men rarely fell from the rigging, of course it did happen, and he had witnessed the horrid sight before. He closed his eyes, trying to wipe the image of the boy's helpless form dangling high above the decking. His eyes had been filled with terror and pain.

Alaric finished the last of his meal. He turned in the wooden chair, looking out the window that sat behind the desk. The waves steadily rolled over each other, sea birds flew around, diving close to the water, their beaks skimming the top as they snapped up the small fish that swam below.

He felt his body go cold, he tried to move, tried to turn but his limbs would not budge. He had to find Benjamin. Alaric knew the boy was in danger; something had gone wrong. Thomas appeared, his flintlock raising. Alaric tried to yell for Benjamin to move. His body was not responding to his protests. A cloud of smoke exploded from the gun as the tiny ball shot from the barrel and met its mark. Alaric heard the distant splash as the boy's body hit the sea below.

He woke with a sudden jolt, nearly falling from the chair.

44

Alaric got up, placing his hands on the table for support. His body was coated in sweat. It was not the first time he had fallen into that dream or one like it, in fact, nearly every time he closed his eyes, he relived that moment. Each time unable to save Benjamin.

Alaric could hear the men bustling about on deck, the shouts indicating they were nearing the island. They once again were anchoring on the side, away from the busier part of the port. Many hideouts and paths were spread out in and around the islands, some used more than others. They made it easy to get on the islands without drawing too much attention to the ship. If they anchored to the docks, their ship would be listed in the logbooks at the port and everyone on the islands tended to know which ships were in the ports at what times. Alaric pulled on his boots, strapping his sword and flintlock on his belt. He reached for the blade that he had sat on the desk; Lucas's father had given them each one when they were lads. The hilt of the dirk had his initials carved into the rich, smooth wood. He stuck it in his boot and headed for the hatch.

"Nice spot for fishin', Capt'n. Do ya mind if we try for a bit?" Gordy asked hopefully.

"Aye, I see no problem in it. Do as Eddie commands though and be ready to sail quickly. You should have time to catch a few." He responded, moving over to where Ol' Shorty and Ethan stood, readying to climb down into the skiff.

"I have a feelin' 'bout this one, Capt'n. Somethin' just don't seem right." Ol' Shorty whispered as they rowed their way to the sandy banks.

"It will be fine, Mate. I don't think we will find Thomas and his crew here this night, or in Tortuga for that matter. I don't believe our luck to be that good. We will likely be dining on a fair bit of fresh fish tonight though." Alaric grinned, his smile wavering slightly. He had been feeling uneasy the moment he had awoke from the sleep. He had attributed it to the reoccurring dream but still could not shake the feeling, especially now that Shorty had voiced his own unease.

They made their way quickly through the dense shrubs and trees, and towards the taverns that lined the paths. Men stumbled through the openings of the establishments, swearing and swinging their fists in the air. One sailor swung too hard, his fist missing its mark, causing the man to trip and fall into the mud-covered path. Sailors around the man burst out laughing, sloshing the ale that filled their tankards. Alaric signaled for Ethan and Ol' Shorty to follow him onto the path, the men that stood about were distracted by the fallen man.

They neared the entrance of one of the taverns, cautiously entering. The door creaked loudly as Alaric pushed it open, no one in the establishments seemed to notice or care.

"A couple ales for my friends and I," Ol' Shorty spoke up to a woman they passed. Her gown cut far too low. Her hair done up in an attempt to mimic the fashions in France.

"Of course, and you just let me know if there is anything else you or your friends might want," her hand brushing against Alaric's arm, her eyes traveling the length of his body.

They made their way to a table near the center of the

room, their eyes never resting too long on a spot. "Do you see anyone you recognize?" Ethan asked, glancing from Alaric to the rest of the sailors that crowded the small tavern.

A woman played a piano that sat in the corner, while another tried her best to sing. Alaric recognized the lyrics, the song spoke of a boy that sank a Spanish ship. Both women were far from on key and the pianist played much faster than the other woman sang.

Alaric shook his head, "I'm afraid not, though that doesn't mean none of these men know of Banning or know someone that might." He reached into his pocket, pulling out several ivory cubes. "Care for a game?" He asked, grinning. He knew that as soon as the dice hit the table, they would have other sailors asking to join in.

A couple men came over, one had his hair hanging low in a long braid. His hair was so blonde, it nearly looked white. "Mind if we join you?" He asked, his voice gruff and none too friendly. Alaric shrugged, waving a hand in the air as if he were enthralled with the game.

"Been on the island long?" Shorty asked the newcomers, not bothering to look up from the dice.

The man shrugged, "No longer than a fortnight or so. What brings you lot here?"

"Looking for a man by the name of Thomas Banning." Alaric replied, noting how the other man's hand suddenly paused over the dice.

"Not many men that would go lookin' for him." The sailor with the braid said. "Only two reasons anyone would seek him out. Either you are wanting to make a fair deal of money, no matter what it cost ye, or you be seekin' him for revenge." His eyes roamed over Alaric and his men. "Which one is it that you be searching him for?"

"We did hear that those that sail with him often find themselves at the bottom of the sea but those that are lucky enough, walk away with a sizeable sum in their pockets." Alaric said, holding the man's gaze. "I take it you've sailed with him. You'd be one of the fortunate ones then."

"Aye, I did, and I'd sail with him again if I knew where to find him. I heard tell, he went towards France. Last he was seen was near Madeira. I reckon he came back here and is around somewhere or headed down the African coast, pickin' up slaves and goods from those parts." The man sat back, glancing at the sailor next to him then back to Alaric. He did not like the look in the man's eyes. "You two don't look as if you are wantin' for money or sound like the others that join Banning's crew." He challenged.

"You are right, we would not normally be seeking such a crew out, to join." Alaric paused, rolling the dice. "But here we are." Raising his head, he locked eyes with the sailor, matching his challenging gaze.

The two sailors stood, gathering up the jewels and coins they won during the game, "There are other ships you could join, perhaps you'd be better suited to a Privateer ship, or even the Royal Navy. No, I don't believe you and your friends would last long under Banning." The man scoffed at his own comments, laughter erupting from his chest. His friend snickered, obviously eager to leave before someone tried taking his earnings from him.

"Perhaps," Ethan commented, watching the sailor's cautiously as the two left the tavern.

"Come, we should be going. I have a feeling those men knew more about Thomas's location than they let on." Alaric stood, a man in the corner near the entrance catching his eye. Ol' Shorty glanced at him, clearly noticing the ragged man as well.

"Can we help you?" Alaric whispered to the sailor. His worn clothes and battered face making it hard to determine just how old he really was. One eye was shut, bruising, and swelling nearly gone, though the eye appeared to still be damaged. A fresh scar ran down the man's arm, partially hidden under the sleeve of the shirt that was rolled up. Alaric cocked an eye at the tattered man. "Looks as if you might need it."

The man shook his head, raising a hand, "no, but you will if you go chasin' after that man with the compass tattoo. You'd do best to stay far from him and ask no more questions bout 'im." His voice was low and crackly, giving away his age.

"How do you know of him? Is this his doing?" Ethan asked, gesturing to the man's wounds.

"Aye, he destroyed the ship I was on. Ran it aground along a shallow reef. He killed the crew, took what he wanted, left the rest. He believed me to be dead, I am not sure how long I was asleep. When I awoke, I took what I needed to the island nearby and set the ship alight. Not long after, a merchant ship came close enough to spot me standin' on the sand, they took me aboard and dropped me off here. Do as I say, laddie. As much as that man needs to be rottin' at the bottom of the sea, fish feeding on his flesh, you stay far from him and don't make any trouble with him." The old man spoke urgently, causing a fit of coughs to erupt from his chest.

"Do you know which way he was headed? Where did he attack your ship?" Alaric asked, his voice as low as the old sailor's. Shorty and Ethan stood at his back, cautiously watching the activity in the crowded room.

"Aye, north, bout two days sailin' from here. I am afraid I do not know where he was headed or how long it has been since the attack." He shrugged, rubbing the mark on his arm. The new skin had only recently formed over the cut.

"I thank you," Alaric said, reaching into his pocket and dropping a few coins in the older man's hand. Without another word they headed from the tavern and into the concealing cover of the trees.

Alaric's head shot up, he had been focusing on the path in front of them, working their way back to the ship. He took a deep breath in and listened carefully. He rose his hand, indicating for the other two to hold fast. Smoke, he was sure of it, the clanking of swords and firing of flintlocks could be heard in the distance. Alaric raced forward, his heart drumming loudly in his ears, blocking out all other sounds.

The men broke through the trees, *The Trinity* sat swaying just offshore, smoke coming from the fallen mast that hung over the shattered railing. A Spanish ship clung to the other side of *The Trinity,* men poured over, spreading about the deck. Alaric raced quickly across the sand and into the small skiff. They quietly climbed the side of The Trinity. Alaric neared the top, he peered over, flintlock drawn. Flipping himself over the edge of the railing and onto the deck. His finger pulled hard against the trigger. Grey smoke filled the air in front of him. A man from the other ship dropped suddenly to the deck, as he fell, his sword was left protruding from the shoulder of one of Alaric's crew members.

Alaric gripped the hilt of the sword, pulling it steadily

from the sailor's arm. "We need to get you to Doc. You are lucky the bastard missed his target," he said, lifting the man up.

"Aye, thank ya, Capt'n." Edward choked out, stumbling along the deck and towards the hatch, Alaric following closely behind him, guarding the injured man.

"Captain, is it?" A voice spoke, the heavy Spanish accent unmistakable.

"At your service," Alaric replied, bowing dramatically. "Shall we," he asked, waving his sword through the air, "or are you quite ready to surrender?" Alaric noted the darkening in the other Captain's eyes at the challenge.

The captain took a slight step back, his shoulders straightening. He tilted his head, lunging forward suddenly, his blade narrowly missing Alaric's neck. He felt the shock of the swords meeting as he pushed the captain's blade downward. His stomach tightened as a boot smashed into his middle. He grinned, knowing the other captain was growing angrier at the fight. Clearly, he had not expected such a challenge. He had likely spotted their ship and thought to take it as an easy prize, thinking most the crew would be on land or deep into their cups. Alaric watched the captain swing the blade towards him once more, stepping out of the way of the blow, he brought his sword up, slicing the other man's hand. The captain's sword clattered to the deck, a raging howl emanating from the man's chest. With the captain's cry, the fighting around them had ceased. The crews watched on, waiting to see what would become of the Spanish captain.

"Take your crew back to your ship. I will be sending a few of my men ashore to inform the governor of your capture. From there, he can do as he wishes with you and your crew." Alaric said, his voice hard and commanding.

The captain of the Spanish ship motioned for his men to return to their own deck and await further orders. He followed; his hand wrapped in his shirt in an attempt to slow the bleeding.

"Eddie, take a few men with you and get a message to the governor. See if he won't send some men to finish here, we need to be on our way as soon as we can." He said, cleaning his sword with a bit of fabric he had pulled from his pocket, before returning the blade to its proper place on his belt.

"Aye, Capt'n," he said, turning to a few crewmates that stood nearby.

"Shorty, get the men started on mending the railing and the mast." Alaric walked past the older sailor who had already begun shouting out orders to the crew before Alaric could finish. Alaric ran a hand through his hair, he glanced about his ship, smoke still swirled up from the sail that swayed just above the water. They had been lucky, if the sail had fallen about the deck, instead of the salty sea, the ship would have been destroyed. He stepped through the hatch, needing to check the damage belowdecks. He walked through the companionway, staring into each cabin, assessing the damage. He made his way towards the cages and pens that held the animals. Reaching out a hand, he gave one of the goats a reassuring pat. Occasionally he would come down to sit with them, it reminded him of their farm back in Ireland, though the smell from the livestock was far worse on a ship rather than in the open air. He looked the chickens over, collecting a few eggs he found. Keeping the animals on the ship helped greatly with the food supply and allowed them to have fresh milk.

To his relief it appeared the Spanish had aimed high, only taking the foremast out. It would take a bit to replace the mast and sails and they would need to pick up new supplies before they sailed out, but all in all, the damage was minimal.

Alaric stepped through the door and into the small galley. He placed the basket of eggs on the table, "How are you holding up, Cook?"

"Fair enough, thank ya for askin', Capt'n. What of the ship and the crew?" He asked, stirring a spoon through a large pot of broth. "I expect the men could use a bit of a bite to get them through the night. I reckon we have a few injuries though by the sounds of it, the fight did not last long."

"Aye, I believe the broth will do just fine, thank you. I have yet to check on Doc and the rest of the crew. I am heading there now. I wanted to give Doc more time to clean the men up and get a better judge of the worst injuries." He turned to leave, "I will be back for a bowl," he said, pointing to the pot.

Alaric could hear Doc speaking to one of the crew members as he approached the surgery. He had to admit, Doc was the best surgeon they could ask for, especially on a ship. Many vessels had to make do with the carpenter and no real doctor at all. He knew Doc missed Catherine being there to help him during battles. Doc had also told him that he missed being able to go over the surgery books with her and having someone to talk to about new ideas and medicines. Cook had expressed the same at losing his galley hand.

"Looks like you got it all in hand," Alaric said, announcing his presence. "How bad is it?"

"Unfortunately, more injuries than I would have suspected, for such a quick skirmish. The other crew knew what they were doing. No injuries too serious, though. I expect them to be healed within a couple weeks, at most." Doc replied, washing his hands off in a water basin that sat on a table in the corner. The various ointments and herbs sat on a shelf above it.

"How is your shoulder, Edward," Alaric asked, moving over to the hammock where the sailor lie. When he saw the other man over the young sailor, the sword sticking in him, he had been sure the boy would not make it. It was only when he got closer to him that he had noticed the sword was in his shoulder and not his chest.

"A bit sore. Doc has been generous with the rum though, so I am not too bad at the moment." He grinned, before pausing, his face straightening. "We were caught quite off guard, Capt'n. The crew was fishing, we caught a fair amount." He shook his head, "the Spanish gave no warning of attack. In fact, it looked as if they were going to simply sail past, without so much as looking at us. We relaxed a bit, that's when they blasted their cannons. We were able to get a shot off with our ship's guns but no more than that. They were already boarding us, some of the crew did not even have our swords in time."

Alaric nodded, appreciating the honesty of the report. "No one was too badly hurt, and the ship did not take on much damage." He looked over at Doc, "besides, tomorrow morning I expect we will be dining on some rather tasty fish." He smiled, his eyes traveling over the men that lay in the hammocks around him. A cheer went up, causing the air in the surgery to seem less strained. He knew the men felt poorly for not being on guard and more vigilant, but they had done well. There had been no casualties and they gained a prize ship that they had not anticipated capturing.

"Once the men return and the ship is mended, we will be heading towards Tortuga. As we near the island, and once there, we will need to be far more prepared. The closer we get to the ship we are after, the more alert we will all need to be. Tonight, you rest up, I expect we will be weighing anchor in a few short hours." He nodded to Doc, turning, and heading through the hatch and back up on deck to check on the progress.

Several men were pulling hard on ropes, stretching on either side of the mast. Thick planking between the lines and the shattered part of the mast. The sail had been removed, a new one ready to take its place up in the rigging and along the yardarm. Shorty wiped his sleeved arm across his forehead. Sweat dripped from his hairline. The sun had begun to rise, already heating the heavy air around them.

"Take a break. Cook has broth and ale ready. I will take over until you've rested a bit." Alaric said, motioning for the older man to hand him the bit of rope he had been pulling taught.

"Don't mind if I do, Capt'n." He said, gladly handing the line over to the captain and heading towards the galley.

Alaric felt the rough ropes pulling through his hands, the lines had to remain as tight as possible while other men secured the ropes and planking to the splintered mast, in order to mend it. He placed a booted foot on the wood in front of him, bracing against it to get the most force behind it to be able to keep the lines tight. He felt his shirt tighten against the muscles in his shoulders. One of the men fixed the line, tying it in a knot that would not likely come undone unless the rope itself was severed. It was enough to hold the tall and thick mast securely together. Alaric let his muscles relax, calling the crew for a rest, allowing them to fetch grog and broth before the job of raising the mast was to be done.

Captain," Eddie called out. Alaric turned, Eddie and a few of the other crewmates that he had taken with him to alert the Governor were clambering up the side of the hull and onto the deck. They were followed closely by several of the Governor's men. "We are to hand the prize ship and crew over to the Governor's men. They will deal with the rest, and we are able to weigh anchor when you are ready, Capt'n." He said, hastily relaying the message to Alaric.

"Aye, very well. Thank you, Eddie. Go and have some broth and grog with the rest of the crew. We will finish the mast up after everyone has had their fill. We will then head for Tortuga." Alaric replied, heading towards the hatch to retrieve the wood that would be needed to mend the railing. He would rather work a while longer. This had set them back at least a day. He had felt Thomas's presence growing closer. What they had learned in the tavern the night before gave

Alaric hope that they may indeed find Banning sooner rather than later. Now with the attack and the fallen mast, it would allow Thomas to get further from him or even give someone the chance to let Banning know he was being tailed. He let out a breath, dropping the planks on the deck near the broken railing. It would not be able to be repaired until the mast was raised.

Walking to the captain's cabin, tray of broth and rum in hand, he kicked open the hatch. Typically, one of the younger or less experienced sailors would be made to bring in the tray, but he did not see the point in that at the moment. He tore his boots off, followed by his shirt that clung to his skin from the hot and sticky air. He lowered his head into the water basin, letting the cool water soak his hair and face. He did not move to grab the fabric that sat next to the basin, no sense in trying to dry off when the thick air would only wet it again.

There was a knock at the door, "come in," he said. Almost relieved for the chance to distract his mind once more from the anger and frustration he felt for falling behind.

"It was a good lead. Still is," Ethan said, as if reading his thoughts. "Banning rarely leaves these waters unless he is headed for Africa. We know that is not likely, as it seems he only returned to the West Indies around the same time we did. He would not be wanting to head back out on such a voyage after just returning from one and you know his men would not either. Not after what they witnessed these last several months. He likely has had to recruit a new crew as well." He reasoned, bringing another thought to Alaric's mind.

"Aye, I suppose you are correct in all that. I wonder, perhaps we have been going about this the wrong way." Alaric sat down at the desk, Ethan following suit on the other side. "In Tortuga, we will not ask about Banning or his ship at first. We will ask after a ship taking on new crewmates. After all it does follow the story we told in St. Kitts, so if word gets out, it will appear that we are simply doing just as we say. With any luck, he will be taking on new crew in Tortuga. Who was it that signed you onto Banning's ship before? How did you join?" He asked, sitting forward slightly.

"His first mate, Grady. He would do anything Thomas asked, though I could not say why. I am not sure if he fears him or respects him, but he would never go against Thomas's word. I did just as you said. I was looking for a pirate crew to join, I heard about Banning and his crew, he fit the description of my sister's attacker. So, I sought him out by continuing to ask about crews to join and that I had heard a man by the name of Thomas was hiring men on. It did not take long. I was told to head to a tavern where Thomas's first mate was staying. Grady asked me a few questions, but nothing much. Next thing I knew, I was aboard the ship and heading after *The Trinity,* though I admit, I did not know that at the time." He grinned, sitting back in the chair, and looked out the window that sat behind Alaric.

"Very well, when we reach Tortuga, we will ask after a ship that is taking on a crew. Even if he is no longer there, someone is likely to know of where they headed to and how long ago." Alaric concluded.

"What of the logs that the docks keep? Would he register his ship in them by anchoring at the island's ports or would he be doing as we have been and use the hideouts?"

He nodded, "aye, he will be using the hideouts, after all he has done over the last few years, he will not want his name, or his ship being registered at any port if he could help it."

7

Thomas grinned, the smell, sound and temperament of Tortuga was what he enjoyed, almost more than taking ships. A group of men sat at a table in the tavern near him, they were placing bets on who would win a game of checkers, he did not care for the game much, but he recognized one of the men that sat at the round table, hunched in concentration over the small wooden pieces. He was a sailor on his ship, he did not remember his name but knew the sailor had been with him for a couple voyages now. He also remembered he was a skilled fighter and had not backed down when they took a ship a few days before. Thomas rested his feet on a table, his tankard in one hand and his flintlock in the other. As much as he enjoyed the island and its ever riveting atmosphere, he knew well that there were many men who would not hesitate to run him through as quick as he would down them.

"Mave, give me another, luv, then come sit here for a spell." He ordered one of the women who had walked past, several cups in her hands, her dress was frayed and slipping off one of her shoulders, exposing more pale flesh than was considered proper. She responded with an obedient and hopeful smile, setting the cups down and returning to him with a full tankard. Grabbing at her, Thomas pulled her onto him. Letting out a squeal and giggle, she settled onto his lap. Thomas's gaze went back to the game in front of him, his pistol still in his hand as he wrapped his arm around Mave's waist.

The sailor from his ship stood up, flipping the board over and off the small table in anger at losing. Thomas raised his flintlock, not bothering to aim properly, pulling the trigger steadily back until smoke erupted from the barrel and a loud crack sounded, echoing through the tavern. Through the chaos that ensued he saw he had hit his mark. The rough man that had beat his sailor lay still on the ground, blood seeping from a wound in his chest. Thomas sneered, grabbing harder at Mave, burying his face in her neck. Some sailors had run out, others broke into fights, using what they had on hand as a weapon. One sailor, a larger man, his hair reaching down his back in a long, black braid, reached for a table, lifting it above his head and slamming it down on another man. The man sank to the ground unconscious, the table splintering apart.

"Grady," Thomas said, approaching his first mate. He rubbed his hand across his face. The night before in the tavern had been a mistake. He had enjoyed himself but had awakened with his head feeling as heavy as the cannon balls. "Make the ship ready to sail. I ain't stayin' here any longer." He had many enemies and could not linger, he also suspected Harding and his first mate would be searching for him soon.

They would want revenge on him for killing the boy. He had plans of his own, he was heading north, out of the waters they would be searching for him in.

"Aye, Capt'n, the new recruits have already loaded the supplies, e'erything is ready, Cap." Grady spoke, spitting on the ground and wiping his arm across his mouth.

"I'll be in my cabin, see that the crew is all there and give the order to weigh anchor." He replied gruffly, scrunching his face at the morning sun. He walked through the busy dock, crates being loaded and unloaded, causing men to slam into one another from lack of seeing where they were going. There was a screech from behind, he turned, seeing a young woman with flaming red hair.

She kicked at a sailor, the point of her foot meeting the burly man between his legs. He nearly collapsed, curling into himself, his grip finally releasing its hold on the girl. She whipped around, slamming right into Thomas. "No need to fear, I've got you now." The sound of his voice taking away any trace of kindness he had meant to display.

"Somehow I doubt this is any better." She squirmed, "let me go or suffer the same fate as your friend." Her head jerking in the direction of the sailor that was slowly gaining composure. Her foot came down hard on his. He laughed, releasing his grasp on her, and holding his hands in the air. He gave a dramatic bow and turned, heading for the path that led to his ship on the other side of the island, shaking his head, and howling with laughter. He had anchored far enough from the docks to avoid registering but close enough where he did not have long to trek to reach it.

He stepped from the skiff, climbing up the side of his ship. He hollered for a cabin boy to bring him in a bucket of water, he needed to clean his flintlock out and ready it in case they found another ship they could take. He had heard how profitable the colonies were becoming, especially with trade. He suspected there would be an abundance of vessels traveling the trade routes to the colonies, as well as plenty of passenger ships. He grinned at the thought of the number of women left unaccompanied, except for a maid or mere footman, headed to meet their husbands that await them at their plantations or large estates. He wagered their men would be willing to pay a hefty sum to return their womenfolk to them.

He heard the hatch open to his cabin, the young cabin boy walked in, struggling under the weight of the bucket full of water. Setting the bucket down, he stood straight, waiting for further orders to be made. Thomas looked the boy over, he did not recognize him and guessed him to be one of the new recruits Grady had signed on. His last cabin boy had not made it through the previous battle, and he had not intended to continue on without a new one. He did not fancy the idea of having to retrieve his own buckets of water or clean his cabin and clothes. The only reason he cleaned his own weapons was because he did not trust being left without them or trust anyone else to clean them without tampering with them in some way that may cost him his life.

"That'll be all, for now." He said, then thinking on it more, "see that Cook has started my meal and that more rum is brought to my cabin." He finished, sitting in his chair, and pulling his flintlock out. He did not miss how the boy shivered.

"Aye, Cap." He replied, rushing through the hatch.

Opening a drawer in his desk, he pulled out the strips of thick, fibrous cloth that was used to clean the barrel. There were only two or three strips left, enough for one more cleaning. He had meant to purchase more in Tortuga but had not remembered in all the ruckus. He would take what he needed from one of the crew if he must. He dipped the strip into the bucket of water, soaking it thoroughly before pushing it into the barrel of the flintlock. Drawing it out, it was thick with black smoke and powder residue. Repeating the process and running a dry strip through, until the barrel was sufficiently rid of the remanence. A small bottle of sweet oil sat on his desk, pouring droplets on the metal, he smoothed it over, until the pistol brightened. The dull, worn color vanishing below the slick coating. He turned it over in his hand, placing it on the table as the cabin boy returned with a jug of rum.

"Just in time." He grinned, "Tell me your name, lad." He ordered, motioning for the boy to place it on the desk.

"Jimmy, Capt'n" he replied, his eyes remaining on the flooring.

"And how old are you, Jimmy? Where is your family?" He asked, yanking the cork from the bottle and spitting it on the ground.

"I will be twelve soon, Cap. I do not have a family." He replied simply, shrugging his shoulders.

"Neither do I." Thomas said, the boy raised his eyes, meeting Thomas's briefly before nodding and leaving the cabin.

Alaric stepped from the skiff, another dense forest of trees and bushes lay in front of them. He glanced back at *The Trinity,* hoping that no ship came upon them again in the night. He doubted it would happen again, most ship's captains, no matter how unforgivable they could be, they tended to stick with the general rules of the sea. Attacking an anchored ship was not something even the most ruthless of captains would usually do, not unless that ship caused the other to be run aground. Alaric looked ahead on the narrow path, sharp rock faces occasionally broke through the trees. On many islands, these rock structures provided the perfect refuge for pirates to store their treasures in or to hide away for a while from the Navy or privateers that might be hunting them. Caves were strewn about in the rock, some going on for miles with various chambers set in them.

The shouts, gunfire and laughter were unmistakable. No other island was quite like this one. Alaric rested his hand on the hilt of his sword. The men and women on the island seemed to all but seek out fights, firing into the air or at passing sailors, just to watch the reactions of the men around them. As they broke through the trees and onto the muddy path that led to the taverns, Alaric nearly stumbled over a man that lay sprawled out across the path, his face half sunken into the dirt, a bottle still tucked into his meaty hand.

"Let's start here," Alaric motioned. Men sat about on barrels outside the establishment, some of them throwing knives at a piece of wood that had drifted onto the beach from the sea. Alaric stepped forward and through the door. Making their way through the maze of sailors, women, and tables. They found a spot near the back where they would be able to watch the scenes in front of them unfold. Most of the sailors were far too into their drink to be of any use to Alaric or his men.

"Excuse me," Alaric held out a hand, stopping a woman as she walked past, carrying a couple tankards to a group of men that sat at a table nearby. "Do you know if any of these men are taking on a crew?"

"I might have heard something," Her eyes brazenly traveling over Alaric's figure. "I would be willing to tell you. For a price that is."

He cleared his throat, "you best get those men their drinks," he replied, inclining his head towards the table of sailors that was growing impatient waiting for their ale. The woman placed the tankards in front of them, hardly taking her eyes from Alaric.

"As I said, I'd be willing to tell you what I know, for a price." She placed a hand on his chest.

Alaric gently gripped her wrist, lowering her hand and

turning it over. He placed a few coins in it, "now how about that ship?" He asked, his voice low.

She smiled up at him, hiding the coins in the folds of her dress, "there was a man in here a couple nights ago, he was taking on men."

"Are they still in Tortuga? What was the name of the ship or Captain?" Alaric asked, steadily growing impatient at the woman's impudence.

She stepped a bit closer, "The fella that was signing on the new recruits was a man by the name of Grady. I seen him and his Captain in here before, but if you want the name of this Captain then it will cost you a bit more." Her voice matching the look in her eyes.

"Thank you, you have told me all I needed to know." He looked over at Shorty, "guess we will go see if Grady and Captain Banning are still here." He did not try and hide his smile as the woman scoffed, pursing her lips in a brusque defeat. Turning, she strode back to the table of men nearby.

"I don't recognize any of these men, Capt'n. Let's try closer to the docks, they may be gathering supplies." Shorty suggested.

"Aye," Alaric replied, moving forward through the crowd once more. He noticed, more than one sailor in the room eyed them cautiously. Alaric instinctively placed his hand back on the hilt of his sword. If a fight broke out in the middle of the tavern, there is no telling who the enemy would be. The sailors around them would simply begin firing as they wished.

He drew in a deep breath once his feet hit the muddy ground outside the building.

Walking further down, the sounds of the docks grew louder, men prepared to sail in the early morning hours. The sea birds were waking up, hoping to pick up scraps from the fisherman's nets that were coming and going in the breaking light. The ruckus around them did not diminish as they approached the busy area. Men still laid about, bottles in their hands as they snored where they had fallen the night before, some continuing with their drinking and games. Alaric caught movement from the corner of his eye, his footsteps slowed as he eyed the men around them.

"Stein," a cold voice called out behind them. "You are Captain Harding's brother, ain't ya?"

Alaric and the others stayed their steps, turning to see who confronted them. "Aye, I am, though I don't recall ever meeting you before." He said, raising an eyebrow at the man. His clothes were cleaner than most on the island and he did not appear to have enjoyed himself as much as the rest of the sailors around them had. His beard was dark, reaching down towards his bare chest.

"You and your no-good brother took a ship a few years back, *The Drogo*. It was my ship you took that day. See, I had been wounded in a battle that had taken place a few weeks before. I was sick with fever, could no' see past my own hands. My crew thought to protect me by not saying who the rightful Captain was. They said I had died in the last battle, when you and your brother had come down the hatch to tell my crew you had captured my ship." He raised his hand in the air as he spoke, anger, and despise evident in his voice. The captain watched Alaric and the others as he paced in front of them. A few other sailors had gathered, standing behind the enraged captain.

Alaric let out a groan, "I apologize you were unwell, and therefore unable to speak up at the time. As I recall, you and your crew were released and pardoned." Alaric challenged, knowing the man did not care about their pardon now, but about his lost ship. There was not much Alaric could do about that, it had been the governor's decision and the captain, being unable to request a meeting with the governor at the time of his ship's taking, had caused him to lose all but his life.

"You see, I feel that ye didn't take my ship fairly. You had an unfair advantage o'er me." The man watched Alaric, judging his reaction.

He crossed his arms over his chest, returning the gaze. "What's it you're wanting to do about it then?" Alaric did not see much point in trying to talk the man down.

"First blood," he answered, taking his gun belt and sword off. He drew a knife from the inside of his vest. His grin showing a gold tooth that glinted in the rapidly rising sun.

Alaric unfastened his belt, handing them to Ethan, who flung it over his shoulder, freeing his hands in case he needed to step in. Alaric knew Ethan was most likely not used to this sort of behavior still. Being an officer in the Royal Navy meant he would be with several other officers at a time if they found themselves in port and a challenge like this would have caused the pirates to be arrested and tried to hang if they were not shot first. He pulled the dirk out, feeling its familiar weight in his hand.

"I have not seen Captain Harding in some time, don't tell me he was finally cut down?" The captain asked, feigning sympathy. "I am only sorry it was not my blade that did it."

"On the contrary, he is doing quite well," grinning, he carefully circled the other man. He knew the comment would only anger the burly sailor more. "We could do this for hours, but I have other engagements and would like to continue on with my day," he let the words hang in the air. As much as he did not wish to fight, he had to admit, the frustration that had been building in him in not finding Banning had been getting nearly too much for him to take. "I have to ask, did you ever gain another ship, or after all of these years, are you still pining after the one you lost?"

As he expected, his words did the trick, the man sprang forward. Alaric gauged the lunge, moving only enough for the pirate's blade to catch the sleeve of his shirt and nothing more. Alaric stepped forward, acting as if he were about to make a move. The man brought his small blade up readying to block the blow he believed would come. Alaric stayed his hand, just enough, the sailor took his chance, aiming for Alaric's exposed leg. He brought his dirk down against the captain's shoulder, just deep enough for the droplets of blood that sprang forward to soak through the thin sleeve of the sailor's shirt.

Alaric did not miss the look that passed through the other Captain's raging eyes. "You won again this day, but do not count yourself lucky just yet. Your time will come, and your brother's." The man stood up straighter, wiping a sleeve across his face.

Alaric made a thought to check the logbooks when he returned to the ship. He needed to know the name of this captain; in case he did hold true to his threats. "Let's go, we've wasted enough time." He said, walking them closer to the docks. "Ethan, you take the tavern over there and Shorty you go to the opposite one. I will ask the sailors loading crates. We will find each other in a short while. Meet by the edge of the trees, behind the buildings."

9

"Captain?" A soft voice spoke from somewhere in the crowd. Alaric looked around, it was not unusual for women to be in the docks, especially in Tortuga. They were often asking for sailors to take them to a different island or waiting for the men to come from the ship, hoping to earn as much coin and jewels as they could. He felt a hand rest on his arm, looking down he saw a young woman, dressed in that of what a housemaid or more astute tavern maid would wear.

He raised a brow at the hand that still rested on his arm. The young woman's face suddenly flamed, "Can I do anything for you, Miss?"

"I apologize, it's just that, I saw you fight that man just now. I am hoping to gain passage on a ship." She must have seen the look on his face, as she hastened, "I have coin, not much, but surely enough to pay for passage." She explained, a look of determination and desperation in her eyes. "Please, I cannot stay here."

Alaric let out a chuckle, he had been right. She was look-ing to book passage and was hoping to have a protector on the voyage. "I'm sorry Miss, I cannot take on any passengers this voyage. If you will excuse me," he said, attempting to politely walk past her and to a group of crewmates that looked to be searching for the correct ship.

"Please, you do not understand. I mean what I say. I cannot stay here another day." She stepped in front of him again. A look of fear flashing over her face.

Alaric looked her over, something about her struck him, she was not the typical lass that was seen down at the docks, trying to barter for passage. "Lass, I am sorry, we do not know yet where we are headed to next or how long we will be at sea. It is far too dangerous." He looked at her apologetically. "Bringing you along would mean risking your life, and that I will not be doing." He managed to step around her before she could respond. He ran his hand through his hair, he was not entirely comfortable leaving her at the docks, knowing any sailor might try and take advantage of her but he also knew he could not simply take her aboard his ship either.

"Capt'n," Alaric swung around, he heard Shorty call for him but could not quite pick him out through the crowds. "Capt'n, o'er here." He managed to spot Shorty's meaty arm flailing in the air. "Capt'n, him was here and not too long ago. Him and his crew sailed out just this morning. They is headed North like." Shorty breathed out, his face red with excitement at the news. "I reckon they might be headed for the colonies. I've heard tell the plantation owners pay hefty prices for the proper goods."

"Well done," he clapped the older man on the shoulder. "Let's get Ethan, we will head back to the ship. Ready to sail as soon as we touch the decks." They turned, walking through the crowd and towards the trees that lined the edge of the jungle. Out of the corner of his eye he caught the movement of a lass with red hair. He cleared his throat and quickened his pace, still unsure of what to make of the girl. He tried shaking off the feeling of unease that was steadily growing stronger.

"Blast these roots," Ol' Shorty let out a gruff curse when his feet caught again on another root that stuck out precariously in the middle of the path. They neared the outer edge of the jungle; Alaric's whole body was on alert.

"Quickly, lads, we want to get sailing. Morning broke some time ago and I'd rather not spend any more time on this hellish island." He spoke as the men jumped into the skiff, he followed, after pushing it further into the waters.

He let out a sigh as his feet hit the planking of the deck. The orders went out to weigh anchor before he even had time to breathe the words aloud. He headed for his cabin, he wanted to have a look at the maps, see which islands Thomas may be heading for next.

Alaric's fingers wrapped around the handle of the hatch, pressing it open and stepping in, he froze. The feel of a small, sharp blade pressed against his neck. He swallowed, feeling the knife press harder against his skin. He turned his head slowly, careful not to cause the blade to slice into the thin flesh of his neck. He felt his opponent remove his flintlock and sword, tossing them loudly to the side. He raised his hands in the air in mock defeat, "careful there lass, throwing a gun down like that can cause it to fire." He whispered, the shock of realizing the small knife against his throat was being held by the girl from the docks was still strong. He could feel the blade shake slightly when he spoke. He knew she must be terrified and half out of her mind to attempt such an attack on him. Her words from their first meeting came back to him, he had seen the desperation and terror in her eyes then but had disregarded it as a mere ploy.

"You said that taking me aboard would be risking my life and you were not prepared to do that but leaving me on that island would have been far worse." She said, her voice barely audible.

Alaric gently pushed the blade from his neck, causing the girl to jump back. She held the small knife out in front of her, both hands gripping the handle hard enough to cause her knuckles to whiten. "How did you get aboard my ship? And how did you get into my cabin unseen?" He asked, crossing his arms over his chest.

"Twas not that difficult. I saw you go into the trees; I know that path and found a quicker one." Her voice a bit louder now.

"That does not answer my question about how you got into my cabin." He stepped away from the wall.

"I waited until the crew was distracted with your arrival," she answered quickly, eyeing him cautiously and not daring to lower the blade.

"Clever," he said, walking over to the desk and pouring a small glass of rum for each of them. He knew she would likely not touch it, but he edged the glass to the far side of

76

the table in case she changed her mind. "You said before that you could not stay on the island any longer, why is that?" He doubted she had done anything too unforgiveable, though judging by the way she had snuck aboard his ship and held a knife to his throat, he was beginning to guess there was more to her than her being a simple housemaid.

"I did nothing wrong," Her voice sounding shakier than before. "I can promise you that, but I could not stay. I do not wish to tell you, not yet at least." She lowered her eyes, glancing about the cabin as if some creature from a child's nightmare would appear at any moment.

Alaric took a step closer, causing her to flinch and her eyes to widen, "I apologize," he held his hands up, "as you may recall, I am the one that is unarmed." It of course was not entirely true, but she did not need to be reminded of the dirk he still carried.

"Men do not need to be armed to cause damage," she said, holding the knife a bit higher. Something in her voice sent a chill down Alaric's spine.

"You have my word, not a soul on this ship will cause you any harm." His voice barely above a whisper. "Seeing as how we are already underway; you may stay aboard my ship." Though every part of him knew that even if they had not yet set sail, he would not have returned her to Tortuga. Clearly something or someone had scared her. "You will have my cabin. I will see if cook can make you a meal and I will send Doc in." Turning, he added, "you do not have to worry about either of them, they will not hurt you." Her stance relaxing slightly, though she never released her grip on her knife.

Alaric ducked through the hatch; he ran a hand along his jaw. He had not expected to find her in his cabin, and certainly not holding a knife to him. His chest rumbled as he let out a low laugh. He had felt uneasy as they left the island but thought it was from his encounter with the captain of *The Drogo* Alaric walked through the companionway towards Doc. He wanted to be able to reassure the lass as well as see if Doc could find any more out about her or if she was injured in some way.

Alaric knocked on the door to the surgery, there was a scuffle and what sounded like books dropping to the floor, followed by a low curse. "Come in," Doc replied, his voice hitching as he bent to pick up the fallen books. "I am trying in vain to reorganize my collection," he said, gesturing to the stacks of books, lists and diagrams. "What can I do for you, Captain?"

"I need you to come to my cabin," Alaric said, watching Doc, unsure of how to continue. "It appears we have a bit of a stowaway, a rather feisty one at that."

Doc cocked his eyebrow, "Oh? And who or what might this stowaway be?"

Alaric realized he had entirely forgotten to ask the lass her name, "I am not sure," he flipped open a book, not really looking at the pictures scratched into it. "I met her at the docks, she claimed she could not stay on in Tortuga any longer and asked to buy passage. I had thought she was feigning her fear at the time, but it would appear she was telling the truth. The lass held a knife to my throat as I entered my own cabin," he scoffed in disbelief as he retold the story out loud.

Doc let out a loud laugh, "Finally met your match? A young woman that did not swoon at the sight of you?"

He scowled at the teasing, "I am afraid she has been harmed somehow. I would also like to get to the bottom of why she is willing to risk coming aboard an unknown ship to escape." He shut the book he had been flitting through. "Maybe she will be willing to talk to you. She might relax a bit, though I warn you, she is armed with a rather sharp little dagger." He grinned, thinking of how she had dared to threaten him on his own ship.

Doc shook his head, "You and Captain Harding are far more alike than you realize."

"Why do you say that?" Confused at why the doc had said such a thing.

"When Miss Catherine was first aboard the ship, on that first day when we believed her to be young Allen, he came to me, asked me to get to know Allen and see what I could find out about why she had stowed away in the first place." Doc explained, remembering Catherine. He indeed had gotten to know her; they had become good friends and he had trained her well.

"I see," Alaric cleared his throat. "This is an entirely different situation, and we will likely be meeting with more than one fight. I cannot risk having this lass aboard."

"No, you are right, but like Captain Harding found out very quickly, you cannot simply drop her off at just any port, especially before you find out the reason, she risked boarding this ship." Doc explained, "If you drop her off at the next port, you may be putting the lass into far more danger than allowing her to stay aboard."

"I suppose you are right," He sighed, "Come meet her and look her over, if she'll let you." Alaric said, baffled at how his life had suddenly become far more complicated.

"Cook, I am sorry to ask, but would you mind fixing a tray up of whatever you are able? Oh, and please bring it to my cabin yourself." He saw the confused look on the cook's red face, "you will see what I mean." Alaric nodded to him, leaving him to prepare a meal. Alaric knew Cook had plenty of supplies, they had not been from Barbados long and the fish the men had caught the other night had held them over well.

Alaric headed towards his cabin, this time more prepared, he knocked, then nudged the hatch open, peering in the best he could as to avoid the chance of possibly being stabbed by the red headed housemaid. "Doc will be in soon and Cook is bringing a tray in." He said, fully entering his cabin, annoyed at the fact that he had been so cautious. The girl stood behind his desk, she had been looking through the small window, watching Tortuga fade in the distance. She no longer held the knife in her hand, but he had no doubt she still carried it on her person. There was a light knock on the door, Alaric did not miss how the girl suddenly stiffened. "Come in," he said, not taking his gaze off the young woman.

"Ah, it is a pleasure to meet you, Miss…?" Doc let the sentence hang in the air, the girl shuffled her feet uneasily, glancing between the two men.

"Molly Maclean, Sir," She whispered.

"You may call me Doc," he said, walking into the cabin a bit further. "If you should need anything, you just let me know." He smiled in an attempt to reassure her.

"I thank you, Sir. All I wish is to sail far from Tortuga and never go back." Her gaze flitted to Alaric, "Back at the docks you said you do not know where you will be sailing next or how long you will be at sea, but you will be leaving the West Indies, won't you? At least for a time?" She asked, ringing her hands together, her eyes meeting his briefly.

"Aye, we are headed north, though we may not head far from here, or we may be gone for several months." Alaric looked her over, watching for any signs of regret at boarding his ship.

"That's good," She nodded, "I thank you Captain for letting me stay aboard your ship. I will do what I can to earn my keep. Perhaps you would be kind enough to show me what I can do. You mentioned a cook, so I do not suppose you need me to help in the galley, is there anything else? Mending sails? Scrubbing the decks?" She let out a shaky breath.

"Aye, you could do those things, I am sure the crew would be grateful for the help, but I don't intend to make you work." He replied, surprised at her offer. "What is it that you did back on land?"

"I was a housemaid for one of the plantations," She stared at the floor, not willing to meet his eyes.

"Seems a fair enough job," Alaric stated, willing her to elaborate. There was only one or two reasons a lass would run from a position such as that. A shiver ran down his back at the thought of what the girl might have had to endure during service.

"I suppose," Her voice barely audible.

Doc cleared his throat and shot Alaric a look that said he had come to the same conclusion, "why don't I go see where Cook is with the tray?" Reaching for the hatch as another knock sounded on it. Doc opened it, allowing Cook entrance.

"Oh," his deep French accent making the word sound more like a strangled noise. His eyes moved from Alaric to Molly. He placed the tray on the desk that separated her from the rest of them. "C'est un plaisir de vous rencontrer, Mademoiselle." His round cheeks moved up, causing his eyes to be nearly nonexistent as he smiled. "It is a pleasure to meet you. I hope you'll enjoy the food I have prepared for you." He gestured to the tray, "Please, if you should need anythin', you let me know."

Alaric rolled his eyes at the dramatic display put on by his cook. To his surprise, Molly laughed softly. "Thank you, Cook. The food looks wonderful." She said, returning the man's smile.

"Ah, very well. Let's let Miss Maclean alone to enjoy her meal, why don't we?" Doc said, stretching his arm out in a way of dismissing himself and Cook.

Alaric moved to the chest of maps, he still had not had a

chance to look them over. He was very much aware of Molly and how she was watching his every move, her eyes guarded. He did not wish to intimidate or scare her, but he could not very well move all his supplies into a different area of the ship just to make her more comfortable. Moving the tray Cook had brought in for her to the other side of the table so he could lay the map out. He placed a small weight at each corner of the map, preventing it from rolling back in on itself. He ran his finger along the map, finding their current location and examining the islands around them. They knew Banning had moved north, if he had just recruited so many new sailors, he was likely going out for some time. Alaric scouted out the islands they would be passing. He doubted Thomas would stop again so soon but he needed to know what islands were closest with plenty of resources in case they needed to anchor at any given time.

"There are so many islands, I had no idea." Molly whispered, she had stepped closer, examining the map he had laid out.

"Aye, many of them are inhabited by sailors and plantation owners. The larger ones have forts and big houses where the Lords and Ladies entertain the Navy and high-ranking soldiers. This is Nassau, I am sure you have heard of it. It holds one of the larger forts, Fort Montagu." He glanced up at her before turning his gaze back to the map.

"And the smaller islands? What do they hold? Do only pirates go to them?" She asked curiously.

"Aye, pirates use them, but we do as well. As well as enemy ships that need to hide supplies that they will collect later." He explained, standing up, stretching his back. Her eyes widened and she stepped back to where she been standing before, a blush showing on her cheeks.

"Why do you use the smaller islands?" She finally said, collecting herself. Alaric felt a pang of regret for startling her again.

He shrugged, "many of the islands have fruit and fresh water that can be collected. They have fair hunting and are prime locations to stop at and make repairs when needed. They also help privateers find pirates and enemy ships, they can host a lot of clues and hideaways if one knows where to look."

"And you know where to look?" She asked, a hint of challenge and curiosity in her voice.

"Aye, lass, I do." He grinned, walking away from the desk and to the far corner in the cabin. He pushed on a plank causing it to slide open.

"Incredible," Molly tried peering around him, but not approaching.

"There are many hidden compartments in the ship." He said, knowing he was piquing her curiosity further. "During a storm or a battle, the ship rocks, and bucks, whatever is not firmly tacked down or secured in a compartment, will be tossed around in the fray." He pulled a hammock out that had been folded up. Grabbing a rope, he began to string it up in the corner. Molly must not have realized what it was at first, she gave no inclination as to how she felt or what she had thought until he began tying up the other end of the hammock. He pressed down in the middle making sure it was firmly secured. He heard a gasp from behind him, he could not help but grin. She obviously believed he would leave his cabin entirely to her. "Don't fret, lass, I will be sleeping in the hammock. You may take the bed," he said, gesturing to the bed and not bothering to wipe the grin from his face.

Anger flashed in her emerald eyes, "How dare you," she exclaimed, the knife appearing again in her hands. Her hair falling about her shoulders, making her appear far more dangerous and wilder than she had a moment ago.

"So that is where you hid your little weapon," his arms crossing over his chest. "I told you before, you have nothing to fear from me. I will cause you no harm, though, I'm not sure I can say you feel the same way. How am I to know you will not use that blade on me whilst I sleep?" Trying desperately to appear concerned for his fate.

She let out an exasperated and unladylike sound. Alaric raised a brow, "Very well, I'll put me knife away but do not dare think of coming near me, do you hear?"

He looked her over, her wavey, copper hair and bright eyes giving her Irish ancestry away. Joseph, one of the younger sailors on his ship was also from Ireland and had the same flaming hair, his accent was not near as strong as Molly's though. Joseph's family had moved from Ireland before he had been born. He had expressed to him and Lucas before, that it had been hard for him to find work, especially onboard ships. He wondered if Molly was finding herself in the same situation. Alaric let out a breath. "You may do as you wish aboard the ship and explore as you wish. As Doc and Cook have already expressed, you are welcome to join them anytime." He said, unsure of what else to say. He headed for the hatch, ducking through it.

10

"Do you know how to play chess, Captain?" Ethan said, speaking to Alaric as he emerged from below deck and onto the quarter deck. He sat on a crate; two more crates angled in front of him. The middle crate held a chess board. Ethan was gathering the pieces and setting them atop the wooden board. The small squares making a pattern of dark and light.

A squawk sounded from above as a large sea bird followed alongside the ship, its slender dark wings, hardly moving as it glided along the breeze. It's bright red throat, being the bird's defining feature. He was not sure what kind of bird it was, but knew it was a common sight around the islands. It dove down towards the deck, hoping to gather up a fallen morsel. "I do, though I will not hesitate to tell you that I haven't played in some time and may not be much of a match." He admitted, taking the seat across from Ethan. His eyes traveling the board, he gently moved a pawn forward.

Ethan grinned, many of the men in the navy knew how to play the game, but only a few of them thought their moves through thoroughly or planned their impending victory, he was curious to see which type of player his captain was. "So, is what I heard true? You have a friend that decided to join you?"

"She's not a friend, in fact, I believe she rather be an enemy at the rate she is going." He lifted his gaze to Ethan's. "Did they tell you what she did?"

Ethan chuckled, "She snuck into your cabin then held a knife to you?" He laughed harder, keeping his eyes on the board. "I would give all my coin to have seen the look on your face."

Alaric scowled, "I admit, I was shocked when I felt the blade, even more shocked when I realized the hand that held it was tiny and delicate, not rough and covered in muck." Alaric moved his knight, capturing Ethan's Rook.

He raised his brows in surprise, he had not anticipated the move. "What would cause a girl that is clearly terrified of being aboard this ship, board it in the first place and insist on staying?"

Alaric shrugged, "I am not entirely sure. She only kept saying she could not stay any longer and that leaving her there would have put her into more danger than taking her with us would." He ran a hand along his jaw. "At first, I did not believe her. She approached me at the dock, and I thought it was all a ploy, but seeing the look in her eyes and how desperate she was, an hour or two ago, I am inclined to believe her. Whatever happened to her or whomever hurt her before must have been after her."

"A husband perhaps? A father?" Ethan inquired, trying to piece it together.

"I am not sure who the person was or if it was more than one man, but I intend to find out." He glanced over at Ethan, "She offered to help out around the ship and to pay. She was a maid on one of the plantations. I am wandering if with her thick accent and her hair the color it is made her life more difficult than it already was. I don't suspect she's had a good go of it from the start, and not just because of her birth."

"Mayhap this plantation owner is the reason for her running away." He said, focused on the game. "Check."
Alaric let out a grunt in response. Reluctantly moving his king to the only remaining space he could. "And that's check mate, Captain. I am impressed, you nearly had me at one point." He said, grinning at Alaric who was staring at the board trying to figure out how he lost the game so suddenly.

Alaric shook his head, "you play a good game, mate." He said, looking about the ship, making sure all was in order. "When we were in Barbados, you mentioned you had to speak with your Admiral."

Ethan walked up the steps of the fort, it was the largest on the island and where the Admiral of the Fleet was currently stationed at. There had been news of a French fleet nearing the islands and his commander had sent word to Ethan asking if he would be available to captain one of the Navy's ships to better scout the area. He felt guilt building inside, he had sworn to protect his country and its allies, at all costs. His duty to his sister's memory, however, was far greater at the moment. He would not rest until he found the man responsible for the attack that night.

Two officers stood at the top of the stairs, just outside the large doors. Their rifles leaned against the stone walls that towered up above them. Ethan tipped his head at them as they saluted. He wore his Captains uniform, a strange feel now that he had gotten used to the lose shirt he wore while aboard *The Trinity* and Banning's ship. The two officers reached out, pulling the heavy doors open and allowing him entrance. Several officers stood in the center of the courtyard, their Lieutenant drilling and training them. He remembered doing much the same when he had first entered into the Navy. He had surprised himself and moved up the ranks faster than he had anticipated he would.

"You must be Captain Clarke," a young Midshipman approached him, saluting, and standing at attention, awaiting Ethan's response.

"That is correct, I am here to speak with the Admiral. Would you please take me to him?" Ethan said, the young man in front of him barely reaching his chest. The lad could be no more than fourteen, he himself had not been much older when he had joined.

"Yes, Captain. Right this way." The Midshipman led the way through the stone fort, gallows stood behind the officers that were training. Ethan had seen his fair share of hangings; he had been responsible for sending more than one pirate to them. He clenched his jaw at the thought, it was never a welcome memory. Reasoning with himself he always came back to the conclusion that if he had not taken those men, they would have killed and plundered more than he wished to imagine.

The Midshipman knocked on a door that stood near the end of the corridor, a deep, commanding voice spoke from inside, bidding them to enter. "Captain Ethan Clarke, Admiral," the boy saluted once more, closing the door behind him as he left.

"I am glad to see you doing so well, Captain. I trust you have not found the man you were looking for?" He asked, cocking his head to the side.

"No, Sir. Unfortunately, I have not had much luck in my search. I joined the crew of The Amity, the Captain of said ship matched the description and temperament of the attacker. He even wore the bracelet I had given Helena before I had left. It could not be him though, Admiral." Ethan explained, he hoped the Admiral would not order him to give up the search for the time being. He had already been on leave for some time and if there was indeed a fleet of French ships heading towards the islands, the Admiral would have just cause to make Ethan stay.

"And why is that? How is it proven he was not the same man?" The Admiral asked, bending over his desk, his hands flat on the map he had been studying. A stern and questioning look in his eye.

"Thomas Banning, the Captain of *The Amity* was just off the coast of Africa during the time of the attack." Ethan took a step forward. "While aboard Banning's ship a fire broke out, I took the blame to spare a young lad from the whip. I was tossed in the brig until *The Trinity* came along to rescue their Captain from Thomas's hold. I was set free with him and allowed to remain part of the crew on Captain Lucas Harding's ship. Not long after, *The Amity* attacked our ship. During the battle I snuck aboard Thomas's vessel, in order to confront him about the bracelet. He was nowhere to be found, however his logbook laid upon his desk. I took it and later saw the proof that he was not in Barbados during that night." Ethan returned the hard gaze, unwilling to waver, the memories of Thomas and his crew causing the anger to rise once more in him.

"I see, and I am thinking you wish to continue your search?" He asked, his bushy brows making his eyes nearly impossible to see.

"Yes, Admiral," He responded simply.

"Follow me, I would like to see if anyone has news on the French fleet as of yet." The Admiral walked around the desk, opening the door and beckoning Ethan to follow.

They made their way up and into the bright sun. The ocean spanning the distance, ships dotting the vast blue horizon. Officers stood positioned at various points, looking over the waters, waiting to spot enemy ships. The large, black cannons were angled in such a way that any ship coming close enough would feel the cannon's gaze on them.

"I admire and I understand the duty you feel towards your sister's memory. I will respect it and allow you to continue your search for her assailant." The admiral turned, meeting

Ethan's steady gaze. "You are a fine Captain and I believe you will easily make Admiral, yourself one day. On your voyage, do not forget who you are and your promise to the Royal Navy." He spoke firmly, his voice holding admiration and reverence.

"I thank you, Admiral. I greatly appreciate your understanding and support in what I must do." He looked out at the sea. "I will try and stay in contact with you as best I can. I could not tell you where we are headed to first or how far we will go but I do know that Captain Stein will not stop until Thomas Banning is found and brought in." In truth, he believed that Alaric would kill the man as soon as he got the chance and would not hold to bringing him in, but he was not about to let the Admiral in on that. "If you do not mind, I will take my leave. I would like to visit my estate a little longer and make sure business there is taken care of before we set sail."

"Of course, I will not keep you any longer. I wish you luck on your journey and may you be able bring this Thomas Banning in to see that he gets what he deserves." They saluted one another, the Admiral turning to speak with one of the officers on duty.

"Is that Captain Clarke I see?" A drawl voice emanated from one of the rooms behind Ethan as he walked through the corridor towards the courtyard.

Alaric let out an exasperated voice. He had hoped to avoid Lieutenant Mason. He turned, facing the officer. "I thought you'd be out patrolling the waters, searching for that French fleet." He said, watching the man push himself off the wall.

"Then again, seeing you here," he waved a hand through the air, "I take it you still have not been made Captain, shame." Ethan replied in mock sympathy.

"Watch it, Clarke. There will come a day where I out rank you. I have been here, doing my duty for the crown while you have been in the company of pirates." He stepped closer, the air in the corridor suddenly feeling heavier. "The admiral will not allow you leave again." His voice challenging and filled with contempt. "I will be keeping a close eye on you while you sail about, one mistake and they will bring you back, you will be stripped of your commands. Perhaps even tried as a pirate yourself."

"You may do as you wish, but know that when I return for good, you will not find me nearly as accommodating." His gaze not wavering, "I hope I have made myself clear, Lieutenant." His voice holding just as much disdain.

Ethan was glad to leave Charles Fort for more than one reason. He and Lieutenant Mason had become officers about the same time. Mason had always disliked Ethan and had tried on more than one occasion to get him in trouble with the commanding officers and had failed. That was not to say the Lieutenant did not have his fair share of allies and followers amongst the ranks. He had done nothing but caused an ongoing headache for him. The other reason he was pleased to leave the fort was a much harder one. He had not spent as much time at his estate as he should, the guilt and pain of the loss of his sister and the rest of his family weighed on him more heavily when he was there. He planned to spend the next couple of days getting the estate's files updated and in order and he did need to collect more clothes and supplies.

He also wanted to bring along his chess set, he rather hoped Alaric or one of the other men aboard T*he Trinity* would know the game.

He was looking forward to sailing out again and was anxious to begin. He knew they would be at sea for some time and was not entirely sure where they would head or what island they would start their search at. Ethan had enjoyed his time on Lucas's ship and knew Alaric was just as good of a Captain. He walked down the dusty path, away from the fort, waving down a carriage to take him to his estate, it was a bit too far to walk although he was glad of the small chance to enjoy some solitude and time to think. He guessed that after the wedding they would sail out. Once on the ship, there would be little time to think or escape into one's thoughts.

"Aye, he gave me leave to continue the search, though I am not sure how much longer he will permit it. There was a fleet of French heading towards Barbados. The Admiral had hoped I would Captain one of the ships to investigate." He shook his head, "if I am unable to identify and locate Helena's attacker by the end of this voyage, I am afraid I will not be able to continue the search."

11

A shout came from up in the rigging, "Ship sighted, Capt'n!" Joseph called down as he began his descent. Molly's head snapped up, her hands gripping at the latch to a compartment she had been rifling through, hoping to find more out about the Irish captain and his crew. They certainly seemed far more respectable than other sailors she had met and neither the captain nor his crew had given her any reason to doubt it thus far. Despite the reassurances though, she was curious to know what business Captain Stein had on the seas. Her fear of falling into another hideous situation terrified her more than she could admit. She remained as still as she could, waiting to hear more, but the mumbled voices from above were too quiet. It was as if the entire deck had frozen. The footsteps above, stalled, all she heard was the waves lapping against the hull of the ship.

The hatch flew open, Captain Stein stood in the entrance. His intimidating figure darkened by the light behind him that filtered brightly through the companionway. The words he spoke, warning her of the upcoming battle and to keep her dirk on her made her body run cold. He had warned her of the dangers of the voyage, but they had not seemed real until that moment. She had fought off the Master and had managed to keep the pirate at the docks off her but doubted she would have the ability or strength to do it again.

The captain's eyes were dark, something hidden in their depths that she could not explain. She shivered, nodding and doing as he told her. Her fingers slid over the bolt that locked the hatch to the cabin. It did little to calm her nerves, but it was a start. Molly could not help but think of what might happen to her if the Irish captain and his crew lost. What would the enemy ship or the pirates do to her if they took the ship? Would they even have a chance, or would they sink The Trinity to the depths without a second glance? She had never been in a ship battle before. She had seen sailors fighting when she was on the island and had heard the shots from their flintlocks, firing in the night. The sounds of the taverns and docks would filter up to the plantation, filling her ears with the terrible ruckus.

"Sharp shooters, to your posts!" Molly heard Captain Stein shout. He had told her that he doubted they would enter into a battle but even when he spoke the words, she knew they were false, and he had known it too. Molly's stomach did a small flip. He had also told her to keep her dirk on her, she realized he had not tried taking it from her, even after she had held it up to him that first day. She felt in the layers of her dress for the knife. Now more grateful than ever that she had taken it. At the time she felt guilty from stealing it from the stall at the port. She had walked right passed the stall, readying to head through the trees and find the captain's ship, when she spotted the knife just lying there on the table at the stall. The keeper of the small shop, know where to be seen. Molly had realized then that she had no means of protecting herself if the captain and his crew turned out to not be the men she hoped. The knife would do little in her untrained hands but at least it was something, more than she had made with before. She grabbed the dirk from the table before she could change her mind, stowing it away in the folds of her dress. It now rested in her hands once more. A blast sounded, but nothing happened, the crew had grown silent once more and it did not seem as if the heavy iron ball had reached the ship, the splash confirming her thoughts. Pressing her ear against the hatch, she listened carefully. *What was happening? Why was it so quiet?* The ship lurched, pressing herself against the hatch, trying not to lose her balance. She had been surprised when she first came on board, just how different it was walking on the planks of the ship. She had forgot how it felt at first, but now remembering having had a hard time keeping herself upright on her voyage from Ireland to the West Indies.

Another blast sounded, this one far louder, making the ship buck slightly. Her ears rang. They had fired. This was it; any minute now cannon balls would splinter their way through the ship, killing or harming more sailors than she wanted to think about. She did not know most of the men and had only met a few of them briefly but she did not wish to see any of them injured, or worse. *What would happen if the captain did not make it through? Would the crew be as welcoming to her as they had been?* She hesitated to admit, her heart and mind telling her not even to think it, but Captain Stein had shown her nothing but kindness. She did not want to think of the possibility that he may get hurt or killed. Pressing a hand to her stomach, she suddenly felt sick. She could not focus on any of it, it would only cause her heartache and fear. Closing her eyes, she backed away from the hatch until she felt her body push up against the far wall. The cannons kept firing. It felt like the terror and carnage would never cease.

"Ready to be boarded!" The words were unmistakable. The rumble of feet and weapons being drawn, drowned out any other words that might have been said. Swallowing hard, she tightened her grip on the dirk in her hand. It's solid, dark hilt making it easy to hold, despite her uncontrollable shaking. Closing her eyes against the sounds above, she wished she could drift off to a peaceful sleep and wake only when it was all over. A tear slipped down her cheek, quickly wiping it away, she stood straighter, she could not give in to the fear, it was only her in the cabin, she was once again all alone. Biting her lip, she took a deep breath in, she had to keep her courage. If a pirate came through the hatch, there would be little she could do. She knew the bolt would not hold for long if they wanted in.

The heavy air around her felt sticky and hot, the sweat beading down her body. Footsteps neared the hatch, raising the knife, she held it out in front of her. Pointing it in the direction of the door, not daring to make a noise. A knock sounded, followed by a familiar, deep voice. A strangled sob escaped her lips, she had not realized how relieved she would be when she found out he was alright. Rushing to the door to unbolt it, she retreated quickly back to her spot in the corner, in case any men from the other ship had hidden below, waiting at a chance to defeat the captain.

The door slowly creaked open, the quiet almost eerie against the sound of the metal hinges straining to open. Captain Stein carefully stepped in, his arms raising. She had not even realized she was still holding the blade, lowering it slightly, but unable to completely relinquish it. She stared at the captain as he approached, his broad shoulders and stormy face frightened her, she would be no match for him. His hand rested on hers, lowering the dirk even more. A small voice inside her telling her not fear him, *if only could believe, if only she could let herself,* she thought.

He coaxed her out the hatch and into the fresh air. It penetrated her lungs with much needed relief. The stifling cabin had been getting too much for her to bare. Her eyes adjusting to the light, traveling over the scene in front of her. Molly did not miss the various looks that were shot her way by the sailors, she suspected it was not common for them to have a woman aboard their ship, especially not one with hair the color of hers. On her voyage from Ireland, she recalled several sailors making comments about her being a woman was bad enough, a woman with hair the color of hers was bound to bring bad luck upon their vessel. The only reason she was not thrown overboard that journey was because the captain had wanted his share of the pay from Lord Willington for delivering her safely. Tucking the tendrils out of her face as best she could, she did her best to ignore the looks and focus on the ship. She had to admit, it was an impressive vessel and larger than the one she had been on before.

Passing through the companionway, Molly could not help but investigate every cabin, and compartment, her curiosity getting the best of her. She felt Captain Stein's presence near her, watching her every move, somehow it felt different. Not like when the butler at the plantation watched her, making sure she did not miss a moment of her work or how her uncle had kept his eye on her, scrutinizing her every movement. The way the captain watched her, made her feel emboldened. She wanted to prove to him as much as she wanted to prove it to herself that she could do this, that she is capable and that there is more out there than the horrors and trials she has had to live.

Brushing her hair from her face, she walked ahead, something smelled familiar. She could not quite place it. It was not like the rest of the smells aboard the ship. It did not smell of stale air or unwashed bodies. Stepping into another cabin, this one much larger than the others they had passed, she let out a gasp. She had not expected to see animals aboard the ship.

"I did not realize…" She whispered, taking a slow step forward, not wanting to startle the beasts. She felt her heart lighten at the sight of the animals. She had not thought she would see another animal from the barns in quite some time. She took a deep breath in, now realizing what that familiar scent had been. She could feel the smile slowly appearing on her lips. Molly sensed the captain's eyes on her. For once she did not mind, she felt at ease and safe. Reaching a handout, she stroked the cow's velvety nose.

12

Alaric ducked in through the hatch, a quick knock before he entered his cabin. Molly jumped, one of the panels in the wall was open. Her face turning pink at being caught snooping. Alaric raised a brow, trying to suppress a grin, he had guessed she might do as much.

"A ship is heading for us; I suspect there will be a battle. I ask that you stay in here, you will be safe." He said, not sure if he was trying to reassure the lass or himself. He had no doubt that they would be able to take the ship that was heading for him, but he was worried about the possibility of a stray cannon ball tearing through the cabin. "I take it you still have that knife hidden away somewhere?" He asked, his eyes traveling the length of her. "I don't believe you will need it but do keep it on you," he added. "Bolt the door behind me," he said, turning and glancing over his shoulder, he wanted to comfort her, but did not know what more he could say. Her eyes were wide with fear, she held tight to her middle, her flaming hair cascading about her shoulders as he left the cabin. He paused just outside, waiting to make sure Molly locked the door as she had been instructed to do. She was no fool, he knew that, but he feared she would try and do something brave or reckless and end up putting herself or his crew in danger.

Alaric blinked, his eyes quickly adjusting to the light, the sky was as blue as the waters around them. "Pull 'em in! Half sail!" He shouted, passing the crew as they yanked the sails in, slowing the ship down. Approaching Ethan, he grinned, as different as it was on a Navy ship, he could tell Ethan was in his element and just as ready for the battle as he was. He heard the blast from the pirate ship, the smoke filled the thick, damp air. His grin broadened; he knew very well that the shot would fall short. Turning towards Shorty, he gave the signal. The sails flipped down; Eddie yanked the helm. *The Trinity,* turned to the side, it's cannons now aimed directly at the enemy ship. "Fire!" Alaric bellowed, the planks beneath his feet shook.

Alaric's jaw clenched; the shots were high from the enemy vessel. He gauged where the next shots would hit, if he was right, it would strike directly in the middle of the hull. Not only would it cause far more damage to their ship, but it meant it was more likely a stray shot would rip through his cabin. His hands now gripping the helm, the water pulled hard against the wheel. He could feel the ship shift to the side, the shots fired once again, he yelled for his crew to get down. The heavy shots sped over the deck, narrowly missing the crew and masts. He let out a breath, they were now close enough to board, it would soon be over. Leaping down, he readied himself for the battle in front of him. The men from the enemy ship scrambled across the planks and swarmed the deck of *The Trinity*. Alaric glanced about the ship, keeping a close eye on his crew, he noted Ethan next to him as the captain pirate strode across the plank, his face hard and focused on Ethan and Alaric.

"Which one of ye be da Capt'n o' this vessel?" The man spat out, his voice as rough and grainy as the sandy beaches. His sword tight in his grip, his eyes, stone grey and fixated on the two men in front of him.

Alaric shrugged, "Why don't you fight us both," he said, waving his blade in the air between them, "and then tell us which one of us you think is Captain." His grinned broadened, Ethan groaned but could not hold back his own smile. He had seen Lucas and Alaric antagonize the enemy on more than one occasion, causing the already fierce and angry man to get far more furious.

Ethan watched the other captain, his dark hair long and unkept. A chain hung from his neck, a large medallion dangling from it. The man laughed gruffly, the sound more like a strangled gurgling noise. "Verra weel. If that be what you wishin'," he replied, carefully circling the men, like a large cat, readying to pounce. Ethan adjusted his stance. He had fought many men like the sailor that eyed him now, as part of the Royal Navy, he had to take on countless pirates and other enemy vessels, though typically they fought ships from enemy countries and let the privateers take on the pirates. The enemy captain grunted, spitting on the wooden planks that they stood on. Alaric spun his sword around in his hand, the blade making a whirling sound as it sliced through the air. Ethan stepped forward, not quite lunging but enough of a movement to cause the pirate to block. The captain made his move, jabbing his blade towards Ethan's chest, he jumped back, not bothering to bring his sword up, knowing the blade would not hit its mark.

"Going to have to make more of an effort than that," Ethan chided. Stepping to the side, raising his sword in the last moment, deflecting the other blade off his own.

"The grip on your sword is much too tight," Alaric added, drawing the man's attention to him once more. The pirate raised his blade, bringing it down with such force it made Alaric take a step back, their swords meeting, the metal clanging together.

Ethan slapped the flat end of his blade against the enemies back, the pirate spun around, slicing his sword at Ethan's belly, the blade catching the fabric, his shirt gaped open. Ethan raised a brow at Alaric, "that was not very nice of him."

Alaric roared with laughter, "no, I don't believe it was, mate."

Ethan lunged at the pirate, their blades screeching together. Ethan flinched at the eerie sound. "Have you made your guess yet? Which of us, pray tell, is the captain?" Ethan spoke between clenched teeth. Shoving forward, into the sailor, he was able to pull his sword free from the force of the other blade.

"Aye, I have. I don't much care for either of you bastards though." He said, pulling his flintlock from his belt and aiming it at Alaric, his blade still at the ready in the other hand. Ethan leapt forward, kicking the hilt of the sword into the pirate's middle, the shot fired, followed by a howl. The pirate captain staggered back, Alaric pressed closer, a look of rage on his face, the tip of his blade firmly pressing into the throat of the captain. A trickle of blood dripped from the area. Ethan moved forward unsure of what the pirate might try next, his arm covered in crimson blood that steadily flowed down, dripping onto the deck. The battle around them had ceased, *The Trinity,* the victors.

"I will only ask you once and I expect you to think hard on your answer." The pirate's back pinned against the wall near the hatch that led below, Alaric's blade leaving him no choice but to stand and listen. "Have you seen a ship, *The Amity,* captained by a man named Thomas Banning? They are said to be headed north, the very direction your ship sailed from." Alaric gripped the man's shirt, forcing his captive to swallow hard against the blade.

"Aye," he choked out, "they be headed that way and I ain't tellin' you more." He eyes unwavering.

"Very well," Alaric grinned, patting the cheek of the pirate. Ethan nodded, knowing that was all the information they needed anyway. "Ethan, Shorty," Alaric said, "take our captain friend and his crew to the brig of their ship. Lock them in it, then gather any supplies we might need to repair our ship." Alaric commanded, releasing the captain from his grip.

Ethan nodded, his flintlock pointing at the pirate captain, his blade in his other hand. He had wondered at what Alaric would do; he knew Alaric did not wish to waste any time sending the prize ship back. It could take a week or more to bring a prize ship in and meet with the governor. Locking the crew in their own brig left them at the mercy of any other ship that might pass. With their colors still flying, a navy or privateer ship would be able to easily spot them and take them in themselves. And seeing as how the navy was patrolling the waters more vigilantly, expecting to find the French fleet, it was likely they would stumble upon the captured pirates.

He dismissed his crew to lock the remaining pirates up and to begin repairs. He was anxious to make sure Molly was unharmed. He grimaced, he had never considered having to guard and protect a woman aboard his ship before and was not entirely sure he was enjoying the responsibility. Even when Catherine had been aboard *The Trinity,* most of the duty fell upon Lucas, though he would never have let harm come to her, it had not been his concern. There was only one other time he had been tasked with taking care of and protecting a lass. It had been when he and Lucas were commissioned in the Royal Navy. An admiral's young and beautiful daughter was on her way back to England to spend the season with her aunt and uncle. Her younger cousin was being presented at court and needed another chaperone. Alaric had been charged with the task of being her sole protector on her journey. He had certainly not minded at the time and had rather enjoyed their flirtatious banter along the voyage. It was late at night when the bells rang, shouts called to beat to quarters. A pirate ship had been spotted. The shots screamed out, he stood in the cabin with the young woman, not doubting for even a minute that his shipmates would be able to fend off the enemy. It was not long after he heard his captain yell out orders and preparing the men for the upcoming onslaught that he heard the swords clanking together and muskets being fired. There was a banging at the cabin door, his sword was drawn. The latch would not hold, Alaric had known it, it flew open, allowing a rough, disturbing sailor to enter the small cabin. He had easily defeated the brute and knew they could not stay in the small cabin any longer, if more men came, there was not enough room to fight. He had peered around the frame of the door, making sure no one else had found their way down. Alaric quickly yanked the young woman down the passage to hide amongst the spare sails, something the pirates would be less likely to look twice at, but it had been too late.

"Molly," He called out, knocking on the door. "It's over, lass. You are safe and can unlock the hatch." He heard a shuffle from behind the door before the metal scraped across the wood as she undid the latch. He expected her to open the door, but it remained shut. Carefully opening the hatch, he slowly entered the room, spotting the girl standing in the corner, her dirk pointing directly at his chest. He groaned; he was beginning to feel tense about the lass repeatedly point-ing a weapon at him in his own cabin. He clenched his jaw, raising his hands in a feeble attempt to calm her. "It's alright. The battle is over, and the men are repairing the ship as we set off." He looked her over as best he could in the dim cabin light, "Are you unharmed?" He asked, gently taking a step forward, he could see the blade shaking fearfully in her hands.

Nodding just enough for him to catch the slight movement. He moved forward, his eyes not straying from hers. "What of the pirates?" Her voice barely audible, the knife slowly lowering, though not enough for him to feel comfortable.

He came up beside her, gently placing his hand over hers. The knife seized it's shaking. He realized her fingers had long since lost their tightened grip. "They are all locked away in the brig of their own ship and we have already pulled away from them." He replied in a husky whisper. He felt a mixture of frustration and guilt at the look of fear on her face and did not know how to take that away or if it would be wise to try. He stood and held out his hand, "come, why don't you come on deck and get a bit of fresh air, it will make you feel better, and I can show you around the ship, so you do not have to stay in here the entire voyage."

She gazed up at him, hesitating, she nodded, though refusing his hand. Placing the knife on the desk, he led her out the hatch. She blinked at the sunlight that cast down upon the deck of the ship. A few of the sailors paused their work to catch a glimpse of the lass that had stowed away on their ship. Alaric's gaze turned as stormy as the waters beneath them, warning the crew to keep to themselves. He led her to the bow, lines crossing this way and that as the men about them scrambled up and down the rigging, repairing the damage that had been done.

"There are so many ropes," her voice holding more than a little surprise. "How do they know what rope goes to what part of the ship?" She asked, gently running her hand along one of them.

"Aye, the sailors learn fast enough. It does not take long before they know the lines like they know their own body. Each man has a specific place they are needed, task that is assigned to them. They all know the running of the ship and all work together to make it sail correctly. Not much different than how a large plantation estate is run, I suspect."

Molly scoffed in reply, "aye, we all know the runnings of the estate but do not all work together." Frustration and pain in her voice.

He heard a small gasp escape her, he followed her eyes, spotting what had caused her brief shock. "He will be alright. See the rope tied about his middle?" Alaric pointed to the sailor that was dangling precariously over the water from the bowsprit. "If he were to fall, he would get nothing more than a slight soaking before his shipmates pulled him up."

"But what is he doing out there?" She asked, taking a step closer to get a better look.

"Fixing the spot where a cannon ball hit." He explained, his eyes focused on the lass next to him. "Would you like me to show you the rest of the ship?" He offered, holding his arm out in front of him as he turned.

"Oh aye, tis much larger than I had thought." She replied, staring up into the rigging and amongst the sails that billowed above them.

Alaric grinned, "I thought you would have become well aware of how big the ship was when you climbed up the side of it to sneak into my cabin." He looked down at her, her face now matching the shade of her hair.

"I…well…that is, I suppose I didn't get a good enough look at the whole of it." She murmured, twisting her hands together and watching her feet move her forward across the deck and to the hatch that led below.

"Ethan," he called out, causing Molly to halt in surprise. Clearly, she had not thought he would introduce her to any of the crew. "I'd like to introduce you to Miss Molly Maclean." He said, not missing the teasing look on his friend's face. "Captain Clarke here is one of the highly esteemed Captains in the Royal Navy," Alaric raised a brow, was the lass merely intimidated by the other captain or was it something he had said the brought the fear back to Molly's eyes?

"The pleasure is all mine." He said, bowing at her, only causing the shock on her face to spread. Once you get fully settled in and used to the ship, I hope that you will join me on deck sometime and tell me just how surprised our captain, here, looked when you held that blade of yours to him."

"Oh, I…" her words suddenly cut off.

"Don't you be worryin' none about them two boys, lass." Ol' Shorty said, giving a stern look to both men as if they had just been scolded by their father. "If they be buggin' you any, you just come tell me and Ol' Shorty here will set them straight." He said, tucking his hands into the pockets of his pants, his eyes traveling between the three of them.

Molly choked out a laugh, quickly placing a hand over her mouth and looking down at the deck again. "I thank ye."

"Yes, thank you," Alaric said, sarcasm ringing in his voice. "If you two *gentlemen,* will excuse us, we will finish our tour of the ship now." Alaric said, quickly leading Molly down through the hatch, the two men left howling with laughter.

Alaric watched Molly take in all the ship, he did not miss

the small shutter that wracked her body as they passed by the cannons that sat at the ready. "Try not to worry much." He paused, realizing he was about to tell her he did not except many more fights, but knew it was not the truth. He wanted to comfort her and calm the fears he saw rising in her. It would not be right of him or fair to her though if he did not tell her the truth. Letting out a breath, he continued, "I told you before, that this particular voyage was not going to be an easy one. We do not even have a destination at the moment. I expect there to be many more battles and likely ending in a rather more dangerous one." He watched the emotions fade from her face, a hint of fear lingering in her eyes, a look a determination taking over.

Her chin sticking out slightly, "Aye, you mentioned that. I will no be changin' me mind though. Right now, the farther we sail away, the longer I am on this ship, the safer I'll be." Pausing she swallowed, standing up straighter, the top of her head still barely reaching above his chest. "Even with all o' the battles you expect, it'll be safer still." Turning, she continued down the hall, not giving him a chance to argue. He ached to learn the reason for her fleeing. To feel safer on a ship full of men she did not know, to willingly stay aboard a vessel destined for battle, not many reasons came to mind at what would cause her to choose that path. He followed her as she glanced into each of the cabins, examining briefly the contents inside. Mostly, spare cloth, lines, sails and cannon balls lined the rooms. Crates and barrels filled with various goods and supplies were stacked neatly together, secured by netting to be sure they would not be flung around in a storm or battle.

"Oh, I hadn't expected…" her words faded as she slowly

approached the cow that stood in a stall in the middle of a large cabin. She looked about the room, walking from the different pens, holding out her hand for the goats to stiff. "I had no idea animals were kept aboard ships." She exclaimed; excitement clear in her voice.

"Aye, we have chickens, goats and the cow. When we reach land, we try and let them out to stretch their legs and move around. It helps with the milk production and keeps them healthy." He looked her over, her hands now on either side of the cow's face, their noses near to touching. "Do you have much experience with animals, Miss Maclean?"

She shrugged, "a bit, I guess you can say." She replied, moving over to the chickens, "I used to hide in the barn at the plantation I worked at. There were times when I could not risk going back up to the big house. I spent many nights, curled up next to the horses." Her shoulders dropped slightly, "the animals are the one living thing that has no tried to harm me." Alaric raised a brow, surprised at the confession. "The ol' man that took care of the animals on the plantation taught me much about them. I enjoyed it." She let out a squeal, "Well, look at that, I suppose you'll be eating these to break your fast in the mornin'." She said, holding up three freshly laid eggs.

Alaric chuckled, unable to take his eyes from the sight in front of him. "Aye, I suspect I will." He replied. He had not expected her to be so fond of the animals. Cook of course used the animals for the eggs, milk, and meat, he even tried making cheese with the milk from the goats, but it was one of the younger lads that was always tasked with cleaning out the pens and seeing to their wellbeing. It was often a joke amongst the crew on who would end up with the duty that day as none of the sailors were fond of it; usually saying they took to sailing rather than farming. "If it suits you, you are welcome to spend as much time with them as you like."

She glanced between him and the chicken she now held in her arms. "Aye, that'll suit me well, I imagine. Thank ye." Her eyes remained fixed on the plump bird that lay perfectly contented in her arms.

Alaric cleared his throat, "Would you prefer to stay here a bit longer? I can take the eggs to Cook." He offered, turning his body towards the cabin's exit.

"I should like to say hello to Cook again. If you'll show me to the galley, I can bring him the eggs," she responded, placing the chicken back down on the straw filled pen. Small boxes sat at the back for the hens to roost and lay their eggs in comfortably.

Alaric simply nodded, turning fully to lead the way to Cook's.

13

"Please don't do this. You can 'ave anything you want aboard my ship." The man pleaded. His arms held out in front of him as he laid on the planking of the deck, half propped up against the railing. His leg had already been badly sliced from the short battle that had preceded. Men were sitting or lying about the deck, if not already dead, then severely injured. Thomas's crew had spotted the frigate, a mere merchant vessel, hanging low in the water. They attacked the unprepared ship without warning, all but sinking it to the depths. The only reason it had not fully sunk was for the shallows that lay just off the shore of the small, tree lined islands.

"No, you are correct," Thomas waved his flintlock through the air dramatically. "I should not kill you, after all, what could you or your crew do to me and mine?" He asked, raising his brows, his gaze sweeping the deck of fallen sailors. "Mink, see to it that anything of value is taken from this ship and taken directly to my cabin. I wouldn't want any items missed," he said, looking at the sailor that stood next to him, turning to give the order to the rest of the crew. Thomas looked back at the merchant captain that lay on the deck, fear still showing in his eyes, but slowly being replaced by relief. "Oh, and Mink, make sure there are no survivors." The sailor nodded, signaling to the rest of Thomas's crew to obey the same order. Raising his pistol once more, the shot fired, followed by several more and the sounds of swords digging deep into the fallen men.

Turning, he looked about the ship, they had taken a couple others before this and did not need any more provisions. Often times though, merchants were tasked with bringing, jewels and items of great value with them, as well as the occasional passenger. He did not wish to miss out on any precious cargo that might be aboard any of the vessels they encountered. He watched his men rummage through the pockets of the dead sailors and scavenge the ship for any possible treasures. Stepping across the planking and onto his ship he glanced up at Grady who had been watching the scene unfold from the helm. "Be sure they do as directed, once done, prepare to continue North."

"Aye, Capt'n." He replied, a smile spreading across his malicious face.

He ducked in through the hatch and into his cabin, tearing off his sweat and blood-soaked shirt he tossed it aside. He'd have the cabin boy try and clean it later. He doubted the blood would wash away, as it usually stuck to the fabric like a dye, but it would keep the lad from getting up to mischief. Something in the boy's expression had reminded him of himself not so long ago. Reaching for the pitcher of water on the table that sat in the corner, he poured the contents over himself, ignoring the sailors that came and went, bringing anything of value to his cabin for him to examine.

"Cap," a gruff voice sounded from behind him.

"What is it, Mink? Is all the needed cargo off the other ship?" He asked walking over to the pile of goods that had been brought in.

"Aye, though not all of it be in your cabin, Capt'n." He replied, his gaze unwavering.

Thomas stepped forward, "What do you mean it's not all in my cabin?" He asked, his expression hard.

"I mean to say, Cap, that one of the crew took a bit for 'imself." His said, his voice just as stern, his fingers wrapping around the belt that stretched across his wide waist.

"Which crew member?" Thomas's face was now inches from the other man's.

"Cam," Mink replied, "I saw 'im clear as day, taking a jeweled ring from the merchant captain's desk and pocketing it."

"I see," Thomas said, his face turning a cruel red color. "Take me to him." He spat between clenched teeth. Mink nodded, turning and leading Thomas through the narrow hatch. Thomas felt his rage surging. He did not take to being defied or challenged, the sailor would pay the price and any crewmember that stood up for the unfortunate soul would be punished alongside him. Mink did not hesitate, he grabbed Cam by the shoulder, whipping him around to face Thomas who stood there, his arms crossed against his chest. "I hear tell that you have something that is in fact, mine." He challenged.

The sailor's eyes grew wide, he glanced between the two men that stood facing him. Mink squeezed his shoulder harder, digging his fingers into the tender flesh. "Answer your Capt'n." He snarled.

"I...I don't know what you mean, sir." The sailor stammered, wincing at the pain being inflicted on his shoulder.

"Empty your pockets!" Thomas bellowed, quickly losing his patience. "It'll be far more painful for you if Mink here, has to empty them for you." He jerked his head in the burly man's direction, a slow smile spreading on his face.

The sailor dug his fingers into his pockets, pulling out a bit of string, worn cloth and a ring. "I only meant to keep it safe, I had planned to hand it directly over to you but did not get a moment to and then, well, then I forgot." He said in desperation.

"Now you have your *moment*," he replied sardonically. "I suggest you hand it over at once." Thomas held his hand out to the man. Quickly placing the ring in Thomas's hand, he tried in vain to move back, and out of range of Thomas's wrath, but Mink's hold was firm. Thomas let his gaze travel over the sailor. He recognized him as being one of the men that did not pull his weight as well, and was no skilled fighter, making him near useless in his mind. Now he had an excuse to rid the ship of him. "Strap a pair of cannon balls to his feet. Hang him from the bowsprit and let the sea monsters below get a few good whiffs of the coward." He watched the man pale, as the ropes were wrapped tightly around his ankles. The crew carried him towards the bowsprit, where they tied the other end of the rope to.

"You are a bastard, Thomas Banning. You are no Capt'n, just another bloody bastard like the rest of us!" Cam shouted out, lifting his head, just enough to lock eyes with Thomas. A splash sounded, followed by the commands of the men yanking the sailor up, his body bloodied from the barnacles that clung to the bottom of the ship. A strangled moan barely audible over the waves that engulfed him once more.

Thomas twisted the ring around in his hand, grinning. It would fetch a more than fair price, that is, if he chose to part with it.

14

"Alaric," Ethan said, heading towards him. "I hope you do not mind me saying, but during the battle, I had noticed a few of the sailors that were manning the cannons, were not completely sure on what they were doing and a couple of times, even fired too early or too late." He paused, clearly judging Alaric's reaction. It was bold of him to confront a captain about his crew's skills, but Alaric knew he was growing restless and needed to keep his mind occupied and off how he would find Helena's attacker if Thomas does not speak up or if he does not even get a chance to. "I would like to assist the Master Gunner in running the sailors through a few lessons, practices, if you do not mind. I expect we will see more battle and I would like to help get the crew ready."

Alaric nodded, "Aye, I did notice that as well." He replied, tilting his head towards Ethan. He had no problem with Ethan helping to better prepare the men. "I would be glad to have you work with the crew on speed and accuracy. They certainly do seem a bit rusty, a few well-honed practices will do them good." Looking about the ship, watching the crew move about the deck and rigging.

"Thank you," His gaze falling over the men around them, "I will have the Master Gunner call his crew to quarters." He said, turning and heading towards Jim, his boots scrapping against the wooden planks below his feet. Alaric saw the relief and excitement on Ethan's face. He had been doing as much as he could around the ship, but it was not enough.

"Jim, gather your gunnery crew" he said, approaching the man who was elbow deep in black powder from cleaning the many guns on deck. He wiped his arm across his face, causing the black to smear from the mix of sweat and gun powder. The young man raised his brows, setting the musket he had been cleaning, down, "we are going to run them through some practices to better their time and aim." Ethan explained.

Jim nodded, "Aye, Sir." He replied, clearly just as exuberant as Ethan was about getting the men better prepared. If the gunnery crew was the very best, they could be, it would mean the difference between loss and defeat. He had watched his crew, these last few battles. Alaric knew how well the entire ship worked together and knew even the slightest signals, he gave during battle, not many vessels moved the way *The Trinity* did under command of even the most skilled captains. It was impressive and intimidating, and he was proud Ethan wanted to be a part of it. Ethan had spoken of how he had captained ships many times but never had a crew so competent, and if he could help these sailors better their gunnery skills, he would do everything he could. Heading through the hatch, Alaric looked over the cannons, they were very well taken care of and in near perfect condition. The sailors began pouring in through the hatch, lining up, a few crewmates at each cannon. A couple of the youngest sailors, not yet ready to handle the cannons, readied themselves for gathering the powder and cannon balls. Ethan nodded his approval, looking over the crew and to Jim. Alaric stepped off to the side, anxious to see what knew tactics Ethan could bring to the board.

"During the last battle we were in, I noticed, a few of you, lads, aren't quite matching the timing." He said, his arms crossed over his broad chest, a dark vest buttoned over his lose fitting shirt. His voice echoed through the long cabin. "Our Captain expects to see quite a few more battles before this voyage is done," he paused, his gaze traveling over the crew in front of him, a few of the sailors squirmed uncomfortably as his eyes rested briefly on them. "If we expect to see ourselves through these next few months, we need to be the best gunners we can. Our shots need to be accurate, and our timing cannot fail us." His voice grew louder as he spoke.

"Right, you heard the man," Jim bellowed, "git the powder and ball ready." He said, pointing at the younger sailors that stood off to the side, nearly hidden in the shadows. "The rest of ye, let's show 'im what you've got."

Ethan watched, observing every movement the crew made, judging where they slowed and what areas they needed to show improvement in. Long, wooden rods pushed the powder filled bags to the base of each cannon. The supplies were well stocked, and the canvas cloths were filled adequately with the powder. "Faster!" His voice thundered through the cabin, causing one of the younger lads, to jolt, nearly tripping against the hard cannons. "On your feet!" He said, the boy's face flushing, "in battle there will be many distractions and terrors, expect them and prepare for them." Ethan said, walking down the passage, watching each sailor do their job in getting the heavy guns loaded. "Those cloths are too big," he said, pointing towards a piece of old fabric that was meant to go in next.

"What, happens if the cloth is too big?" A young lad, no more than seventeen asked. His shirt was torn at the shoulder and needed mending. His hair loosely tied back. He stood to the side, waiting to pass an iron ball to the loader. Alaric smiled, any sailor that asked questions and showed initiative, was bound to be a well-trained and trustworthy crewmember.

Ethan turned his attention to the lad, his voice still loud enough for all to hear. Alaric appreciated the question and knew most of the men on these ships, even on navy ships, learned what was needed to be done, even mastered the skills but did not know the reasoning behind the tasks and skills. "Optimal pressure is wanted, to fire that ball," he said, pointing to the rounded iron in the lad's hands, "as deeply and accurately into the enemy's ship as possible. For that to happen, every bit that goes into the bore needs to be measured with just as much accuracy." He grabbed the cloth, ripping a strip of it off, handing it to the sailor next to him, then looking at the lad, "better the cloth be too small than too big." He nodded to him, encouraging the men to continue. The cannon balls slid to the back smoothly, awaiting their shattering exists.

Ethan caught sight of one of the sailors, readying to fire, "Hold fast," he said, stepping forward, his hand up. "Sailor, I did not see you puncture the powder bag. Ian, is it?" Alaric stepped forward, eyeing the sailor.

"Aye, Sir," he replied, his feet shuffled uneasily, glancing over at Alaric.

"Best of luck trying to get it to fire properly." His eyes traveling over the crew again. "Do not skip any of the steps, lads, it could cost yourself and the crew their lives." He said, his voice stern. Nodding to Ian who quickly punctured the powder bag. Ethan turned to Jim, "give the order, Master Gunner."

"Fire!" His voice traveling down the hall, each cannon, roared as the ball was expelled with such force, it caused the cannons to leap backwards, stopping only once they hit the ropes that restrained them and readied them for the next set of loading. A few sailors rushed forward, wet cloth and sponges set on the end of long, sturdy sticks. They quickly wiped the barrels clean, making it safe once more for the next set of powder and ball.

"Well done," he grinned, several of the men cheering in response. He pulled his watch out from the pocket of his vest, "Now, let's see if you can better your time."

"You look pleased," Alaric said. He had stayed and watched the first round of the practice. Ethan walked through the hatch and into the cabin. "I take it the crew did well the remainder of the session?" He let out a laugh, I could hear your commands from in here, I reckon you had the younger lads just about pissing themselves in fear."

Ethan smirked, "not quite, though a few trembled a bit." He pulled the chair out from the desk, opposite Alaric, "Where is the fair Miss Maclean?" He asked, looking around the room for any sign of the lass.

Alaric shrugged, "she has taken to the livestock. Apparently, she has a soft spot for the animals and often sought their solace at the plantation she worked at." His brows furrowed, "she mentioned how she would hide in the barn and spent many nights in there. I'm beginning to truly wonder if the master of the plantation caused her harm."

Ethan accepted the glass of whiskey his captain held out to him, "It is very likely, many of the plantation owners are unkind and often times brutal."

"She does know more than a bit about the animals, I told her she is welcome to care for them as long as she is aboard the ship. She was pleased, and it will give the lads a break from having to deal with the beasts." He explained, raising the glass to his lips. "You didn't happen to bring your chess set with you, did you?"

"As a matter of fact, I did." Pulling the rolled-up set from the inside of his vest and laying it out on the desk in front of them.

"So, Captain? What next?" Ethan asked, his eyes still fixed on the small wooden figures on the board.

"Keep heading north, confronting the ships we can. In a few days' time we will be near some islands, we can let the animals out to graze and mayhap there will be signs of *The Amity*." His fingers gripping a small player, moving it forward to strike its enemy. "There are several hideouts on the islands, if Thomas stopped at any of them, we will see the signs."

"Aye, he certainly seems to leave his mark wherever he goes." His voice hard, the pink, raised lashes on his back had healed better than he expected, thanks to the efficient work from Doc and Miss Catherine, but he knew the light scars would always be there. Not to mention, more than one sailor they had spoken to the last several days had talked about Banning's destruction.

"I doubt whatever we may find will be a pleasant sight, not if Thomas had a hand in it." Alaric added.

"And what if we see no signs of the man? What will the plan be then? According to the pirates, we are on the correct course, but who's to say Banning doesn't make a turn to circle back to the West Indies?" Ethan knew they had little choice, stay the course until another ship came by or they see signs of Banning at the islands they would be stopping at in a few days.

"Not much we can do. Hope to meet with other ships, though I rather not do many battles, I doubt we will have any other choice. Other ships and the coming islands are our best bet, from there, I will make a decision if we have no further information on the bastard." A grin played on his lips, "check, Captain Clarke."

A laugh emanated from the man sitting across from him. "Our supplies are well stocked and once we reach the islands, it is probable there will be sources of fresh water to replenish our barrels. We could continue the search without having to return to the West Indies." He said, turning the subject back to their voyage. He was reluctant to return, if he did, his commander would get wind of the news that he was back and would not allow him to return to *The Trinity* to continue his search for Banning.

"Aye, and I do not think Thomas will return there so hastily. He will still be wanting to keep in the shadows a bit longer." Alaric eyed the board; his opponent having out maneuvered him once more. "Even when distracted by thoughts of vengeance, you play a good game." He said, sitting back in his chair, "I actually thought I had you a moment ago." His eyes fixating on the hatch as it slowly opened.

"I apologize, I did not realize you were in here." Molly said, her face flaming, fumbling with the hatch in an attempt to close it and flee the cabin.

"Miss Maclean, it's perfectly…" Alaric's words fell short as the hatch clicked shut with such force, he was sure the bolt would come off.

"A bit skittish, I'd say," Ethan laughed, shaking his head. "I'll leave you to it." He said, rolling the chess set up again.

"It's rather infuriating if you ask me." He replied, annoyance in his voice. "I have been nothing but civil, yet the lass acts as if I've taken a belt to her backside."

"I admit, I am a bit surprised. I was under the impression from Lucas that you were the one that always charmed the ladies. It would appear, either your brother lied, or you have lost your touch." Ethan said, doing his best to keep the grin from his face.

Alaric grunted in return, pouring himself another generous glass of whiskey. "We will see about that."

15

"I thought you might have fled back down here." Alaric said, his voice low. "You needn't fear me or any of the men aboard my ship." He knew it was futile to say so, as he had told her it before, but he felt the need to reassure her once more. "Ethan and I were but playing a game of chess. As I said before, you are welcome to roam the ship as you wish, though I do suggest you stay clear of the men's sleeping quarters." He tried lightening the mood, "it is not the most pleasant of areas, I expect our little farm here," he said gesturing at the animals around them, "smells better than that lot." He cleared his throat, placing a hand on the cow's snout. He watched Molly, her flaming hair falling in thick waves about her shoulders, a spotted colored hen resting comfortably in her lap, her face remaining somber.

"It wasn't that you and Captain Clarke were sitting there," she replied, her words barely audible. "It was that I disobeyed. I should never have entered your cabin without permission. I apologize. I had not meant to interrupt." Her body visibly shaking.

"Without permission?" He asked, shifting his weight,

moving closer in order to hear her better. If it was not for the fear on her face he would have laughed. "I seem to remember you already did enter my cabin without my permission once before and nothing too terrible happened after." He raised a brow, waiting to see if she would challenge this. Her sudden fear of being reprimanded for disobeying baffled him. She had not seemed to care much in the past and he did not believe for one minute that was what truly caused her reaction.

"Aye, but that had been different. I had been desperate!" Her voice strained and pleading, as if she were afraid that he would now change his mind and not be so kind about her stowing away. "I had no other choice then. Tonight though, I entered, knowing you might have been in there. Knowing it is your cabin and I did no' even knock." She stood up, her arms rigid at her sides. This time it was her that held the challenging look. She opened her mouth about to say more but thought better of it. Her outburst causing the hens around her feet to scatter. "It will not happen again, Captain. It t'would be best if I stay down here. I thank you for offering to share your cabin, but I am better suited to stay in here." She explained, lifting her chin just slightly. "I will be out of sight and out of the way."

Alaric stood motionless. He had not anticipated the terror in her voice or the suggestion she presented him with. He was appalled he even considered such a notion. How could she believe for one moment he would allow her to remain down with the livestock? To take her meals and sleep with them. It was perfectly alright for her to tend to them, but he had not suspected she would say such a thing. Alaric felt his own emotions rising at the look on her face. Her eyes told him a lot, but the tears spoke louder. "I see." Anger being the greater of the emotions that ran through him. She was keeping more than merely her past from him. He would wager it was far more complicated than he had originally thought. The fear upon her face when she had spotted him and Ethan in the cabin was enough to confirm his growing suspicions.

"How can you? You know nothing. Nothing of me, nothing of what those Lords are capable of. Nothing of what I have had to do or live with." Her voice quavering with distress.

He stepped forward, his jaw clenched, "you are correct when you say I know nothing of you or what has happened in your life to make you fear so." He let out a breath taking another step nearer her, her eyes widened. She glanced about the room. Her only way of exiting, laying behind the captain.

"I'm not going to harm you." His voice coming out in a husky whisper. Alaric slowly stepping back, hoping to settle her. "Miss Maclean, I cannot understand you or protect you unless you tell me what you are running from or what it is you have had to do." Saying the last bit pointedly. "I also will remind you that you are aboard a privateer ship, Miss Maclean, not a passenger ship. I do not believe any of my crew will harm you, but I cannot allow you sleep or eat in here." Her body shook, more tears flooding her eyes, a small noise escaping her lips, causing the cow next to her to spook in surprise. Alaric looked her over, unsure if her tears flowed out of relief or fear.

"Shhh, I'm sorry lassie, it's alright," Molly whispered, stroking the heifer.

A grin spread across Alaric's lips, "I couldn't have said it better." He leaned himself up against the wall, goats walking about his feet. His eyes traveling over her, puzzled at how the spirited young woman he had witnessed before could change so rapidly into a gentle, carrying lass, now hiding behind the cow that stood between them.

"I cannot say." The sound of her soft accent breaking the silence. "That is, I don't 'ave the words, not just yet."

"I can understand that" he paused, "but when you do, have the words, I am just as good at listening as your animals are." He said, stepping away from the livestock and towards the companionway. He waited, seeing if the lass would follow him. A smile playing on his lips as she emerged from behind the large cow, carefully stepping through the gate, being sure not to let any of the goats escape. "I'm going to see what meal Cook has waiting for us, would you care to join me, or would you prefer to wait in the cabin?"

"I should be the one fetching the tray for you, Captain. I will see to it." She responded. Her eyes riveted to her feet.

"Very well, if you wish," he said, continuing down the companionway. "I have not had a chance to speak much with Cook though, so I will accompany you this once." He said, annoyed at the growing need to make her understand she was safe in his presence. He needed to find out what happened, and where he could take her. The sooner she was off his ship the better it would be, for her, the crew and himself. Knowing his crew would not lay a hand on her did not make it much easier, he had heard the men speaking of her and had caught more than one of them casting glances her way. He could not blame them of course, but he despised himself for allowing her emotions to get to him.

"Are you and Captain Clarke very close?" She asked, as they made their way up the companionway.

Alaric furrowed his brows, *what was it about Ethan that worried the lass so?* "Aye, I'd say so. As close as I am with many of the men on board." He had not known Ethan long, but he did enjoy his company and he felt as if he had sailed with him for many years. He watched Molly's reaction, but she simply nodded in response, making no move to elaborate on her question.

"Oh, you've brought the fair lass back to see me," Cook exclaimed, his eyes twinkling. "Tonight, I have made a most delectable fish with a white and creamy sauce to go over it." He explained, pointing to a tray, a large fish laying atop it, surrounded by oranges and lemons that decorated the tray with such color, it almost looked more like an item to adorn a fine house, rather than something to be eaten.

Alaric chuckled, "a fine job you did, Cook. It looks and smells wonderful. The crew will be envious, what are they having?" He asked, knowing that though Cook enjoyed creating lavish meals, he rarely did so unless they had guests from another vessel. Since Molly Maclean had been aboard the ship, though, Cook had made a point of making each of her meals splendid.

"Ach, well, you know. They are having fish and sauce as well, same as you, with biscuits and potatoes, it is over there." He said, jutting a thumb at the narrow counter behind him. Alaric stifled a laugh, the food was thrown onto different plates, ready to be put on the tables for the sailors, and lacking every bit of elaborateness, his and Miss Maclean's meal held, though he suspected it tasted just as well.

Wiping the grin from his face at Cook's quick and stern look he added, "we will be reaching some islands in a few days, let one of the lads know if there is anything you are needing. We will be letting the animals out to stretch a bit, while we look about the island for any signs of *The Amity*."

"Oui, oui, that'll be fine." He said, waving a hand at Alaric. He picked the tray up, placing the last plates on in it. "Here my dear, you take that and enjoy your meal." He beamed down at Molly, "and when those hens lay more fat eggs, you bring them to me."

Molly carefully took the tray from Cook's rough hands, "I certainly will, and I'll bring you the milk up first thing in the mornin'," she assured him, turning, and leading the way to the cabin.

Alaric watched her enter the room slowly, unsure of where to place the tray. His desk was still covered in open charts and maps. Rushing over to it, he cleared it, gesturing for her to place the tray on the desk. He realized they had not actually shared a meal yet; she had been eating either with the animals or in Doc's surgery. Alaric had walked in one evening to check on Doc and see if he had seen her, since she had not been belowdecks where he had expected her to be. Her and Doc were laughing and discussing how animals and humans are not so different, that many techniques and remedies used on people, could be applied to the livestock below. Until Molly had arrived, it had only been Doc that tended to the animals, even Miss Catherine had not done much healing on them, she had stuck with the helping the crew.

"Please, have a seat," he said, waving a hand at the chair, opposite where he sat at the desk.

She made no move forward, instead stared at her feet once more, ringing her hands. "I don't think I should, Captain." Her voice hard, her body ridged.

Alaric let out a long breath, "I will not hurt you. I've said it before," he said, sitting himself in his seat. He reached for the serving spoons, dishing up a healthy portion for each of them.

She raised her chin, her body still rigid, showing her uncertainty and fear. Coming forward she slowly sat in the chair opposite him. "Mmm," she exclaimed, delicately lifting the small silver fork to her lips, a slice of fish atop it. "He really is a good cook. I have never tasted food like this before." Her eyes fixated on the delicious meal in front of her.

"He certainly is. Judging by his speech, I am sure you have figured already that he is from France." Alaric said, dishing himself up more potatoes, swirling them around in the white sauce that pooled on his plate. "What is it that you mainly ate while at the plantation?" He asked, hoping to learn a bit more about her time spent there.

Molly shrugged, her hand reaching up to tuck her hair behind her shoulder. "Mostly soups and stews. They were good and filling but nothing like this. We'd have bread and cheese as well, to go along with our meals and porridge in the mornings."

"That's not too unlike what we have when our supplies run low. Cook is, imaginative, he makes even the smallest scraps into fine dishes, but don't get too comfortable with this sort of meal." He chuckled, his chest rumbling. "Once our provisions become low, we have to live on heavily salted meats and dry biscuits with whatever gravy Cook can conjure up in order to soften the meat and bread. If gravy is unavailable, we have to soak our food in the remaining grog." He said, judging her reaction. He could not help but wonder if the trials and hardships of the voyage would cause her to quickly change her mind about remaining onboard or if it would affect her at all.

"Then I shall savor every morsel of the fine meals he serves, while they last." She replied, happily placing another bite between her lips. "And I will no' mind it when the food stores lessen. I have gone without, many times." She said assuredly. "How long have you been captain of this ship?"

He grinned, happy she was willing to continue the conversation and had not yet held some form of weapon towards him. "Not long. A few weeks, actually."

"Really? I had thought you were captain a long time? You seem so sure and the crew, they respect you so." She said, her brow furrowing.

"Aye, I have been aboard *The Trinity*, many years. Captain Lucas Harding was the captain before me. His parents took me in when I was a very young lad. He and I were part of the Royal Navy before The Trinity." He replied, taking a bite. "What of you? I am guessing you have not lived in the West Indies all your life."

135

"No, I haven't. I lived in Ireland with my mother. I was very small then." She said, swallowing hard.

"I am sure you miss her. I lost my parents, lived with my aunt for a bit, until she also passed. That was when Lucas's family took me in. They became my parents." He said, understanding a little more of how she felt. "Where did you go to live after that?"

"My ma and I lived in a small cottage for some time. The landlords took it from us though. We could not keep it and our crops were failing again. We had not had a good crop in a long while and had already done all we could to keep our home. Did you know, near Ardara, there are many caves? They can be dangerous. You have to be mindful of the tides and be sure not to be near the caves when the waters rise."

"Aye, I have heard tell of the caves. There are many like them on the islands around here." He said, wondering what brought them up.

"Mother and I lived in them after the cottage was taken from us. She fell ill and sent word to my uncle, who I had never met. A carriage was sent for me one day, bringing me to him. I never saw my mother again. I received a letter saying she did not make it another fortnight." The words rushed from her, as if they needed to be heard, needed to escape.

"What of your father? Where was he?" Alaric asked, frustration mounting at the landlord that took their home from them and anger at the man that should have been there protecting his wife and child.

Molly's shoulders lifted, "I never met him, he went back to Scotland to his clan. His kin needed him and my mother did not know she was with child when he left. He told my ma he would send for her once he was settled again, but he never did. He had met her on his way back from France. She tried sending word to him about my birth, but it was during the rebellion. Mother never heard from him again. I am sure he was killed in the battle or taken prisoner, like many others." Her fork sliding the food around her plate while she spoke, not once looking over at Alaric.

"I am very sorry, Miss Maclean." He said, studying her silently. Pleased that she had trusted him enough in that moment to tell him a bit more about herself. He had heard of the rebellion in Scotland and knew that many of the men that fought in it did not make it out alive and if they did, they were branded a traitor and shot on sight.

"I mentioned, Captain Lucas Harding, before." He said, pausing to take his last bite. "He got married a day before I left on this voyage. He and his wife own a large plantation in Barbados." Falling silent at the sudden ashen look on her face. The paleness bringing out the small freckles that dotted her features.

"What are they like, the captain and his wife? Do they know many of the other plantation owners?" She asked, her voice shaking.

"I suppose Catherine's, that is, Lady Harding's father knows several of the owners around the islands. Whether he knows the man you worked for, I could not say." He replied, knowing now his suspicions regarding the Lord she had been a housemaid for, were correct. Nodding, she did not say another word. Alaric decided it was best for him continue with what he had been saying. "Lucas and Catherine are good people and are considerate and understanding plantation owners, I know that many are not." He added, a knowing look on his face. "You will also not find a more skilled farmer or surgeon anywhere near the islands."

"The captain is a farmer and surgeon as well?" Surprise replacing the fear that had remained in her eyes.

"Lucas and I both know our fair share about farming. That is what our family did back in Ireland. We worked the lands around our cottage since we could first lift the tools to do so. As for Catherine, she and Lucas met aboard this very ship." A grin spread across his lips at the memory. "The little chit had snuck aboard this ship, not unlike yourself, Miss Maclean. Only difference was, we all were under the impression that she was a new and very young recruit, not a Lady by any means." Alaric laughed at the expression on Molly's face.

"You mean to say that she pretended to be a lad? How long was it until the captain found out that she was not a young lad?" She asked, sitting forward, her hair falling over her shoulders, framing her face with coppery waves.

"Several weeks into the voyage there was a storm, a rather terrible one in fact. She was worried for the captain and wanted to help. She disobeyed his orders to stay below. It nearly cost her, her life. She was injured, that was when it was discovered she was in fact a Lady." He explained, "she discovered she has a mind and an eye for doctoring. She learned a great deal under Doc and tended to the wounds of

138

the crew, myself and Lucas included." Alaric glanced down, the memory of that night, flashing before him. He relived that moment every time he closed his eyes at night. Swallowing, he continued, avoiding the rest of what had happened during that battle. "Catherine now is able to affectively treat and take care of the folks that work the plantation's crops, before, they had to do what little they could for themselves. It was not much and many of them, unfortunately did not make it." Alaric said, "so you see, we have had one other lass aboard this ship. She became a valued part of the crew, ask any of the shipmates and they will tell." Alaric hoped, that by telling her about Catherine that Molly may feel more at ease, safer, especially in his presence. There was something about not being able to make her feel more comfortable that irked him. He sat back, watching the lass across from him, timidly eat the delectable food. Alaric knew she had suffered in the past and understood she felt she could not trust those around her. Something in him feared this knowledge, it made him want to prove to her that she could trust him, that she could forget what had happened to her and no longer feel the fear she still felt. Running a hand through his hair, he stood. "I'll leave you to finish your meal." He said, needing some air and wanting to give her privacy to get settled for the night.

16

"Doc?" Molly cautiously knocked on the hatch to his surgery. She had just come from feeding the animals below, she noticed one of the goats was not acting quite itself.

"Come in, Miss Maclean." He said, opening the hatch and beckoning her into the small cabin. "How are the animals fairing today? We are nearer the island, and I am sure they will be just as pleased to step foot on land for a bit as the crew will be."

"That is just what I have come to speak with you about." She wrung her fingers together, she had quickly grown fond of the animals below, knowing full well they may not make it through the entire voyage. The fact was, she could not simply sit back and watch any of them be in pain or unwell. "I wondered if you might come down and see one of the goats. She has gone off her feed and is staying away from the others as best she can." Molly explained, hoping Doc would not object to examining the beast. She had an idea of what it might be but wanted his opinion on it.

"I don't mind at all," he said, adjusting his spectacles, a

friendly smile resting on his lips. "Lead the way Miss Maclean and I shall follow."

Molly smiled back, pleased he had so easily said yes to accompanying her. She was beginning to slowly feel more at ease with some of the men on the ship, though most of the crew she still tried to avoid, particularly a certain Irish Captain. Even Captain Clarke did not make her feel so unsettled, and he should most of all. He had all the right to hand her over to the authorities if he found out what she had done. A shiver ran down her spine, rubbing her arms trying to take the bumps away that had formed on her flesh. Even with that knowledge though, it was Captain Stein that made it hard for her to speak and think when he was around. A new type of fear formed in the pit of her stomach, every time he was near her. His presence making it near impossible to sleep with him swaying silently in the hammock across the cabin from her. It did not help that she had to sleep in his bed, a bed that smelled strongly of his masculine scent.

"Well now, Miss Maclean. What can you tell me about the poor beast?" Doc asked, bending low, his gaze traveling over the goat that stood alone in the corner.

"She has gone off her feed and as you can see, she won't go near the others. At first, I thought her hooves must be the cause of the discomfort, but I don't think they are. I was feeling around and well, if you feel just there, where her milk comes out. One is swollen and feels much warmer than the rest." Blushing, she quickly looked down, pushing the straw around with her foot.

Doc simply nodded, brushing a hand gently over the goat,

examining it much as she had done a moment ago. Molly watched closely, anxious to see if her diagnosis had been a correct one. "Miss Maclean, I believe you are right. Tell me, did you encounter this problem with any of the livestock on the plantation?"

"Aye, once, the man that cared for the animals would give them dried kelp, to prevent this from happening. It did not always stop it though." Molly explained, her hand resting on the goat's head. She calmly stroked the soft fur beneath her fingers, wanting to make the animal feel better.

"Kelp?" Doc asked, standing straighter, "I will have to read on that, I had not heard to do that before." Doc smiled, "and what was the treatment for the goat on the plantation?"

Molly shrugged, "I only recall him giving the goat more of the dried kelp, then keeping a warmed cloth on the udder, and trying to milk her until the milk flowed once more."

"Aye, that is one of the ways it is done, and usually quite effective. We do not want this getting worse though, so I suggest we do a bit more." He said, glancing from the goat to Molly. "Why don't you go and ask Cook to heat some water for us, then meet me back in my cabin. I will show you what more we can do." He said, dismissing her to get the water from Cook, as he made his way back through the companionway.

Trying not to spill the hot water over herself, she slowly made it down the steps and into Doc's cabin once again. Placing the bucket on the narrow table in the cabin, she watched Doc rummage through the bottles of herbs and tinctures. "Ah, here we are." He said, holding up a sealed bottle of yellow flowers. Handing it to Molly for inspection and scooping out a portion of the water and placing it in a bowl. "We will be letting those flowers there, steep for some time in the water." Gesturing for her to undo the bottle. "Go on then. Just a few, mind you. We will save the rest in case we need to make more."

Molly did as she was told, carefully rolling one of the soft, round flowers in her hand. The islands were filled with beautifully bright flowers, usually larger than the one she held now. This one was softer than anything she had felt before, she barely even felt it resting on her palm. The small ruffles that formed the yellow ball, each perfectly spaced. She placed a few in the water, dipping them gently under with a spoon that had been placed near the bowl.

"While those steep and the ointment from it sets up, we will tell Ol' Shorty to be on the lookout for kelp. I would like to give it a try, as I have never used it before and am quite curious what other ailments it might cure. We also need to get that goat of yours to eat a few of these, it will help to keep the infection from spreading." Doc explained, holding up a few cloves of garlic. Molly scrunched her nose at the smell. "You certainly did not seem to mind these when Cook used them with your meal last evening." Doc said chuckling, handing over the garlic to Molly.

"She won't be liking that garlic much, you'll have to make her swallow it all at once." Doc said, "and be mindful of her teeth, I don't want you to become a patient of mine because she crushed your fingers." He warned, watching Molly slowly approach the goat.

Reaching a hand out she spoke quietly, whispering to the scared animal before her. Gently stroking the goats head and neck, she reached another hand up, towards the corner of the animal's mouth. Prodding the mouth open, she quickly popped the cloves of garlic in her mouth, continuing to rub the goats face and head.

"Remarkable," Doc beamed down at Molly, "Well, done. Very well done." He said, "Now, we will need to alternate between the ointment we have made up from the flowers and warm compresses. Perhaps we shall try expressing the milk as well, once we've given the ointment and warmth a little time to do its job." Doc instructed.

Molly reached her hand into the ointment, gathering up a fair amount. Gently rubbing it over the goats utters. "Shhh," she said, petting the furry back with her other hand as the goat lifted her leg in protest. "I know it hurts, but you will soon feel better, wee lassie." Molly did her best to sooth the upset creature, not wanting to cause the goat anymore discomfort than she already felt. Molly could feel the warmth under her hand, from where the injury on the udder was. It was much warmer than the rest of the utters and was an angry red color. Running a hand along the soft, brown and white fur, she felt the animal relax a bit. It would be several days of constant care to free the udder of infection. Molly did not mind though, she was finally beginning to feel as if she had a purpose, as if she almost truly belonged somewhere.

A generous amount of ointment lathered the goat's red and swollen udder. Molly stood up, looking the other animals over. They appeared to be doing perfectly fine and had grown used to her company. When she knew no one was near, she often sang to them, songs her mother had taught her long ago. She remembered curling up on her mother's lap, they would sit on the old wooden chair her father had built, rocking and singing, in front of the fire that burned warmly inside their modest cottage. Their home had been small and had not been much but the memories she had of it were the last and only fond memories she held within her.

A shout sounded from above, footsteps could be heard rushing around. Molly looked at Doc, she knew by the expression upon his face he suspected another battle was underway. "I should stay with the animals." Her voice shaking with nerves, "what if she gets worse?" Molly asked anxiously, nodding at the goat that had made herself as comfortable as she could against Molly's leg. She could hardly bare to leave the animals, even knowing they had seen more sea battles than she had. Knowing they would likely be perfectly fine on their own. The thought of leaving the already injured and scared goat at her side caused an aching in her chest.

"It would not be safe for you to stay down here. It would be best if I took you to the Captain's cabin. I am sure the goat will be perfectly fine for the few hours the battle will likely last. It is more important you are safe, lass." He coaxed, "come, she will be alright, we've done what we can for now. I need to be preparing the surgery." His arm was stretched out, beckoning her to lead the way up the companionway.

Molly stepped forward, glancing about the straw that filled the large area. The animals were perfectly at ease, munching on the grain they had been given. A noise emanated from the goat by her side as she tried stepping through the gate, the goat following closely. Molly let out a sigh, "I am sorry Doc, but I must do something." She said, glancing apologetically at him. Reaching for a rope that hung on a hook just above the fence, she wrapped it securely about the goat's head, leading her from the gate and up the companionway. Molly caught a glimpse of Doc's grin as she passed.

17

Alaric stood near the railing; his telescope held to his eye. The ship he had in his sight was too near the island and appeared wrecked, though he did not want to take any chances. He could not be too sure it was not a trap and wanted his men to be prepared. "Beat to quarters!" He bellowed, glancing about the deck, he had only just checked on Molly not long ago, as he had suspected, she had been with her animals. It would not be safe for her to remain below, there would be no protection or place to hide if it did turn into a battle and the enemy managed to get below. "Shorty, will you see to it that Miss Maclean is safely locked in my cabin?" He commanded, the image of the other young woman he had failed to protect those years ago, flashing through his mind. Shaking his head, he cleared his throat, taking his sword from one of the younger lads that had fetched it for him.

His eyes traveled the length of wrecked ship, something about it, did not feel right. There had not been a storm recent enough that would have caused the ship to wreck against the island and no captain would have sailed close enough to have risked it. Even if a less seasoned sailor had taken command of the ship, they would not likely have wrecked. "The damage it sustained is from far more than just a wreck. It was in a battle before it ran aground." Alaric said, he had heard of a strategy pirates used on occasion, they'd attack a ship relentlessly, chasing it closer and closer to the shallows until it had no way of escaping or maneuvering out of the range of shots. The pirates would then have the full advantage, easily taking their prey down and looting the ship of all its contents.

"Aye, and by the looks of it, and the few men I can see in the water and aboard the ship, it is not more than a couple days since the battle ensued." Ethan added, lowering his own spy glass. "It does not look like many of the men are alive, Mate." His voice somber.

Alaric nodded, clipping his glass shut and handing it over to Gordy. "Eddie, get us as close as we can." He said, nodding to the man at the helm. "Be prepared for a fight, it looks to be a mere merchant vessel, but we can't be sure what happened here or if the ship that attacked them is still in the area."

He caught sight of Shorty coming back on deck, looking pleased, "is the lass locked in my cabin?" Alaric asked, an uncertainty creeping up. The look on Shorty's face made him feel even more uneasy than he already did. The wreckage had him on edge, he needed to be sure the lass was safe before they reached it.

"Oh aye, she is safe and quite comfortable in your cabin, Captain." Shorty said, wiping a sleeve across his face trying to hide the smirk. Quickly turning his back to Alaric, Shorty found his position on the deck.

Shaking his head and rubbing a hand over his hair he

focused his attention back on the merchant vessel. Bodies of fallen sailors bobbed in the shallows, swaying with every small wave that passed. Lines and splintered wood were strewn about, washing up on the sandy beach. More sailors laid about the deck, not a sign of life remaining on the vessel. Alaric tightened his grip on his musket, his eyes trailing over the horizon, looking for any sign of the enemy ship.

"That's 'bout as close as I can git her, Capt'n." Eddie said, signaling for the men to bring the sails in fully.

"Aye, that will do. Eddie, you stay and man the helm," he said, "Henry, climb up and you and another lad keep an eye on the horizon for any other ships, call down immediately if you spot sails." Walking to the railing, he untied the ropes to the skiff, "Joseph, fetch Doc as quick as you can, we may need his assistance. Shorty, Ethan, Edward, we will go in the skiff and see if there are any survivors." He said, glancing at the hatch that led to his cabin. Clenching his jaw, he made his way down the ladder and into the wobbling skiff. The sound of the lapping waves against the hull of the ships would have been a soothing sound any other time, now it was broken up with the sounds of fallen wood, clanking against the ships and the sight of pale, lifeless bodies floating helplessly in the waves. Alaric shook his head at the sight, grateful Molly was in his cabin and not able to see the sight before them. Something in him he could not quite explain, made him want to shelter her from seeing or having to be a part of anymore terrible happenings. The thought of wanting to protect her, made his stomach flip, he did not want to care, did not want to have to try and protect her, knowing he may fail again.

Alaric climbed up the side of the merchant vessel, closely

followed by Ethan and the others. Cautiously peering over
the tattered railing, he looked for signs of life. His boots
echoed eerily across the bloodied deck of the merchant vessel.
Clearly the men of this ship had not stood a chance against
the pirates that had attacked them. Placing his arm over his
nose and mouth, he tried taking a breath in, the smell from
the heat and the bodies was nearly unbearable, even in the
open. The breeze was slight and did little to waft the stench
away. Waving a hand, he gestured for his men to follow him
onto the ship. Stepping away from the railing, Alaric looked
over the sailors as the others joined him on the deck.

"Look around, see if there are any survivors. I'd like to
find out who did this if we can." He said, angered at the
sight in front of him. He had dealt with a countless number
of pirate captains, no matter how terrible or ruthless they
were, not many of them would have gone this far. A merchant
vessel was typically no match for any pirate ship. There
would have been no reason they needed to slay the entire
crew to loot the ship.

"Shhh," Ethan said, holding a hand up. The men stayed
their footsteps, listening carefully. "I was sure I heard a
voice." He whispered, his brows pulling together.

"Shorty, Edward, go below and see what you can find.
Remember, stay alert and see what, if anything was taken,
goods and supplies or if everything was left." Alaric said, he
had a sickening feeling that the pirates did not take much,
instead just attacked and killed the merchants just to fight.

Kicking at a gull that had landed on one of the fallen
sailors, Alaric carefully went from man to man with Doc,

checking to see if there was any life left in even one of them.

"Captain, if you please," Doc spoke up, his face grim. "This lad is still breathing." Doc said, rummaging in his pack for a pair of scissors to cut the dry, blood-soaked shirt from the young sailor's body.

Alaric strode over, looking from the gaping wound to Doc. Seeing his friend shake his head just enough to know the answer to his unspoken question. Kneeling, he gently placed a hand upon the lad's shoulder. "Can you hear me?"

A moan escaped his lips. Trying to wet his dry mouth to speak, his eyes fluttering open, attempting to adjust to the bright sun.

"Here, take a slow sip of this," Doc said, holding a bottle to the lad's mouth.

A few drops of the rum falling on his lips, just enough to wet them and prevent them from sticking together once again. "It was a pirate and his crew. The pirate, his chest..." Swallowing, he continued in a raspy voice, "they came upon us fast, we tried to fire back." He shook his head, closing his eyes, "They ran us aground. He..." The sailor's words falling short.

Alaric nodding, squeezing his shoulder in order to give the young man what comfort he could. Reaching for the sailor's arm, he felt for the pulse he already knew he would not feel. He stood up, "Check the rest of the men, I will order the crew to prepare these men for a proper send off." He said, his anger rising. The lad had mentioned the pirate's chest.

Alaric knew what the lad had been trying to say, by the look on Doc's face, he had caught it as well. The tattoo Banning had was unmistakable. "Red," he hollered over at the men on *The Trinity*. "Red, gather some of the crew and fetch the hammocks below. Gather the dead and prepare them." Alaric commanded, heading for the hatch to check on the crew that had gone below, they had been gone long enough to have checked on the rest of ship. The vessel was not a large one, it would have taken mere minutes for the pirates to have looted the ship and for his own crew to check the damage done.

"Shorty," Alaric called down the companionway. Drawing his flintlock once more, he cautiously made his way past the small cabins, peering into each one as he passed them. Muffled voices traveled down the hall, coming from the small galley.

"Slow down, mate. Just try and remember what was said, where the ship went." Edward spoke softly, bent low over a small figure in the corner, between the stove and several crates and bags, still filled with provisions.

"What's this?" Alaric asked quietly, not wanting to scare the child any more than he already was.

"This young lad says he's the galley 'and. Says the Cook told 'im to stay hidden til' he returned for 'im." Shorty explained, his face grim. "He appears unharmed, though rightly shaken. Edward's been trying to coax the lad out." He said, gesturing towards the sailor and the small boy.

"Right," Alaric said stepping forward, the boy shrinking further back, as if he planned to become part of the planking that made up the walls. "It's alright, you are safe now." As he spoke the words his mind shifted to the lass he knew remained safely locked away in his cabin. Breathing out a long breath he continued, "Do you know where your vessel was headed to?"

The boy nodded slowly, "them colonies, Captain."

Alaric smiled, "very good, smart lad. Tell me, the ship that attacked, do you know which way they were heading?" He doubted the lad knew, seeing as how he likely had not moved from that spot since the attack.

The boy shivered, "I heard them talking. Thems said they'd be heading to the colonies too." The boy looked up at him, his eyes filled with dread. "You don't suppose they will attack the folks at the colonies, do you?" His voice shook, his lips beginning to tremble.

"No lad, I don't think they would. The folks in the colonies don't have much trouble with them." He replied, doing his best to smile down at the child. "Do you have family there?"

"Aye, me auntie." He said, a bit happier. "I was workin' as the galley hand to pay my way." He explained, pride lighting his face as he sat a bit straighter.

"I see. I am sure you were a fine help too. We have a Cook that could use a strong lad like you." He said, pointing to the young boy's chest. "Would you be willing to work for our Cook for the rest of your journey?"

The lad scrunched his face, taking into consideration the

offer he was being granted. "Aye, I say you've got a deal." He finally replied, shoving his hand out, "names MacKay."

Alaric choked back the laughter that was threating to bubble up, "Welcome to the crew. I'm Captain Stein. I'll leave you with your shipmates to get your things moved over." He said, jutting a thumb at Shorty and Edward. Turning he whispered to Shorty, "Take your time gathering the boy's things and other provisions. He shouldn't see the carnage. Give it a few minutes, by then Red will have had the fallen sewn in their hammocks." Alaric said, turning and heading back up the companionway. Clenching his fist, his stomach felt heavier than the rocks on the shore. What he and the rest of his crew had just witnessed was only more proof of what Thomas was capable of and why he needed to find him even faster. Alaric had no doubt that if the boy had disobeyed or been too frightened to hide, Thomas would not have spared him.

Alaric watched as Red stitched up the last of the hammocks, the board that the bodies would be placed on, sat at the ready. Alaric waved a hand in the air, signaling for them to sail to deeper waters for the burial. "I'm going to check on Miss Maclean. When we are far enough out, gather the crew," he said.

"Aye," Ethan responded, a hand resting on the young boy's shoulder. The lad looked about the ship, his eyes wide in wonder.

Alaric headed towards his cabin, swallowing back the lump forming deep in his throat. MacKay reminded him of Benjamin as a wee lad. He is a bit younger than Benjamin had been when he had found him, but in just as much need of help as he had been. Seeing the boy curled up in the corner of the galley had brought back an image he would never forget. Benjamin's small and frail body lying on the cold stones near a building. He had been too weak and cold to even lift his head. When he had first spotted him, he had thought the lad already dead. His clothes had hardly fit and were torn and stained in multiple spots. It took Alaric and Doc several weeks to get Benjamin strong enough to walk and clamber around like other kids. By the time they reached Barbados again, he was healthy enough to keep up with the other children at the home. Alaric ran a hand over his face at the memories that he could not keep from replaying in his mind.

Knocking on the hatch, he waited to hear the bolt move over, bidding him entrance. His brows furrowed at the sounds behind the door, *what on earth was the Lass doing?* "Miss Maclean, it is safe. There will be no battle." He added, just as the door opened a crack. Lucas slowly pushed it open further, weary of what he might find. Shorty had sounded odd when he told him the lass was perfectly safe and comfortable in his cabin.

Whatever he had expected, it had not been the sight presented before him. His mouth falling open. "What...I..." He stammered, looking from the lass to the furry animal that lay curled up against his desk. He took a tentative step forward, adjusting his stance, unable to think of what to say or do.

"Please, Captain. I beg your pardon, but the thing is, she isn't feeling well and has a painful injury on her..." her words stopped abruptly, her face turning scarlet, "well, that is, she has an injury and I couldn't bear the thought of her staying below in pain and being afraid of the battle. Doc would not allow me to stay with her, so I brought her in here to tend to her during the battle." She finished, the words spilling from her at a rate she did not even realize she could speak at. Crossing her arms over her chest and standing taller, she awaited the scolding she was sure to receive.

"I see," Alaric finally spoke, letting his breath out slowly, trying to recover his dignity after gaping like a fish trying to breath out of the water. "Seeing as how there is no battle to come anytime this day, I suggest we get your friend back down to her kind and out of my cabin." He said, looking Molly over, stubbornness and caution equally visible upon her face. Her hand resting on the goat that now stood protectively by her side. Laughter bubbling in his chest at the sight in front of him. He cleared his throat, "best get going, I am needed on deck and perhaps you should come too, though it is your choice." He said, a grin still playing on his lips.

"What is happening? Doc and I heard you call the crew to quarters." She asked, placing the rope around the goat's neck once more.

"There was a wreckage at the island we were going to stop and let the animals out at. Unfortunately, we will no longer be able to do that. Though I'm sure you have the beasts well in hand." He smirked, knowing it would only be a matter of hours before the entire crew knew the lass had brought a goat into his cabin. "The wreckage had many dead and we will be giving them a proper burial." The look of understanding and shock on her face made him wonder if he should have told her or not. "Like I said, it is your choice to be present, no one will think ill of you if you stay below." He added, wanting to take the sadness from her eyes.

"No, I'd like to be on deck, if you do not mind." She said, not looking at him but rather the creature next to her. "I will take her down now," she said, tugging on the rope until the reluctant beast followed her past Alaric and through the hatch.

Watching the pair head down the companionway and out of sight. He was quite proud of Miss Maclean; he had not expected her to agree to come on deck for the ceremony and would not have pushed her to. The bodies would be covered, and she would see no more than the canvas hammocks, however, it was still a sobering sight.

Alaric waited for the crew to be gathered around. A few of the men, selected to place the bodies on the boards, stood silently at the ready. Clearing his throat, he began, "We therefore commit their bodies to the deep, to be turned into corruption, looking for the resurrection of the body, when the sea shall give back her dead, and the life of the world to come…" his voice echoed across the ship. The only other sounds were the squawks from the sea birds above and the splashes that followed after each body was delivered into the sea. Finishing, he watched the final body be placed upon the board and covered in the flag. The men lifted the board onto the railing, tipping it enough for the canvas to slip from the wooden planks. Looking over at Molly, who stood next to Doc, he thought he could see a tear making its way down her cheek but could not be sure.

18

Molly did not know or had even seen any of the men that were sewn in the canvas hammocks, but her heart went out to them and their families. She knew it meant someone out there had lost a husband, a father, or a son because of duty. It made her wonder if her father had not needed to return to his clan, if it had been safer, would her mother still live? Would she have been sold to Lord Willington?

"Not to worry, Miss Maclean, all will be well." Doc assured her, patting her shoulder. "How is your furry patient doing? Any improvement?" He asked, changing the subject, steering her away from the rest of the crew and leading her towards his surgery.

"Aye, I believe she is a bit better. I would like to check on her in a bit. I want to give her a chance to rest before applying the salve and warm cloths." Molly replied, looking over her shoulder at Ethan, his hand still resting on the small boy's shoulder. "Was the wee lad on the merchant vessel?" Concern filling her eyes.

"That he was. He was hidden safely away behind a few

crates and bags of spuds." Mister Clarke will be bringing him in for me to look him over." He said, opening the hatch to the cabin.

"How terrible, what horrors he must have witnessed." She said softly, her mouth opening to speak more on the matter when Ethan and Mackay knocked on the inside of the cabin door. Molly felt her body begin to tremble, *surely Captain Clarke could see she feared him* so, she thought. Stepping slightly behind Doc, pretending to flip through the pages of one of his many books, trying to keep the Naval Captain's eyes from her. A sketch on one of the pages catching her eye. It showed a man with a dark mark on his face, just below his eye. His face appeared swollen and distorted. Fat worm like creatures clinging to his flesh. She ran a finger along the text. Leeches, that was it. She had remembered one of the slaves on the plantation putting a couple on her face to bring down the swelling and bruising, after Lord Willington had gotten angry with her. She had been avoiding him as best she could, but he had waited for her late one night, hidden in the back stairs. She thought he had gone up already and was in his chamber as all of the maids and footmen had already retired for the night. She planned to sneak up to her room. Molly had been sleeping in the stables the nights before, but a storm had blown in and the Master must have suspected she would seek refuge in her room. Not that it was much warmer than the stables but at least she would not have to trek through the pounding rain and deep mud to the house the next morning and risk her thin shoes being wet and cold the rest of the day. She remembered seeing a figure in the dark, realizing her mistake too late. He grabbed her, digging his fingers into her delicate flesh. The only reason he did not continue his advances that night was because he must have believed he had killed her. Molly tried recalling what had happened next, but all she could remember was his meaty fist hitting hard against her cheek. He must have lost his grip on her then, she had felt her head slam against the stone staircase. The world went silent. The next morning, she awoke in a hut on the other side of the plantation. A woman was bent over her, her face crinkled with years of working in the hot sun.

"Now you lay still, Miss." She gently reached a hand up. Molly felt something wet and smooth slide from her cheek. The gentle woman picked it up, showing her what had been attached to her flesh moments ago. The older woman explained to Molly what the creatures were for. It was days later that Molly was recovered enough to move about the estate, doing the duties required of her. A word was never spoken of the event, though Molly knew all the staff downstairs knew what had transpired. One of them had to have found her lying there the next morning. Bleeding from the back of the head, on the cold stone. They must have feared she would not pull through, therefore placed her in one of the many slave huts, far from curious eyes and esteemed guests that might stumble upon her and see her tattered body.

"Miss Maclean?" Captain Clarke said, bringing her back to the present. "Are you alright?" He asked, reaching a hand out to steady her. Flinching away from his touch she quickly looked away, hoping to hide the fear and shock on her face. She had all but forgotten she was not alone in the tiny cabin; she had been so engrossed in her own memories.

"Yes, I apologize," she finally spoke, regaining her composure.

"What are those?" The boy asked loudly, pointing to the picture of the little beasts.

"Leeches, I believe," Molly replied, smiling down at the boy. "They certainly aren't the loveliest of sights."

"I should think not. Though they can be very useful if used correctly." Doc chimed in. "Why don't you show our young friend here to the galley and help him get acquainted to Cook."

Molly nodded, glad of the excuse to be out of the same cabin Mister Clarke was in. "Come this way. You will enjoy working with Cook and I expect you will be quite the cook yourself once this voyage is done."

"Cap says we be headin' for them colonies. When we get there, I will be with my auntie. I wager she'll be mighty proud when she hears I've been workin' on a real Privateer ship." He said excitedly.

"I'm sure she will be." Molly replied, wondering just how they would find the wee lad's auntie. She imagined it would be difficult finding one auntie in such a big area of land. She had seen the maps in the captain's cabin and had looked over nearly all of them. She herself had not realized how much land stretched across the colonies and suspected the young boy had no idea either. "Did you travel from Scotland?" Curious to know what the boy had to say about it, if he had any memories of it at all. She could tell in his voice; he held a bit of the speech.

"Aye, I never met me Da and me mother passed on before we could leave together to meet my auntie, so I was sent alone." He said, his voice growing quieter.

"I am sorry, I lost my folks too when I was wee." She said, understanding only too well how the boy felt. "What was it like there?"

MacKay shrugged, "cold," he said simply, "it was always raining. There was mud everywhere and many folks did not have much to eat. My Auntie, she wrote and said how she found a place in the colonies to be a sort of tenant at, like back home."

Molly smiled, "Is your auntie your ma's sister?"

"Aye, that she is. Names Elsie MacDougall." He replied proudly. "I'm a MacDougall and will be with me own clansmen soon." His words cut short as they reached the galley. Molly still staring open mouthed at the young lad beside her.

"Ah, but this must be my new galley hand." Cook said, his bushy eyebrows raising. "Just in time to help be prepare this evening's meal." He said, leading the boy into the small cabin, "you are to prepare the biscuits," he said gleefully, winking at Molly before turning his full attention to the lad.

Molly left the two of them to get to know each other. She had no doubt they would do just fine together. She felt lighter, curious. Before, she had felt little connection to her Scottish blood, she had even disliked it, blaming it for the reason her father left her mother those years ago. She had never met another Scotsman since she left Ireland and even the ones she had met in the past, it was only for a brief moment, no more than a fleeting exchange. Molly had marveled at how proud

Mackay had been about his clan. She was going to have to ask the boy more about his clan when she got a chance and about his aunt, for now, she wanted to check on the goat to see if the swelling had gone down any.

Opening the small gate, she stepped slowly into the pen, not wanting to startle the animals. "There, there, lassie," she coaxed, bringing the bucket of warmed water and the salve nearer the goat. Feeling around, Molly could still feel the swelling, though not as bad as it had been. The flesh felt warm to the touch, warmer still than it should. Molly sighed, "I'm doing the best I can, lass. These remedies should help you in no time, now and I am here. You are not alone, not now." She said soothingly.

"Are you telling the goat that or yourself?" A deep voice rumbled through the cabin.

Molly's faced flushed. In truth she did not know the answer to his question. Irritated at herself she turned her attention back to her patient. "I already gathered the eggs and milked the cow and the goats, if that is why you came down here."

"Ah, don't be fooled into thinking you are the only one that seeks solitude with these beasts." He said, leaning up against the wall.

"Be that as it may, don't think I believe that you came down here just to pet the cow." Flinching at her own tongue, she would be lucky if she was not whipped for speaking to him in such a way. Her words had gotten her into trouble many times before and she would not be surprised if it happened again.

A deep laugh filled the room, "no, I will admit, I did not come down to pet the cow." He said, glancing at the beast apologetically. "I spoke with Doc, about the lad. He says he's in fine shape and unharmed."

Molly straightened, somehow, she knew this was not going to be about Mackay at all. "Yes, he is in lively spirits, considering what he has been through." She thought of telling him what she had found out about the lad but remained silent.

"Doc said you seemed quite fascinated by one of his books. I don't blame you, leeches can be rather a sight." Alaric stepped forward, away from the wall. "He also said, you seemed fearful of Ethan. You have no reason to fear him." He said, she could feel his gaze on her, studying her reaction to his questions.

"Aye, leeches are rather nasty wee things." She replied, thinking of what next to say, his gaze making it hard for her to focus on much else. "I got caught up reading about them in the book and had not realized they had been speaking to me." She explained, looking directly at him. Wiping her hands off on the apron she had borrowed from Doc and standing up. "As for being fearful of your friend, I am no more fearful of him than I am of you, Captain." She said, raising her chin, knowing she did not look as intimidating or sure of herself as she meant. "Now, if you'll excuse me, I will begin cleaning the pens." She said, only to realize he was standing right next to the wooden rake that sat against the wall. He must have come to the same conclusion, as he turned and grabbed the rake before she could take a step forward.

"Here you are, Miss Maclean." His voice low and husky, handing her the rake, but not releasing it right away. "I am glad to hear you are no longer afraid of me." He grinned, stepping to the side, and leaving her standing in the pen.

Her hands shook, *how dare that odious man*, she thought, raking a bit faster than she normally would, causing the hens to seek refuge in their nesting crates. In truth she was terrified of both men, though not at all for the same reasons. Worse was that she was beginning to trust and even feel safe with the captain. Chiding herself, she knew she should not allow herself to trust him. She knew that he would probably be dropping her off in the colonies with the lad. It crossed her mind to let him, but she had a feeling that if the Master lived, the colonies would be one of the first places he would assume she would run to. No, she would not allow Captain Stein to drop her at any port, her best bet was to wait her time out on The Trinity. In the meantime, she would have to be more careful about how she presented herself around Captain Clarke. If the Doc had noticed her fear, there was no doubt he had as well and that would only raise more questions.

19

"I couldn't be sure, Capt'n but I thought I saw a ship approaching one of the other islands. Before I could get a better look, I no longer saw any sails and we was already raising ours." Ian explained.

"Could you tell anything else about the vessel?" Alaric asked, irked that he may have missed his opportunity if it had been *The Amity.*

"No, Capt'n. Only that it was no pirate ship, and too large to be merchant." He said, trying his best to recall what he saw.

"Alright, thank you, Ian. Back to your post," he commanded, "And keep a close eye out." Alaric added. He had the feeling they were now the ones being followed, though not by Banning.

"Doc," he called, knocking on the side of the hatch. "How did Mackay appear?" He had no doubt the lad was unharmed but felt better about having Doc look him over.

"Fine, fine," he replied, ushering Alaric into the surgery.

"I was rather more concerned about the lass."

Alaric's brow furrowed, "what about her?" He asked, not sure what Doc could have meant. She was perhaps a bit distraught during the burial, and rightly so, but appeared to be holding herself together when her and Doc walked off.

"Mister Clarke brought the lad in, Miss Maclean was chattering away, that is, until Ethan came through the door. The look of fright in her eyes took me aback. I of course acted as if I had not noticed, but it did no good, she tried standing behind me as if hiding from the man." Doc spoke, concern, and confusion on his face. "I began speaking with him and Mackay, only to find, that by the time I had finished my examining him, Miss Maclean was so enraptured by the picture on the book that she did not hear us saying her name for some time." He explained, "when she finally did look up, Ethan had stepped forward to steady the lass, and the fear from before was back."

Alaric adjusted the chair he was in, sitting forward slightly. "She was afraid of Ethan?" He asked, he had seen the same fear in her eyes when he introduced her the first time to him but had not thought more on it until now. "What was on the picture she was looking at?"

Doc rose his hands in defeat of the perplexing moment, "nothing but leeches. Granted, they were on a man's swollen and beaten face, but she seemed almost lost in thought over the image."

Alaric nodded, "thank you Doc." Leaving the room, he ran a hand over his face. He had only seen leeches used on men before, after battles or fights. They were not like any other beast he could think of and it most likely was a shock to Molly to see such a sketch. It gave no explanation though as to why she reacted the way she did towards Ethan or why she would have been so drawn into herself at the sight of the drawing.

Stepping into the cabin that held the animals, he paused, watching Molly tend to the goat, her hair cascading down her back and about her shoulders. Listening carefully, he heard her soothing the beast next to her. He was still struck by how much she cared about the animals, cared enough to risk his anger, and bring one into his cabin. Stifling his laugh he took a tentative step forward, he was grateful, Doc, Ethan and Shorty had not said a word about the goat to the rest of the crew.

As soon as his voice broke through the near silence of the cabin, he almost regretted speaking. He did not miss the way her body had tensed or how she avoided looking at him. Judging by her reaction to his question, he had caught a glimpse of a different part of her. A part deep in her soul that she was not ready to share with him. Leaning against the wall, he tried holding his grin at bay. He had not expected such a sharp response from the chit but supposed he should not be too surprised. He had witnessed her fire before.

The look on Molly's face when he handed her the rake told him all he needed to know. He had felt her hand shaking before he let the handle go. He knew all too well she feared him, but he suspected it was not for the reason he had first thought.

"Capt'n! Capt'n, them sails is back. It's that ship I saw before, I'm sure of it." Ian said hastily, meeting Alaric in the companionway.

"Right, come on," he responded, rushing the sailor through the hatch. "Beat to quarters!" He bellowed. He did not feel comfortable leaving Molly down with the animals if a battle ensued. He would have to go down before they got too close to the other ship and get her to his cabin. Taking his scope from his belt he looked the quickly approaching ship over. Ian had told him the ship was no pirate vessel. The young sailor had been correct. It was a Royal Navy Ship. Clipping his spy glass closed, groaning. Glancing next to him he saw the expression on Ethan's face.

His eyes hard, "I'll wager the French have drawn nearer. The admiral will have sent for me." Shoving his glass in his belt, he clenched his jaw.

Alaric understood how he felt and knew he would not have taken to being stopped in finding Benjamin's killer. Clapping Ethan on the shoulder, "I'll do what I can to convince them you must stay aboard *The Trinity*, if it comes to that." He shrugged, "they may not even be flagging us down for that." Alaric could not see the navy sending a ship as far north as they had gone, to pick one of their captains up, rather than promoting a Commander. It did not sit right with him or add up.

"Gordy, see to it my cabin is ready for entertaining, and alert Cook that we may have guests." He commanded, gesturing for the crew to bring in the sails and await further orders.

"Ian, fetch Doc and have him alert Miss Maclean of our visitors." He added, not entirely sure she would be as thrilled as the crew was. He wanted to give her fair time to prepare for their guests though. If they planned to dine with them. It would do no good to have her barging into the cabin unannounced with a table of naval officers. He would need to introduce her to them as a guest aboard his ship. If he did not and they discovered her on their own, her reputation would be ruined for sure, and he did not want to risk any of the officers aboard the naval ship to mistake her for a woman of lose morals.

"It's Captain Hanes," Ethan said, his eyes focused on the ship. "If he is Captaining that ship, then no doubt Lieutenant Mason is aboard it, waiting to cause as much trouble and inconvenience as he can." Groaning, he watched the ship move in beside them, the men readying the planks.

"You must be Captain Alaric Stein. We have heard much of you and your brother." The Naval Captain said, "It is a pleasure to finally meet you."

"Unfortunately, I cannot say the same," cocking his head to the side, feigning interest, he added, "I am sorry to say it, but I have never heard of you."

Captain Hanes's face turned hard, "Tis unfortunate indeed, Captain Stein." Turning towards Ethan he said, "Any news yet on your sister's attacker or is the illustrious pirate captain still illuding you?"

"What is it you two want? I can't imagine you came all this way to simply ask how I'm fairing." Ethan replied, unwavering.

"On the contrary, my dear friend," Mason stepped forward, "we were in the area and wished to see how you are getting on."

"In that case, why don't we invite you to dine with us." Alaric offered, knowing it was not as simple as they let on. There was no way they could have known where they had been unless they had been following them the entire time. "Captain Clarke, see to it they are led to my cabin. I will see that the crew has an extra ration of rum, and the whiskey is brought in for us." In truth, he knew Cook would have it all in hand. He had noticed Doc had arrived on deck without Molly. He had glanced at Alaric briefly, slightly shaking his head.

"Did Doc not come down and tell you we have guests?" Vexed at the woman's stubbornness.

"Aye, he did." She replied, equaling his tone. "I do not see it is any concern of mine. A housemaid would not be permitted to dine or even greet guests, why should I be summoned?" She challenged.

Stepping closer, he looked her over, "You may have been a housemaid before, but you are now a member of my crew as you have said so yourself. As a member of my crew, I expect you to follow orders." He really could not see why she was being so difficult. Most women would be pleased to dine in a room full of officers. Shaking his head he turned, looking over the animals that seemed to be staring back at him as if protecting the woman that cared for them in turn. Looking back at Molly, her face pale, making her hair appear brighter in color than it already was. Frustration and fear showing in her eyes. He noticed for the first time, her body was rigid and shaking. Letting out a breath, he slowly turned back to her, "I apologize, I hope you will forgive me."

Shifting her eyes to the ground, she refused to speak. He felt the frustration in himself rising once more. "I will ask that you be my guest tonight at my table." His voice lowering, afraid if he spoke louder, his anger would show. He was trying to protect her; how could she not see it?

"And if I should refuse the offer?" She asked boldly, her face flushing red.

"Then you would be putting your life and reputation in your own hands, and that, I cannot allow aboard my ship." He replied, stepping close enough they nearly touched. "I am trying to help you, Miss Maclean. You cannot stay below or out of my sight even, with a ship full of men I do not know and cannot vouch for their characters. I will let no harm come to you but for that to be possible, I need you to stay within my reach." His voice low and deep.

"Alright," She whispered, hardly loud enough for him to hear, even in such close proximity. Reaching behind her, she slowly untied the apron, draping it over a crate on the outside of the pens, she followed him up the companionway.

"Gentlemen, let me present to you my guest, "Miss Molly Maclean," he announced as they entered his cabin. Ethan and the other two men sat at the long table his crew had put up. Steering her to a seat between him and Ethan he pulled the chair out and waited for her to sit. It was clear she was not used to the chivalry or comfortable having the unknown officers' eyes on her. Pouring her a glass of wine and himself a whiskey, Alaric settled into his chair, anxious to hear the real reason they had flagged them down.

"Tell us, Miss Maclean, how is it you came to be aboard *The Trinity?*" Captain Hanes asked curiously.

"I bartered passage on a merchant vessel from Ireland. I was under the impression it was headed to the colonies. Unfortunately, it was not. I found myself in the West Indies, where I came across Captain Stein, who kindly agreed to take me to the Colonies himself." She explained, raising the cup to her lips, and taking a sip. Alaric sat motionless; he had not expected her to tell such a tale. His eyes shifted from his own cup to Molly. Meeting the large blue eyes, he could not help but notice the pleading look on her face.

"Aye, that is about the way of it." He grinned, regaining his thoughts, "turns out, Miss Maclean has quite a way with the livestock. Without her knowledge and help, we would have lost a valuable goat," he added.

"Aye, that she does." Ethan said, raising his cup to her in thanks.

Ethan poured Captain Hanes more whiskey. Alaric noticed how Mason's eyes kept traveling over Molly, making Alaric's anger quickly rise. He did not care for the look in the lieutenant's gaze and knew Molly must feel even more uncomfortable. Her hair fell about her shoulders, framing her face perfectly in a bronze hue.

Cook opened the hatch, followed by a couple of the younger sailors, carrying trays of food and a pitcher of ale.

"Thank you, Cook." He said, gesturing for the guests to help themselves. Molly made no move, "no time to be shy now," he whispered to her. He was not about to let her peculiar tale go. He was having trouble believing either story now. Which one was closer to the truth? Had she just arrived in the West Indies when she came across him or had she really been a housemaid on one of the local plantations? None of it added up and the one thing that seemed to have remained the same was her aversion to members of the Royal Navy.

"What is the news from the Islands since we left?" Ethan asked, hardly touching the food on his plate.

"None really," Captain Hanes replied, "the French fleet has not been spotted thus far, the only real news is that of a Lord Willington."

Alaric felt Molly stiffen beside him, the color all but gone from her face, even her lips that were normally a lush pink had grown ashen. "What is it that he has done that caused such a stir?" Alaric asked, not one to encourage or care about the gossip of the islands, he was curious as to what the name meant to Molly.

Lieutenant Mason laughed, "he did nothing, it was one of his servants they say. Poor fella was found, blood pouring from a gash on his head."

Alaric cleared his throat, now regretting asking for further explanation. "My apologies Miss Maclean, I am afraid our guest has forgotten he is in the company of a lady." He said, bowing his head towards her in apology, all the while his eyes remaining hard on Mason. Clearly, the name had meant something to the lass or perhaps he simply being a Lord on the islands had made her weary. Fear had even shown in her eyes when he mentioned Lucas and Catherine being plantation owners.

"So, tell us, where are you heading to next?" Captain Hanes asked, leaning comfortably back in the chair.

"The colonies," he said, without further elucidation. "I take it, you will be heading back, nearer the West Indies?" He asked, his tone as hard and challenging as the look in his eyes.

Mason cocked a brow at him, "perhaps, though we need to be patrolling all the water around here. No telling where the French fleet may be or what pirates might be lurking about. Often times, the pirates in these waters hide in plain sight, in disguise of something more honorable." His eyes straying from Ethan to Alaric.

"What exactly are you implying, Lieutenant?" Ethan said, his voice hard.

"I think it is time you and your Lieutenant found your way back to your ship, Captain Hanes." Alaric said, his eyes not wavering from the naval captain seated across from him. He stood, his hands resting firmly on the table.

"I do believe we have outstayed our welcome, Lieutenant Mason." He replied, nodding his head in his friend's direction, his eyes training on Alaric. "Thank you for the delicious meal," turning, he led the way through the hatch and onto the deck.

"Stay here a moment," Alaric said, gesturing for Molly to remain in his cabin. He followed the men on deck.

"The Admiral may be deceived, but your time with pirates has clouded your judgement. You have become one of them. Do not think he will give you leave any longer or be merciful once he hears what you have been doing to the vessels in these waters. You will hang." Mason spat out, "and don't think for one minute your captain here will be spared." He said, jutting a finger at Alaric.

"You forget your place, Lieutenant," Ethan said, taking a step nearer the man.

"Mason, that's enough," Captain Hanes called over his shoulder as he crossed over the rickety planking.

"I told you, I'd be keeping a watch on you," Mason replied, stepping onto the plank, "oh and, give my regards to Miss Maclean." His gaze shifting to Alaric. "It's not often you get to set your eyes upon such a rare beauty out at sea. I doubt there are many women on the islands with hair the color of hers."

The commands from the naval ship rang through the evening air. Their sails dropped, pulling the ship away from *The Trinity*. "The bastard has some nerve." Alaric said, his hands fisted at his sides.

"He knows we did not attack that merchant ship," Ethan said, facing Alaric, "but it will not stop him from sending word to the Admiral."

"What of Captain Hanes? What's in it for him?" Alaric asked, leaning against the railing, watching the ship sail on. Their own canvas dropping, filling with the night's breeze.

"He will play along with Mason's tricks. Word is, I was to be promoted, but if I step down, step out of line or worse, it is Captain Hanes that is likely to get it. So, you see, he will as soon see to it that I am disposed of as quick as Lieutenant Mason would." Ethan explained, his fist meeting the wooden railing. Silence spread across the deck, the men had returned to their duties or found their hammocks. The bell would ring in a few hours, indicating the shift change. It was rather an eerie sound in the black of night. Not that the night watch was always terrible, Alaric had rather enjoyed it on many occasions. It had given him time to think, a chance for some solitude, which was not always easy to come by on a sea fairing vessel. "What of Miss Maclean? What do you make of her story?" He asked, glad to change the subject.

"I cannot say, but I will be finding out," he assured. He did not wish to press her, but her reaction and tale had him doubting even more that his decision of letting her stay aboard his ship was a good one. He had concluded that when he delivered young Mackay to his auntie that he would insist Miss Maclean go with him. He had no doubt the aunt would be able to assist in finding Molly a fair position in the colonies.

Alaric headed below, rubbing a hand on the back of his neck. He had felt pride in Molly's trust in him when she had told her story at his table that night. He had heard the quaver in her voice, knowing she was pleading with him to not give her away. Now, he must confront her and possibly have to break that small bit of ground he had gained. Knocking on the hatch, he cautiously opened it, not waiting for a response.

"I cleared the table and cleaned the cabin from the meal. I was unsure of the table or how to return it to your own. I asked Cook to help, and he showed me how it's done." Molly said, her words coming out quicker with every breath.

Alaric stood, amazed at how fast the lass had cleared the room. He had been gone mere minutes, yet his cabin looked cleaner than before. "Thank you," he said, walking to the desk and pouring a dram of whiskey. Holding the bottle and looking Molly over, he realized she may be in need of one too. He could see her hands shaking, despite her holding them close to her middle. "It'll calm your nerves," he said, gesturing towards the cup.

"He was a brutal man." Her voice barely audible, even in the silence of the cabin. She was sure the captain could hear the beating of her heart. Molly could not make herself look him in the eyes. She did not wish to see his disapproval or anger. She almost wished he would shout, show his anger, the kindness and calm confused her. It only made her feel even worse about her deceit and lie. He and Ethan and spoken up for her, had not given her away when they so easily could have. "They said he was found, laying there upon the floor." Taking a deep breath she continued, "I was tending the fires in the rooms when he came and approached me. It was the day I met you."

"What did he do? When he approached you that morning?" He asked, his eyes dark. Taking a sip from the cup he held, watching her.

"He grabbed at me." She had never told a soul of what she had suffered at the hands of Lord Willington. Not that the other servants did not know, they were well aware, but speaking the words aloud was different somehow. She could not tell if it was relief she felt or fear. "It was not the first time he did so. I knew no one would help me. He knew it too. I still held the bucket from tending the fire. I didn't hesitate. I…" Her words fell, leaving the cabin in silence once more.

"You then fled the estate?" Alaric asked, his body rigid.

"Aye, I did." She replied, the cup he had offered her, remaining in her hands. Waiting, she wished he would say more.

"You then boarded my ship in an attempt to flee from his wrath should he wake."

"Aye, tis true. I also feared what the officers would do, should they find out." The thought, making her stomach turn. He was a privateer and his friend a Naval Captain, they had a responsibility. A duty to bring in those that deserved to hang or pay for a crime they had committed.

"You said it was not the first time he grabbed you. What happened before? How did you come to be a housemaid for Lord Willington?"

Molly turned, facing the bed that sat at the other side of the cabin. "My uncle, he was a greedy man. He sold me to Lord Willington, I cannot say for how much I was worth, but it was an offer that neither my uncle, nor Lord Willington would pass up." Her body shifting, facing the captain once more. "Lord Willington often had a house full of guests. Those nights I was safe from his grasp. The nights he was alone were the ones I knew to stay out of sight as best I could. Those were the nights I stayed in the stables. The worst of the times was when he struck me, knocking me down the stairs and into the servant's hall. It was many days later that I finally recovered. A slave on the other side of the plantation tended to me while I recovered. See, they did not want word getting out of what Lord Willington had done. They feared a guest might come upon me while I recovered in the big house. So, they tucked me away out of sight." She finished, letting out the breath she had not realized she had been holding.

Alaric drained the last drops that remained in his cup, placing it on the desk. "And you chose to keep this from me? You knew the officers or even Lord Willington himself may be looking for you, yet you thought boarding my ship and putting my crew's lives in danger was a good idea?" Alaric stood, facing out the small window that sat at the back of his cabin.

"You will hand me over then?" She asked, swallowing the lump that was beginning to form in her throat. She had told herself she should not put any trust in the Irish captain, no matter how kind he had appeared. He was a privateer and she understood why he must do what was expected of him. Molly had not realized just how much she had begun to trust him or how much she had begun to enjoy being on the ship, caring for the animals and speaking with Cook, Doc and Ol' Shorty.

"No, I will not," he finally replied. "You were doing no more than protecting yourself from a vile man." Stepping closer to her he added, "besides your crime, if you could even call it such a name, was done on land, not at sea." He explained, waving an arm through the air, "and seeing as how you are neither a pirate, nor an enemy of the crown, awaiting to gain information. I see no harm in letting you go free, Miss Maclean." He winked, taking the cup from her hands. "I only ask, that you do not pull your wee dagger on me again, or bring any more beasts into my cabin," his voice low.

Molly nodded; her body numb. She had not expected him to say what he had. She had expected anything, anything else but his understanding and forgiveness. She tried swallowing but the lump would not allow it. "I thank ye, Captain Stein. Though, I promise to not lift my blade to you, so long as you behave, I am not sure I can promise to not bring any more animals in your cabin."

Laughing, Alaric moved to the large chest that contained the various maps of the seas. "Fair enough, Miss Maclean." Rummaging through the rolls of parchment, he found the one he was looking for. Spreading it out on the desk, he placed the sextant on one corner, his dirk and a round pendant, a knot of vines etched into it, on the other corners, assisting in holding the map down, stopping it from rolling back in on itself.

Molly watched the man in front of her. He was by far the most intimidating and confusing man she had ever met. She had known vicious men, loyal men and an amount of kind men she could count on one hand but had never met a man that terrified her yet made her feel safe at the very same time. A moment ago, she had cursed herself for trusting the man, now here she was, feeling even more trusting of him. Even if he promised not to turn her in, what would Captain Clarke think? Would he see fit to bring her in? "What of Captain Clarke? He is bound to find the truth out and when he does, will he lock me up or return me to the plantation?" Her voice shaky, giving away her emotion.

"Not likely, Ethan is a good man and when he hears the truth, he will understand and will not blame you." His eyes fixed on her, briefly looking up from the parchment.

Brushing her hair behind her shoulder as best she could, she took a look at the map. "How will we find young Mackay's auntie?" She asked, wondering what it meant for her. Molly still feared he would try and leave her with young Mackay and his aunt. "I've heard the colonies are no longer as small as they were. More and more settlers are heading there. The servants at the plantation used to speak of the colonies and the opportunities they hold. Are those opportunities what brought his aunt there?" She asked, a rock forming in her stomach. Molly had always enjoyed hearing the stories of the colonies, even though some of them were terrifying and spoke of dangers she would never have imagined. Now she was on a ship bound for those untamed and unknown lands, free forever from the miseries she had known, yet she did not feel any calmer. She had dreamt of the colonies before, of starting a new life there like so many others, to just be another settler. The thought of leaving the safety she had begun to feel aboard *The Trinity* though was nearly too much to bear.

"Aye, I suspect it was part of her reason for going to the colonies, though many Scotsmen were forced to leave their lands or be faced with prosecution and possibly branded a traitor to the crown. When their clan lands and estates were taken from them, many had no other choice but to flee." He explained, still looking over the map. "As for how we will find the woman, I will speak more with Mackay and see what I can find out. We will have to ask around a bit, with any luck, it will not take long to find her. Young Mackay is eager to be reunited and we have to continue our own search."

Molly scrunched her brows, "Who or what exactly are

you in search of?" She asked, her curiosity peaked once more.

"A pirate that goes by the name of Thomas Banning. A vile man that cannot be allowed to sail the seas any longer." He answered, the muscles in his arms tightening.

"What has he done?" Molly knew many men that fit such a description but could not help but wonder what this Banning had done to earn just distain from the captain.

Alaric let out a breath, looking up at Molly, the look on his face made her want to take a step back. Refraining, she nearly regretting asking about what the man had done. "He took something from me that can never be replaced." Standing straighter and crossing his arms over his chest he continued, "he also kidnapped Lucas, threatened Catherine, destroyed merchant and passenger vessels that stood no chance against him. Taking what he wants, caring not for the poor souls that find themselves in front of him." Molly remained silent, listening to the horrors the man had performed. Alaric paused, clearly unsure if he should continue. "He is the one that attacked the vessel young Mackay was on, killing the crew. He also may hold information to the whereabouts of the man that attacked Ethan's sister, not to mention Ethan wants his own revenge on the man for what he did to him." Looking back down at the map, he bent over it once more.

"I am sorry for the pain he has caused." She whispered, wanting to say more, to take the hurt he felt from him but not knowing how.

A knock sounded on the hatch, followed by Captain Clarke entering the cabin before Alaric had a chance to answer. "I apologize for interrupting, but a ship has been sighted. They are headed in our direction. Pirates, Captain." Glancing between the two of them.

"I'll be right up." He responded, immediately moving to the chest that held his sword and flintlocks. Quickly and efficiently loading one, he handed it to Molly. "Don't hesitate to use it if someone comes in," he paused, "just make sure that someone is not me, first." Winking, he strapped his sword and the other two pistols to his belt. "Still have your dagger?"

"Aye," Molly responded, her heart dropping to her stomach at the thought of yet another battle. "Be careful, Captain Stein." She finally breathed out.

"Aye, you as well, lass." With that he turned, heading through the hatch and up on deck.

Gripping the flintlock in her hands, she marveled at the weight of it, turning it over in her hands, she examined it. She had never truly looked one of the guns over before. A shot fired, rocking the ship beneath her feet. *A warning shot,* she thought. She no longer had to grip the table or a chair to steady herself when a blast swayed the ship. She had gotten used to the feel of the ever-moving vessel and the feel of the wooden planks beneath her feet.

She could now hear the orders above being given to the crew. The captain's deep voice commanding his men to prepare for battle. Backing against his desk, she waited. The shots would come ringing through *The Trinity* at any moment. Her grip tightening on the pistol he had given her.

Closing her eyes against the shouts and blasts, she remained still, waiting for the moment it would be all over. The ship bucked. She could feel the blasts rippling through the center of the ship. Her thoughts traveling to the men below, the men firing the cannons, manning the pumps. What of the men on deck? The captain? There was nothing protecting him from a musket shot or a blade. Swallowing hard, she squeezed her eyes tighter. She had seen the men recovering from their wounds from the previous battles. Doc had said the crew had been fortunate, only a life or two was lost in each battle thus far. One of the sailors, a man named Colin, had his arm shattered by a cannon blast. Doc had been unable to save it and had to remove it. Her stomach turned at the thought. She had stayed with the animals nearly the whole night, not wishing to see any of carnage that remained.

Another blast sounded, this one from *The Trinity,* shouts roared out. The sounds of the muskets firing and drumming of feet above, pounded in her ears. The pounding grew closer, Molly opened her eyes, it sounded as if the battle was right on the other side of the hatch. Taking a step closer, she listened for the sound of the captain's voice. The hatch shook, nearly knocking the bolt from its place. Taking a step around the desk, she waited, her ears flooded from the noises above. If it was the captain, she could not hear him say so. Another hard knock to the door loosened the bolt, slipping it from the latch. Molly raised the flintlock, hesitating in case Captain Stein entered.

A dark figure loomed in the doorway, quickly stepping into the cabin, shutting the door behind him. Desperately trying to hold the pistol steady in her hands she pointed it directly at the sailor. He stood a good head taller than her, his chest bare, a blade held firmly in his grasp.

"Stay back," the words falling from her lips, trying to sound firmer than she felt.

A laugh emanated from the pirate, sounding more like a vicious snarl. "No, I'll be quick." He stepped forward, his heavy, dark boots scraping loudly against the wooden planks.

A moment ago, all Molly could hear was the clanking of swords and the cries of the men above, but now all was silent except the pounding of her heart and the heavy breathing of the man in front of her. Backing up, she felt her backside hit the wall. The captain's words echoed in her mind. The burly man stepping ever closer. Feeling her finger curve around the trigger of the flintlock, the pressure grew stronger. The blast sounded, ringing in her ears and filling her senses with thick smoke. Her arms aching, she could not wait in the cabin, for fear another pirate would come in. She had no means of reloading the pistol and if the next man was as large as the first, her dagger would do little good against his strength or his sword. The smoke cleared, the sailor's body lay still and lifeless on the planks. Blood steadily seeping from the wound in his chest. Her hand shook, unable to hold the flintlock any longer. Letting it slip to the ground, she tore her eyes from the pirate, rushing from the hatch and down the companionway. Her vision blurring, she could hear shouts behind her, the battle still raging on. She could not look back, did not want to know if another pirate followed.

A shot fired behind her, waiting to feel the searing pain she knew was bound to come, she ducked into the large cabin, the animals staring frantically back at her. Hiding behind the cow, she shut her eyes, trying as she might to block the image of the man that lay in the cabin from her mind, the way he had looked at her. His face turned briefly to Lord Willington's in her mind. Squeezing her eyes tighter together, Molly rested her head against the cow's smooth fur. Listening to the animal's breathing and trying to slow her own.

21

Feeling the blade drive deep into flesh, he spun around, kicking his booted foot into another pirate's middle. Stopping him just long enough for Alaric to swing his sword over his head and down across the pirate's chest. Moving forward through the fray he caught sight of Joseph, struggling with a much more skilled fighter.

Shoving the young sailor to the side, he blocked the pirate's blade with his own. The force behind the swords caused the blades to screech eerily against one another. Gritting his teeth, he pushed forward, making the pirate stagger back. Allowing the man to regain his footing, Alaric lunged forward, moving his blade down against the sailor's leg. The pirate dropped, gripping the cut that now flowed crimson. A shot sounded, Alaric turned, seeing who fired but no smoke could be seen, no man held their pistol. Alaric felt the blood drain from his body.

Running to the hatch he kicked at it, hoping to feel the resistance but instead it flung open with ease. A man lay on the ground, a pool of blood forming on the planks below him. "Miss Maclean?" Alaric shouted, looking about the room, there were not many places she could possibly hide in the cabin, aside from a chest or two. "Molly?" He shouted again. Noticing his flintlock laying abandoned on the floor. Striding from the cabin he headed down the companion way, hoping with every fiber of his being, the lass has fled down towards the animals and not into the midst of the battle. Pulling his other pistol from his belt he hastened on. Images of the woman he had failed to protect those years ago flashing in his mind.

Alaric listened, he could hear footsteps, echoing down the companionway. Catching a glimpse of a sailor and a flash of fiery hair, he lengthened his steps, "sailor," he spoke, knowing the man was not one of his but not wanting to fire at the man from behind, he raised his flintlock, aiming it at the pirate's now exposed chest. Firing, he did not slow his steps, he needed to get to Molly. No telling how many pirates had made their way below decks or if Molly was injured.

"Miss Maclean?" He asked, his voice loud enough to be heard over the shouts from above, but not enough to draw attention to anyone that might overhear. "Molly," he called out, cautiously stepping closer. "Molly, are you injured?" He asked, coming around the large animal. Her eyes were shut tight, her head lain against the beast. Tentatively lifting his hand, he brushed her waving hair from her face, letting his hand rest gently on her shoulder.

Molly's eyes fluttered open, a look of fear clouding her gaze, slowly transforming into relief as she realized who stood before her. "Molly, are you alright?" He asked again, concerned by her behavior and confusion.

"Aye," she slowly nodded. "I don't think the man I left in your cabin is, though," she confessed.

"No," a deep rumbling in his chest, "no, I don't believe he is, lass." Gently running his fingers over her hair. "You did alright." His expression turning serious once more. "He did not touch you, then?" Alaric asked, almost fearing her answer.

Shaking her head, she replied, "no, he did not have time. I did as you said to. I did not hesitate." She explained, almost searching for self-assurance.

"Aye, you did, and you did right. No one will blame you for it." His jaw clenched and his voice hardening. "I am only sorry you had the need to. I should have kept a closer eye on the hatch. A closer eye on you. I am sorry." He breathed out, the guilt and fear of her possibly being injured or worse, weighing heavy on him. The sooner they reached the colonies, the better. He needed to find a safe place for her. Once he got her and young Mackay settled, he could continue on, without fear of losing her to the hands of a pirate.

"No, you had to be on deck, fighting with your crew and defending your ship and these waters. You are the captain and a privateer. I understand that and I knew the risks when I came aboard this ship." She replied, her tone just as firm as his had been. "I will be safe down here now. By the sounds of it, the battle is slowing. You will be needed on deck, Captain Stein." She answered, the trembling of her body giving away her lack of courage.

"Very well, I will be down in a moment to fetch you." Alaric concluded, his eyes traveling the length of her body,

191

assessing her slender form for any injuries she may be hiding or not even realize she had, in her state of shock. He applauded her courage and bravery; she had done what he had told her to do. Not many women could have, and he knew she needed a moment alone. A moment for her fear and emotions to be set free.

"Alaric," Ethan spoke, coming up beside him. "I sent the crew to lock the pirates in their brig like we had done before. With Captain Hanes not far from here, I am sure they will find them." He explained, walking with Alaric to the edge of the ship, watching the crew take the pirates below.

"Very good, thank you." Alaric nodded, his thoughts still on Molly. "A man broke into my cabin." Letting out a long breath he had been holding, "she used the flintlock I had given her and took off down the companionway. Another sailor followed her. I caught up with them and took care of him before he reached her." Running a hand over his face, the image of a woman lying on the wet planking, her hair falling about her ashen skin.

"Was Miss Maclean harmed?" Ethan asked, studying Alaric's expression.

"No, she was very lucky. She was not harmed, not this time." Alaric answered, his fist pushing hard against the railing of *The Trinity*, the solid wood biting into his knuckles. The crew had come back on deck, gathering up the fallen sailors that lay about the planks. Hammocks at the ready for the upcoming burial. Alaric had spotted three of his crew members laying amongst the dead, that did not mean there were not more below. It was not many, as far as battles go. His crew was skilled and well prepared. Even the younger ship-mates knew their way around a vessel full of enemy sailors.

"What do you mean by that?" Ethan asked, shifting his stance.

"I mean that a ship, especially a privateer ship, is not a safe place for a woman to be. Miss Maclean was very fortunate this time. If I had not heard the shot she fired, I would not have gone to the cabin, would not have headed down the companionway and would not have found her in time. Found her before that man got to her." His eyes dark, he stared into the waters below, shards of wood and bits of canvas and rope still floated about. "While serving in the Royal Navy, I was charged with the care of young Lady. She was on her way to spend the season with her young cousin. Her father knew the captain and asked if she could be escorted by the navy rather than a merchant or passenger vessel for fear one of those may be set upon by an enemy ship or pirate." Alaric looked about, the crew had begun repairs on the ship, it would be a few hours before they could sail again.

"What happened to the Lady?" Ethan asked, a knowing expression on his face.

"She was shot," He replied, "I was in sole charge of her. It was my duty to protect her, keep her safe, and I failed her."

"I cannot believe you did not do all you could." Ethan reasoned.

"Be that as it may, I failed to protect her. Our vessel was attacked. I was in a cabin with her, we had bolted the door, just in case. I did not want to take any risks, despite the fact that I had wished to be above deck. I had felt trapped and uncomfortable not being up with the rest of the crew. It was not long into the battle when the pounding to the door happened. I knew the bolt would not hold long. I was prepared. I took out the men that entered. Knowing it was no longer safe for her in the cabin, I intended to hide her amongst the crates and canvases. I did not realize another man saw us. I should have had her in front of me, but she was in shock and refused to move. I had to pull her along." Stopping, Alaric swallowed, he would never forget the feeling of her hand in his, how hers had suddenly grown limp, the moment his ears had registered the shot. "He had come up behind us and shot her."

"I am sorry," Ethan began, "by the sounds of it though, there was little you could have done. I know it is not much help to say it but there it is." Clapping Alaric on the shoulder, "we have all had a task or duty that meant a lot to us. That for some unforgivable reason, beyond our control, we fail it. Fail the people involved."

"Aye, and if anyone can understand that best, it is you," Alaric answered.

"That does not mean though that what happened to that young Lady will happen to Miss Maclean." A grin spread across his lips, "and from what I know of the lass, she has no problem putting men in their place."

"Aye, that is no lie," Alaric replied with a grin, thinking of that first day when Molly had held the blade to his neck. "I need to check on Doc and the injured," He finished, nodding his thanks to Ethan and heading across the deck. The fallen sailors were sewn into the hammocks, awaiting their final burial. Several men were scrubbing the decks, washing away any traces of battle, as best they could. The rest repaired the ship from where the cannons tore through the planking. They would need to make proper and longer lasting repairs once they made it to the colonies. They also needed to replenish their stores. They had been fortunate enough to have come across plenty of ships that they had not run low on much, except fresh water. Even the food was not spoiling as fast due to the cooler temperatures as they neared the colonies.

"What's the count, Doc?" Alaric asked grimly. Watching carefully as Doc sewed up a cut that spanned the length of the sailor's back. It was not too deep, the man had been fortunate, but no doubt he would need to be on light duties with many of the others.

"Four," Doc replied, looking at Alaric over his spectacles before returning his eyes to the task at hand.

"How are you holding up, Gordy?" He asked, moving over to the man's hammock. A strip of white fabric holding his arm close to his chest.

"Not as bad as some," he said, nodding his head in the direction of the sailor Doc was still stitching up.

"What happened?" Alaric asked, gesturing to the bandage.

"A cannon blast knocked me to the deck, knocking me shoulder out of place, Capt'n. Doc says to not move it for a few days, but I still have me other arm to work with." Gordy grinned, wincing a bit when he repositioned himself on the hammock.

"That you do. Take it easy for a bit. We are sailing nearer the colonies where we will stop in and resupply our provisions and fix the ship up right. You have time to rest."

Alaric walked from hammock to hammock, checking on his crew. Many of the older and more seasoned of the sailors had received just as bad if not worse injuries in previous battles. A few of the younger ones though he knew needed more bucking up. Giving the injured all an extra ration of rum, he made his rounds. The surgery smelled of blood, vinegar, and herbs, mingling together to make an unpleasant aroma. A few of the sailors that were not injured as seriously had already grabbed holystone and water from the sea, washing the blood from the planks and scrubbing the salty water into the grains of the wood. Leaving a cup of rum with Henry who had been shot in the leg, he headed up the stairs, taking in a deep breath of fresh, crisp air and heading back down, to retrieve Molly.

22

"Jonathan, you'll accompany me." Thomas said, adjusting the leather straps that draped across his chest and around his waist, holding flintlocks and a sword. He was to take a river boat up stream to meet a man about a shipment of goods. The man had been secretive and had not wished to meet near the towns, instead choosing a remote cabin. Thomas had previous dealings with other men that did not wish to be overheard before and knew these men could be just as unpredictable as himself. He had begun to trust Jonathan and knew he was not only a skilled fighter but did not have any qualms about removing unwanted obstacles.

Thomas was anxious to get moving and be on his way, he had several more stops to make along the way and did not wish to stay in the colonies long. Once on the pirate round he would be harder to track and not as easily spotted as he made his way to England, but there was little chance of making it out of the colonies in haste. He had already received a letter from the governor in New York, a request to dine with him and discuss important business. Thomas had scoffed when he had read the letter. The governor had been gracious enough to grant Thomas a pardon, had given him his Letter of Marque and repaired his ship for him, but at a price. Thomas now seemed under the ever-demanding control of the man. Not that he minded the tasks the governor had given him in the past, but he had little time to do his bidding if he was expected to take on the shipment under the orders of Liam Jackson.

Walking down the plank and onto the busy dock, Thomas headed towards a set of stables that sat at the edge of the port. The strong smell of manure filling his nose. It had been too long since he had sat astride a horse. Digging in his pocket, he pulled out a coin, tossing it to the man that was tending to one of the beasts. "I need two horses, man."

Pocketing the coin, the man gestured to the horses at the end of the stalls, "Those last two are well rested and fed. You can take them." Turning back to loosening the sinch on the mare next to him and removing the faded saddle.

Thomas pulled himself up onto the calm animal, "which way to the boats that'll take us upriver?" He asked, adjusting his seat.

"Just up that there path. Keep headin' northwest for a bit, follow the banks and you'll reach the docks." The man said, not bothering to look up from his work, scraping away muck and rocks from the horse's tired hooves. The horse's back was dark with sweat, its fur sticking tightly to its exhausted body. It eagerly swooped its head into the trough, taking in the much needed water.

Nodding in response, Thomas steered his horse towards the path, leading the way up the muddy trail. It was not the first time he had been to Charles Town, it had been quite some time since his previous visit. Looking about at the surroundings, he saw a few new buildings, and the makeshift roads held more people than they had before but not too much had changed. Clicking at the horse beneath him, he sped the beast along, not wishing to be caught on the river at night.

Houses, taverns, and shops spanned the muddy paths. Ships of various sizes pulled in and out of the bustling port delivering and trading goods from around the world. Most of the ships, coming directly from the West Indies. Men bringing in furs and skins to barter with and sell, stopped at the shops and trading posts. Breaking through all the buildings that lined both sides of the wide path, the river became visible. Large grasses stuck out from the water, giving the birds around the area plenty of places to nest, and roost while watching for the numerous fish and frogs to go by.

Finding their way to the men that waited aboard their flatboats and packets, cleaning, and gathering supplies and passengers to take to the plantations further up the river. They dismounted the horses, "you there, take these to the stables." Thomas demanded of a boy the stood outside of a small trading post.

Quickly, the boy nodded, fear visible in his young eyes. "Yis, sir," he replied, snatching up the reins and leading the horses to a much smaller stable than the last one. An older man stood near the stable, his hair white with age, a peppered beard nearly reaching his chest. Kicking at the young boy who brought the horses to him, Thomas could not make out what the gruff man was saying but it appeared he was telling the boy to hurry up. Snickering at the sight, Thomas looked back at the boats, the note he had received told him to speak with man named Lewis, he would take Thomas to the cabin where he was to meet Liam.

Walking onto one of the small docks, Thomas kept his hand resting casually on his flintlock that remained strapped to his belt. "Where can I find Lewis?" He called out to the man that stood on aboard one of the nearer flatboats.

Looking up from repositioning bags of grain, crates of food and one crammed with chickens. "Aye, I can tell you but what is it you want with him?" He asked, his eyes cautious and guarded. A large knife hanging from his hip.

"He is to take us upriver to meet a Liam Jackson." Thomas replied, frustration rising at the man's insolence.

"Aye, come aboard then," the man gestured for them to step onto the flatboat. "I be the Lewis you be looking for. Liam told me to be expectin' you, but he said no such thing 'bout yer friend." Lewis grunted.

"Well, if you do not wish to take both me and my friend, then it will be you having to tell Liam you chose not to do his bidding." Thomas challenged, stepping closer to the man.

Spitting into the river, he looked back at Thomas, "I never said, I'd no take him, but I charge per passenger, and your friend there was not in the agreement. I ain't so sure Liam will like being made to pay for an extra fella." He concluded, looking Jonathan over, his lips turned up in what only could be considered a snarl.

Jonathan stepped forward, a knife in hand, "you will take

us to your man now or have the gators chewing on your bones by sundown." He warned, the tip of his blade, pushing against Lewis's middle.

"That's enough Jonathan." Thomas said, "there will be no need for that. I do not want anything coming in the way of getting Liam's shipment and killing his man will likely displease him. Besides, you kill him," Thomas jutted a pointy finger at the boatman, "you will then have to steer this boat and I'm rather certain you wouldn't enjoy it." Sheathing his knife, Jonathan glowered at Lewis, keeping a close eye on the man as he readied the boat for heading up stream.

Thomas gritted his teeth against the chill in the air. He had warm clothes aboard *The Amity* but had not thought to don them. The leaves had begun to change into the brilliant array of colors that would soon fill the hills and mountains. The occasional green leaf could still be seen, the shades of orange or yellow burning their way along the green, slowly engulfing it with a new color. Sitting against the wall that led into a small cabin, Thomas pulled out his knife, whittling away at a small branch he had picked up from the deck of the flatboat.

"Here you are," Lewis said from atop the cabin roof. A smooth piece of wood sticking out from the top, allowing Lewis to steer the boat up the river. Hopping from the top of the small boat, he stepped onto the wobbly dock that stuck halfway up through the shallow water at the riverbank, connecting the boat to the land. Letting out a loud whistle, he gestured towards a cabin that sat a few feet back from the banks of the river, sitting amongst towering trees.

Thomas glanced at Jonathan, feeling uneasy about the

situation. If this was a trap, they would have no escape. He could not help but think of the enemies he had made over the years. A few of which were canny enough to create such an enticing plan. Taking a pirate from his ship would be the sure way to get the advantage over him. The promise of such a high payment for bringing in a shipment, whatever it may be, for the man was too good of an opportunity to forego. Thomas had known the risks when he had agreed to me the stranger and was not about to back out now.

"Ah, much thanks to you Lewis for bringing these men to me this day." He said, tossing a leather pouch at the man as he approached the group, coming from the cabin. A sneer spread across Lewis's face, exposing cracked and missing teeth. Opening the pouch to check the number of coins that rested in it, he nodded, thanking Liam before heading back on his boat. Going below, into the small cabin, to hide away his payment.

"Liam Jackson, I take it." Thomas offered, stepping onto the banks of the river. His feet crunching the long since dead and decaying leaving and sticks that littered the ground.

"Quite right. It is a pleasure to finally meet you Captain Banning. If you will please join me in the cabin," his arm extended, pointing the way to the cabin that blended in nearly perfectly with the surroundings. A silvery ribbon of smoke slipping through a narrow chimney at the top, giving the cabin's location away. "Your friend may join us as well, of course." He added as an afterthought, having caught the look the two of them had shared.

"Is this where you stay?" Thomas asked, seeing nothing

around the cabin to indicate the man lived there, except for a pile of neatly chopped wood that rested against the side of the cabin.

"From time to time. When I have a shipment that I do not want to risk being stolen or when I am meeting a potential business partner," he replied, opening the door to the cabin, and bidding the men entrance. The cabin on the inside was bigger than it appeared. A dug out area in wall at the far side of the cabin where the fire burned, bringing light and warmth to the room. A pot swung above the fire on a metal rod, steam coming from the contents inside it. "Please, take a seat," Liam suggested, sitting in one of the only two chairs in the room, a small, worn table sitting between them.

"In your letter you spoke of a shipment but did not say what. Tell me more." Thomas spoke, wanting to get to the point rather than sitting there, making pleasantries all afternoon.

"Yes, a rather delicate and tricky item to secure, but one that comes with a very generous price if delivered correctly." He answered, glancing from Jonathan who stood near the fire, and back at Thomas.

"Go on," Thomas urged, his curiosity piqued at what such a prize may be.

"There is an Earl in London, Earl Whitby. He and I had a rather nasty falling out, you see, and he did not grant me what was owed to me." Liam explained, leaning back in his chair, eyeing Thomas.

"And what was that? What does he owe you?" His mind filled with the delights an Earl might promise.

"His daughter," Liam said, his voice holding more than a little hint of want.

Jonathan scoffed, "you saying you be wanting, Capt'n Banning to steal an Earl's daughter for you? A heavy a payment indeed."

"I take it you are loyal to your Captain since he brought you here today, clearly trusting you to keep him safe, in case unforeseen circumstances occurred. Therefore, I trust you will not speak of what you hear today to anyone." Liam's threat obvious.

"You misunderstand me," Jonathan replied, feigning insult. "I have no objection in assisting Capt'n Banning in the kidnapping of this man's daughter."

"You have much experience with such things?" Liam asked, now eyeing Jonathan more closely.

"Of sorts, aye." He shrugged, idly stirring the contents in the pot.

Thomas watched the exchange, wondering what Jonathan had meant. He knew little of the man's past, only that he had attacked Harding's woman, causing him to be nearly sent to the gallows if it had not been for Thomas and his men, taking him with them. "He will not speak of the shipment. Now tell me, where can I find this Earl's daughter?"

"Her father spends most his time gambling and drinking at White's so you will not have to worry about him. The family is currently staying in Grosvenor Square and will be there for some time." Leaning forward in his seat, his face unyielding, "the girl will be unharmed, untouched in every way. She is to be for me alone. If I find so much as a finger mark on her, you will not get your payment and you will never be able to touch or even look at another woman again. Is that understood?" He demanded, slowly sitting himself back in his chair.

"Aye," Thomas spat, "will that be all for the shipment? Where am I to bring the girl?"

"You may bring back any slaves and servants you can find. So long as the women are pure and untouched, and the men are strong and able bodied. I prefer to get top price for them, as I'm sure you will as well. Bring the girl and any others you can manage, back here. I'll be waiting." Standing, he moved over to a crate that sat in the corner. Pulling out a book, its frayed spine, barely holding the pages in. Opening it up, he pulled a paper out. "This is the Earl of Whitby's lovely daughter." The sketch depicted a young Lady, her hair piled atop her head, a single ringlet falling over her shoulder, draping down her chest.

"Very lovely indeed," Thomas murmured, gazing down at the parchment.

"Mind you keep your hands and your eyes to yourself, Banning. And mind your crew does as well." He reinstated. "Take the sketch, that way you don't forget what the Lady looks like. I expect you back in no more than a few months' time." He concluded, pausing he listened at the door.

Voices could be heard outside, Thomas recognized one of the voices as Lewis's. The other man's was deeper, more assertive. Cracking the door open, Liam peered out cautiously. Letting his body relax, he widened the door. "It is just one of the fur traders. There are many that come through Charles Town to trade the furs and skins with the merchants and folks in the towns. We have no quarrel with them. They don't mind me and my cabin here, I bring them goods they cannot get in the mountains around here and they bring me furs and meat that keep me going in the colder months." Leading the way from the cabin, Thomas and Jonathan followed.

The two men speaking near the river's edge looked up at the group. "Leon Cutter, good to see you. Any new furs?" Liam asked, showing no sign of unease around the man. He wore the typical boots and clothes most the settlers did but with an added warmth from the animal fur he adorned as a vest.

"Just traded all them in this morning. I'll be going out again to reset the traps and snares. I'll be sure to bring you a pelt and some dried meats." He concluded, his eyes shifting from Liam to the two strangers behind him.

"Forgive me, this is Captain Thomas Banning and his friend Jonathan." Stepping aside to allow the men to meet. "This here is Leon Cutter, no better trapper in the area."

Leon snorted in response, "I know this land and the people better than most, aye, but there are many a good trappers in the region." Nodding his greeting to Thomas and Jonathan, he bid them farewell, making his way past the cabin and disappearing into the vast woods. A tapping noise sounded from above, drawing Thomas's attention. A small bird hammered its beak into the side of a tree, boring its way into the bark. The colonies were far different from any island in the West Indies, hosting animals that could not be found on any of the islands he was used to. Even most of the people were different, despite having mainly come from the islands themselves. The new lands, dangers and opportunities seemed to shape the people in another way, molding them to the lands they now belonged to. It made him feel uncertain and anxious. The prospects these lands and people offered were far richer in many ways but were more of a risk than he liked to take.

"We must be going." Thomas spoke, interrupting Lewis and Liam's discussion of a rice plantation further up the river. Thomas wanted to be away from the river as the evening approached. He remembered a tavern tucked away in the town. It had offered ample entertainment before and he hoped it would again.

23

Molly stood at the railing. Her eyes wide at the sights in front of her. Never had she seen trees with their leaves in so many different colors. They covered the mountains that towered in the distance. Mountains larger than she had ever seen. People bustled about in the town, women carried baskets from stall to stall, walking into the different shops, filling the baskets with the essentials they needed. A chill ran down her body. The air was crisp and cool, a steady breeze blowing dark clouds in from the north. The temperatures had dropped by several degrees and Molly had little protection from cold. The captain had been kind enough to loan her one of his oversized coats, but it would not do. The arms reached down several inches from where her fingertips ended and the length of it was nearly as long as her gown, which in itself had grown dingy, worn and near to falling apart. She had told the captain at the beginning of their voyage she would pay her way, but in truth she had no money of her own, certainly not enough to purchase a new gown or even a cloak.

"Quite a sight, ain't it, Miss Maclean?" Ol' Shorty asked, coming up beside her. The ship had made port and the plank was being lowered to the dock. "You'll never see another place like it, Miss. We will be going ashore soon, so be sure you've got all you need." He concluded, turning to a group of younger sailors who were looking on the port with as much excitement as Molly had been feeling only a moment ago.

When Shorty had told her they would soon be going ashore, she felt a lump forming in her throat, her stomach suddenly feeling uneasy. What if word had spread to the colonies about what she had done to Lord Willington? Would the authorities take her as soon as they realized it was her, not many maids had hair the color of hers in the West Indies. It would be easy enough to identify her. What of the Captain, would he keep his word and not hand her over to them? Her mind ran with questions, still not sure of Captain Clarke either, despite Captain Stein's assurances. She also dreaded to find out if the Irish Captain she had begun to trust and even enjoy his company, would leave her in the charge and care of strangers in this new land. She did not wish to find out, nor did she wish to step foot off *The Trinity* and never feel the planks of the familiar and safe vessel under her feet again.

"I hope you are ready to go ashore, Miss Maclean." The captain said, his sword and flintlocks strapped to his waist, as if he were expecting to go into battle at any moment.

"Do you think we will run into much trouble?" A small, teasing smile on her lips, pointing at the arsenal hanging from his belt.

"Well, no, not particularly, but I will not take any chances with you going ashore. Not everyone is perfectly friendly and welcoming, be sure to stay close to me." He replied, his accent coming out more as his voice deepened.

Molly felt her face warming, despite the chilly air. Never had anyone wanted to protect her in the past, instead, they had all put her in more danger than she had been in before. The feeling of uneasiness creeping up on her once more. "You don't believe the officers here will know what happened back on the island, do you?" She asked, unable to look up at the captain, still fearing she would see disapproval in his eyes. Her breath was shaky, and she began to step back from the railing, "perhaps I should stay aboard. I won't cause any trouble. I can stay below with the animals." She whispered, wanting desperately to go see more of the land and town but not wanting to risk the wrath of the officers that were sure to be patrolling the town.

"Seeing as it happened in the West Indies, I very much doubt the officers here would be bothered with an incident so far south. These officers have enough to deal with as it is. Besides, I do not believe anyone here has even heard of what happened." He assured her, placing his hand on her back, guiding her steadily forward. "You also cannot stay aboard at this time as so many of the men are going ashore to resupply and properly repair the ship. There would be no one to watch over you and make sure no strays sneak aboard wanting to make off with whatever treasure they think they may find. No, I am afraid you must accompany me in town, and I rather intend to make you enjoy it." He finished, smiling down at her.

Looking about, she realized he had indeed steered her off the ship and they were now walking through the muddy port, towards the busier part of the town, Shorty and Ethan following close behind. Molly could feel her thin slippers digging deep in the mud, soaking the thin material through.

Scrunching her toes, in hopes the mud would not pull the worn slippers from her feet. She pulled the captain's coat tighter about her shoulders as a chilly breeze picked up. Molly took a deep breath in, she could smell the muddy paths, the familiar scent of horses and a trace of an aroma she could not pin down. One she had never known before. Closing her eyes against the breeze, feeling her hair moving with it, she took another breath in. The salty sea was strong in the air but definitely a scent she had grown accustomed to. The other was a strong, almost sweet smell. It traveled on the breeze as if coming from the mountains themselves.

They had found the smithy easy enough. Shorty had mentioned he needed to visit one to fix a hinge that had been badly bent during the previous battle and the captain had questions about the town.

"Aye, I can have this ready by the mornin' but it'll cost ye a bit extra. I have orders in front of yours that are just as urgent." He said, flipping the hinge over in his hand, looking Shorty over.

The captain and Shorty exchanged looks, "Very well, just so long as me hinge works again." Shorty shrugged, moving aside for the captain to place a few coins in the smithy's work-worn hands.

"Where can we find a tavern?" The captain asked, stepping back next to Molly. Despite the large coat and the chill in the air. She could almost feel the warmth from his body. He had barely stepped a foot from her since they had landed in Charles Town.

"Aye, there be a few nearer the docks, but none so savory there." He answered, nodding pointedly at Molly. "I suggest McCrady's Tavern. Just down the path some and about the buildings a bit. They serve some fine food and the best ale in town." The smithy explained, grabbing hold of a strip of metal that glowed orange at the tip. Bringing the hammer down, it sparked, flattening the metal.

"My thanks," the captain nodded. "Shorty here, will be back in the morning to fetch the piece." He concluded, pointing to the bit of metal that now sat on a table, waiting it's turn to be mended. Placing his hand on the back of her arm, the captain led her and the others away from the smithy's.

It did not take long for them to locate McCrady's Tavern, a wooden sign hanging above the door. Laughter, shouts, and music flittered out through the windows in the brick walls. Stepping in through the door, Molly braced herself. Not entirely sure what she feared would be inside the tavern, officers perhaps or simply drunken men. She of course had been around the crew when they had been granted extra rations of grog and ale, but she had grown to know and understand the men aboard *The Trinity* and knew none of them would harm her, nor would the captain allow them even a chance to do so. In a tavern though, a room filled with men they did not know, it could be dangerous for all of them. Molly glanced up at the captain, he stood a good foot taller than her, his shirt tight around the muscles that spanned his shoulders and back. She felt him tense next to her as they walked through the door of the tavern.

The captain placed his hand on Molly's back, causing a shiver to run down her spine. "Let's take this table," he whispered, guiding her to a seat. The tavern was larger than she had expected and warmer than the cool air outside. A group of men played various instruments she could not name but enjoyed the sounds of. A woman, wearing a dress cut a bit too low, swayed to the music, her voice fluttering smoothly through the ruckus that filled the tavern. A group of folks had moved to an area of the room, nearer the music, devoid of tables and chairs that would be sure to be in the way as they danced to the tune that played.

Another woman came over, placing cups of ale on the table. "Excuse me, Miss," the captain spoke up, before the maid could turn to another table.

"What is it I can get for you?" She asked, her voice sultry as she stepped closer to him, the skirts of her dress brushing against his arm.

He cleared his throat, taking a drink of the ale, "My friends and I were wondering if a man by the name of Thomas Banning might have visited this tavern? He would have been aboard a ship called, *The Amity*."

"I couldn't say, love." She pouted, "but then again, I can't be relied on to remember the name of every man that enters this tavern." Winking at him, she brushed a hand across his shoulders as she sauntered off. Molly gaped at the open exchange, uncomfortable at the pit that had formed in her stomach when the woman had placed her hand on the captain's back.

"A few sailors in here, most though appear to live here rather than be at sea most their days." Shorty observed, quickly draining the drink in his cup, and raising his hand in the air for another, drawing the attention of one of the maids. "More ale and four of the pies, please."

"Aye, that may be best. If he had dealings with anyone in Charles Town or if he caused a scene, the men in this town are likely to know about it." Ethan added, not taking his eyes from the tables of men that were scattered about the room. Molly took a small sip of the ale, not minding the taste like she had used to, in fact, she found the whiskey and the ale more tolerable than the grog. The smell of the pies stuffed with meat and ale gravy filled her senses. Placing her hand over her stomach, hoping to stem the grumbling. Men sat at the tables, drinking, talking, playing dice and another game she did not recognize. It had small round pieces set on a board. Each player appeared to take turns, moving one piece at a time across the board.

"May I join ya?" A large, burly man approached the table. His clothes were made of animal skins and furs. His face covered in a bristly beard, round cheeks popping out just above it.

The captain nodded, gesturing towards a chair that remained between Ethan and Shorty. "What's your name, mate?" Sitting up straight, he rolled the bottom of the cup in his hand.

"Leon Cutter," He nodded to the group. "I overheard your question to the maid." His statement causing the captain to lean forward in interest.

"And what is it that you can tell us?" Captain Stein asked, eyeing the newcomer.

"The man you are looking for, he has light hair, a large tattoo on his chest and has...well, the look of a pirate about him, aye?" Leon asked, his voice low.

"That'll be him," Shorty said, scoffing. "He was here in Charles Town then? How long ago was this?" Pausing in his questions only for a moment when the maid filled the cups once more.

"Aye, but we won't be discussing this here." He answered, looking about the room as if he held a dark secret no one else could hear. "Meet me at the mouth of the river. There I will take you to my cabin. We may talk freely there." Standing, he nodded to the group, his eyes resting briefly on Molly, "Miss." He added in a way of goodbyes.

"What do you make of that?" Molly asked curiously. There was something in the man's eyes that reminded her of Cook. He seemed kind and honest. Molly raised her brows at her own thoughts, it was not often she even considered someone she met kind. She rarely let herself believe it, even now, with Captain Stein. He had shown her great kindness and generosity on their voyage, but she feared her own thoughts, her own wanting. Molly knew if she let herself trust him, she would only be opening herself up to the possibility of being betrayed once again.

"We don't have much of a choice. He seemed an honest man and we need to find Banning as quickly as we can. The longer it takes us to find him, the more likely it is that he will find out we are on his trail. "Finish your drinks and pies, lads and we'll be on our way." He added, switching his gaze to Molly, "what do you think of the colonies, thus far, Miss Maclean?"

215

"It really is quite different. I would never have imagined it to be so. I've heard stories of the colonies but never truly realized what it was like. The mountains, trees, buildings and even the people and the smells are nothing like I've ever witnessed before." She confessed, chiding herself for showing her aw and enthusiasm for the place. She did not want him thinking she liked it so much she would enjoy staying there for good.

"Very true, Miss Maclean." He smiled, draining the last of his ale. Standing, the rest followed suit.

"Not so fast," a man said from behind the group. "You're a pretty thing," he said, stepping closer to Molly. "How about a dance before you go?" He offered, grabbing her hand, and pulling her towards him. She tried yanking her arm back but his fingers bit into her wrist.

24

"Remove your hand," Alaric snarled, his fingers resting on the dirk that was strapped to his hip.

"I don't think so," the man barked, his breath reeking of ale. "Just one dance with the woman won't be hurtin' no one." Pulling Molly close to his chest, her hands pushing hard against him but doing no good. Lifting her foot, she stepped down hard on his. The man only laughed, gripping her tighter.

"I'll tell you once more. Release her." His voice hard, his jaw clenched tight enough, his teeth ached.

The man smiled, looking down at Molly, shoving her forward into Alaric's chest. His arms immediately moving her behind him, blocking the man's view of her. His eyes dark, he did not take his gaze from the man. A guttural noise emanated from the man's chest. Spitting on the ground at Alaric's feet. He stepped forward, bringing his fist up and into Alaric's jaw. He waited for the man to bring his knuckles down on him once more, grabbing the man's wrist before it met its mark. Twisting the man's arm behind his back, causing him cry out, Alaric shoved him forward, knocking him over the table they had just been sitting at.

"My apologies," Alaric muttered to a woman who had come out from the back when the fight had begun. He assumed by her dress and the stern look of disapproval upon her face that the tavern belonged to her and her husband.

Guiding Molly through the tavern doors, they headed for the river. Alaric forced his body to relax as they made their way closer to the water's edge. He regretted having her come with him but knew he could not have left her aboard the ship alone while he and his crew dealt with business in the town. He had caught several of the men in the tavern glance her way and had been relieved when Leon had suggested they not speak there. What had happened in the tavern only made him worry about what might happen if he found her a place to stay in the colonies. He also knew she would not work at any of the plantations, and he would not force her to. It had occurred to him when she asked about finding Mackay's aunt, if there were any Macleans in the area. If so, perhaps they would be willing to take her in. He feared what might happen if she remained aboard his ship, especially once they found Thomas. He remembered the look of fear in Lucas's eyes when Banning had grabbed Catherine and did not want the same to happen to Molly.

"You shouldn't have done that." Molly whispered, "I am not worth you gettin' hurt." Her eyes on the fresh mark on his face.

"You are under my care, and I would not allow harm to come to you." He answered, his jaw hard. "Besides, it's been some time since I had the honor of defending a lass." He added, reassuring her.

"That's what held you up?" Leon chuckled, pointing to the swollen red spot on Alaric's jaw.

"Aye," Alaric grumbled, rubbing a hand over his jaw.

"Best get aboard," he added, waving his hand in the air for the group to board his flat boat. "Mind your step, Miss, there be a bit of a gap there." Reaching his hand out in case she slipped.

Alaric looked about as the boat slowly pulled from the small wooden dock. Men were busy working in the stalls and shops, women held baskets, many with children in tow as they gathered the supplies they needed. A small boy smiled and waved at Leon, running along the bank as the boat made its way up stream. A man shouted at the lad, calling him back to the horse stalls. Just like on the islands, birds were in every tree and bush, some wading in the water, waiting for a morsel to pass by. The birds in the colonies though were far different, a few having bright colors, but most, were browns, whites, and greys, blending in with the grasses and trees that surrounded the area. He glanced over at Molly, she stood at the other end of the small boat, her eyes wide, taking in all the sights around her. He did not miss the slight tremble of her body as she pulled his large coat tighter around her slender body. He felt terrible she did not have the warm clothes she needed for the much cooler weather they had sailed into. Once on the ship again, it would only be colder and with the dark clouds in the distance, he suspected they would run into more than one storm.

"What is it you do in the colonies, Mister Cutter?" Molly asked, looking up at the man that stood atop the small cabin.

Beaming down at her he gestured to his clothes, "I am a fur trader, Miss. I trap and hunt the animals in the area for their pelts. Many a folk want them but do not wish to do the hard work that is needed to get them. That is where I come in." He explained, guiding the boat steadily up the river.

"I see, and you enjoy the hard work that it takes?" She asked, her brows raised.

Alaric grinned, "I imagine it's much like sailing, it's not an easy life and many would not choose it, but those of us that do, enjoy it a great deal. Even you have discovered that, Miss Maclean."

"Well said, Captain." Leon chuckled.

"Oh look, just there, on the bank of the river." Molly exclaimed, pointing towards the large, scaly animal that basked in the little sun that shown through the clouds. It resembled a grumpy looking lizard with sharp teeth that jutted from the sides of its mouth.

"It's a gator, Miss. There are many of them in these parts. You won't want to go swimming in these waters." The river narrowed a bit around a bend, only to open up into a swamp like area, large green moss hung from the trees like ribbons decorating the branches. The trunks of the trees digging deep into the water below. "Nearly there now," Leon spoke up, his hand firmly on the planking of wood that steered the boat along the river.

Leon steered the boat skillfully towards a small wooden doc. "It is a bit of a walk to my cabin, from here. I hope you do not mind." He said, his eyes focused on Molly.

"Not to worry, mate. She is stronger than she looks," Alaric teased, winking at Molly.

Leon had been correct in saying his cabin was a ways into the woods. It could not be seen from the river and was well hidden, tucked away between trees with leaves of bright oranges and yellows. A shack was set up next to the cabin, a large canvas, one similar to the sails on the ships, draped atop the shack. It protected the wood and other supplies from the elements outside. A fire smoldered a few feet from the cabin, a string running from one post to another hung above it. Leon walked to the fire, quickly striking it full alight once more.

"The fire must be kept going to dry the meat properly." He explained, pulling a thin strip of the meat that dangled from the string and handing it to Alaric.

It was perfectly seasoned and did not taste like the salted meat found on the ships. "What meat is this?" He asked, curious as to why the meat tasted so different.

"It's bear that you be eatin." Leon chuckled, "It makes a fine dried meat, no?" Leon exclaimed, ushering the group into his cabin. It smelled of dried herbs, fire smoke and the trees and bushes that surrounded the quaint home. "Come, have a seat." He insisted, pulling a chair out for Molly who had not spoken so much as a word since she spotted the alligator. Her eyes had been wide with wonder. Alaric had been as mesmerized by the expression on her face as she had been with the sights around her.

"Thomas Banning, what do you know of him? You said he was here?" Alaric began. He enjoyed Leon's company but knowing they were so near Banning, he did not wish to delay.

"Aye, he sailed out last night or early this morning. I could not say which. I met him yesterday at another cabin up stream. I was heading further up the river to reset my snares. He was meeting with a man named Liam Jackson. He is well known in these parts, and you do not wish to cross him. That is why I suggested we talk here rather than in the tavern. Banning left Liam's cabin, just after midday."

"What business does this Liam Jackson do?" Ethan asked, his brows furrowing.

"He gets *'goods'* from various ship captains, then sells them for a hefty price. If he took the time to meet your friend clear up the river, it would be to discuss a shipment he did not want others knowing about." Leon explained, poking at the small fire he had built up in the cabin. "Why may I ask are you searching for the man? He does not seem to be the type one would want to seek out."

Alaric felt his body stiffen, he remembered staring into the waters below *The Trinity*. Ropes, torn canvas, and splintered wood littered the sea. A few bodies lay floating and lifeless, but none of them had been Benjamin's. "He killed someone very dear to me." He murmured, "not to mention, Ethan, here has his own questions for him." He finished, not wanting to discuss it further. "Where was he headed next; do you know?"

"Aye, I heard him in McCrady's Tavern later that evening.

He is to head north. He has further business in other towns in the colonies. I could not say which ones, though."

"Thank you, you have helped a great deal, and I greatly appreciate it." Alaric said, standing and reaching a hand out to Leon in gratitude. "If I can ever repay you, let me know."

"I'll bare that in mind when I find myself in need of a favor. In the meantime, allow me to gift Miss Maclean with some furs." He said, wagging a finger in the air as he located the pile he was searching for. "These were given to me by a woman from one of the local tribes. Her young son had fallen in the river. It had just rained, the ground on the banks were unsteady and the waters were high and fast moving. I managed to pull the boy out before he was swept under the waters. As a thanks, she gifted me these. I of course have no need of them, but I hope you may find use in these."

Unfolding them, Molly ran her fingers along the furs. They were lightly speckled greys, white and blacks and were softer than even the finest material she had seen on the women that visited the plantation. Taking the large coat off, she slipped her arms into the vest and pulled it tightly about her body. It had clearly been made for a woman of slight figure and not for a brawny man such as Leon. "I don't quite know what to say. I thank you." She whispered, unfolding the other set of furs, revealing a large blanket that had been made up of similar matching furs. "It is truly lovely. Thank you." She said, beaming at Leon, then glancing over at Alaric as if searching for his opinion on the gifts,

"You look just as lovely. They suit you." He remarked, uneasy with Ethan and Ol' Shorty watching the exchange, not

223

bothering to hide their grins.

"Well, I say, that'll do it. Let me take you back to Charles Town before it grows late." Leon concluded, opening the cabin door, and escorting the group to the river.

25

"Doc is going to be with you. He has assured me he will not leave your side. Ol' Shorty, Eddie and most of the rest of the crew are now aboard again. So, you will be well guarded." Captain Stein assured her. "I need to get some things in town before we continue on. I won't be long." He concluded, his eyes traveling her body, as if he were going to say more but did not know how.

"Thank you, I'm sure I'll be alright. I promised young Mackay I would teach him how to milk the goats." Molly smiled, thinking of how excited the boy had been at the idea. He enjoyed the animals almost as much as he enjoyed being in the galley.

"That's good of you. I'm sure that lad will like that. I will be asking around in town about his aunt. I hope we can find her for his sake." He said, taking his leave of the cabin and leaving Molly in the silence of the room.

Molly groaned, her and the captain had dined together on more than one occasion though she still felt more comfortable eating her meal with Cook or Doc. They even slept in the same cabin, the thought making her uneasy. She was a servant and always would be. He was a gentleman and a highly reputable sea captain, their stations in society were vastly different and she had still felt as though she had no right speaking to him so freely and by the awkward exchanges they often had, he clearly felt the same. Shrugging her thoughts out of her mind, she headed for the galley to find Mackay.

"Oui, now the butter be meltin', add the sugar, powder, salt and a bit o' the milk in that there bowl. Mix it good like, then put it atop the melted butter in the pan." Cook nodded as he watched Mackay carefully add the ingredients. The flour puffing up in a plume of white dust as the boy poured it into the bowl with the other ingredients. "Oui, now mix together the rest of those there ingredients and most importantly the blackberries." Cook instructed, "come in Miss, young Mackay here is making you and the captain a delicious blackberry cobbler." He explained, rubbing his middle.

"You sure be learning a lot, Mackay. Once you are done with your duties here, I'll show you how to milk the goats. Then perhaps you can have a slice of that cobbler with some fresh milk." Molly suggested.

The young lad turned to Cook, beaming. "Could I really have a slice?"

Cook laughed, his cheeks turning a brighter shade of red, "Oui, oui, I can no see why not. So long as you finish your chores in here and help Miss Molly." He said, wagging a finger at the lad.

Molly smiled, watching the boy bound down the companionway, towards the animals. His cobbler had turned out well and he had been more than proud of himself. "Now remember what I've said before, Mackay," she called after him.

The boy stopped abruptly, bowing his head slightly, "sorry, Miss Molly. I remember." He apologized; his steps now far slower than they had been so he did not startle the animals.

Molly crouched beside one of the goats, stroking her hand along the soft body. "Right then, sit next to me." She patted the ground beside her. "This here is where the milk comes out of, much like the cow." She explained, nodding towards the tall cow that stood in the next stall over. "Just place your hand here," she grabbed his small hand in hers and placed it on the utter. "Now gently squeeze and pull down like." Guiding his hand until he had the hang of it.

Mackay let out a small laugh as he watched the milk spray steadily into the wooden bucket. "It's not so bad, Miss. I be figuring it'd be harder." He exclaimed, delighted with his newfound skill.

"You are a fast learner, lad. Your Aunt will be proud of how much you have learned during your voyage." She said, standing up, brushing the straw from her tattered gown. There really was not much material left on it and it was made for the warm, humid temperatures of the West Indies. She had been thankful for the fur vest and had not taken it off since she had received it. It did a fare enough job warming her shoulders and chest but did little for the rest of her body. Picking up the rake, she began cleaning the stalls, scooping up the remnants left by the animals and placing it in a bucket to be dumped into the seas below. A fresh bundle of straw and buckets of grain had been brought down. They had even managed to find a large barrel of dried seaweed to help with the goat and cow's diet and milk production. Thankful for the new supplies, for the planks beneath the old straw were beginning to show through. Molly grabbed a handful of straw, stuffing them gently in the nesting boxes, careful not to break any eggs that might be in there.

"The bucket is near full now, Miss Molly." Mackay announced, pushing the last goat away from the pale.

"Very well," She replied, continuing to lay straw about the stalls. "Best get yourself back to the galley for that slice of cobbler." She said, lifting her head from her task, beaming at the lad.

"Oh, thank you Miss Molly," he exclaimed running from the large cabin and up the companionway.

Finishing the chores with the animals, she made her way to Doc's. He had asked her to stop by his cabin to see a book he had found in Charles Town. Her curiosity had peaked, she could not imagine what book he may have found that he believed she would be interested in.

Giving a light knock, the door opened, Doc looked down at her through his spectacles. "Come in, come in, Miss Maclean. I have been bursting to show you, my find. Here, have a seat, and since we have been in such a bustling town, I have been able to stock up on my supplies and a few I believe you might be interested in, Miss Maclean." He explained, pouring the both of them tea and placing a couple of biscuits on their plates. "Take a look at this," Doc said, placing a book on the table in front of her. The cover looked untouched, the binding firm. She ran a hand along the rough cover, opening it, revealing the first page, it read, *A Knowledge of the Animals*. Molly flipped a few more pages into the books, a sketch of a cow showed arrows pointing to various parts of the body, naming each one, the page explained what each part did, common ailments and how to treat them.

"This is incredible," she whispered. She had never seen a book like it. When she was little, her mother had no more than three or four books that she had read to her. She had taught her to read, though once their home and all that was in it had been taken from them, she had little chance to practice her letters and reading.

"I am pleased you like it. It is yours." He smiled, his hands folded together, watching her study the book. "And now that you have that to study, and I am in need of my expulser back," chuckling he continued, "I have one more gift for you." He explained, sliding a narrow box towards her.

Molly slowly lifted the top, revealing a metal hook of sorts with a handle made of wood that had been sanded down, so it nearly shown. Gingerly, she lifted it from its place in the box. "A proper pick," her words barely audible.

"Aye, now you will no longer be needin' to use my expulser, which I must say, I will have to clean several times over, so the men do not smell the manure upon it." Doc laughed, taking a drink of his tea. "I am pleased you enjoyed the gifts, though they are not much. You have shown great courage during this voyage and have been more help than you could know." He finished, leaning forward and grabbing the book he had given her. Flipping through the pages he found one with the image of a hoof. Turning the book to her, he allowed her to look the image over, before going over what it was discussing.

Molly could hardly contain her excitement over the gifts. She had never owned a book of her own and had never imagined she would ever get another chance to read or have the chance to learn more about the animals she loved so. Holding the book tightly in her arms and the pick in her hand, she headed below, once more, eager to begin reading.

Molly tucked her legs up against her body, trying to stay warm as she slowly read the book. It had been so long since she had practiced, she had only been a child the last time she held a one in her hand. She had not made much progress but was enjoying what she had read thus far. It was an introduction about the different areas a veterinarian or farrier might encounter, how to act around certain beasts and what noises or body movements they may show and the meanings of them. She looked up from her reading, as footsteps approached. Quickly standing up, still holding the book and pick, she stood against the wall, waiting to see who might be coming down.

"We are weighing anchor," Captain Stein said, walking into the cabin.

Molly shuffled her feet about the straw, she did not want him knowing she had been struggling with reading. "Did you find all you needed in town?" She asked, hoping to keep the topic. She had noticed as soon as he had spotted the book.

"I did, yes. Was there something you needed?" He asked, a brief look of concern on his face.

"No, Capt'n. I have all I need," she replied, unable to look directly at him. She could do with warmer clothes she thought but was content with the ones she was in and felt happier than she had been since her mother had been alive.

"I see Doc gave you the gifts he found." He stepped forward, reaching a hand out to see the book and pick. "He was mighty pleased with himself when he found them." Captain Stein smiled, looking at her a moment before examining the gifts.

"I'm very grateful for them. It was kind of him." She whispered, not quite sure what else to say.

"Are you enjoying the book?" He questioned, his head slightly tipped to the side, trying to see her face better as she kept her gaze on the ground.

"Aye, it's full of things I never thought I could know," her voice low.

"And the pick, it will keep the goats and cow from getting any more injuries in their hoofs, I suspect." He added, handing both the book and the pick back to her.

Molly nodded in reply. The cow had been standing oddly and not wanting to be milked or moved. She had first thought her utters were tired but quickly found the problem was the hoof. It had been caked with manure and straw, causing a sore to build up under the mess. Doc had given her the expulser to use to clean the area. He assisted her in washing the hoof and stripping it of the pus that had oozed from the wound. When washing the swore hoof they found what had really caused the injury. At first, they had believed it had just simply been too clotted with manure, but a small splinter of wood had found its way into the cow's hoof, causing great pain to the animal. They had bandaged the injury and allowed it time to heal. Having a pick, she could now keep the hooves of the goats and cow cleared daily so no unwanted matter could build up.

"I am going to head up for my meal. I suggest you do the same, it is getting cold down here and the cabin may be a bit warmer," he suggested.

She could see his breath as he spoke and he was right, it was far colder than it typically was. "Aye," Molly answered, placing the pick on a nearby crate and looking back at the animals. "Will there be a storm?"

"I should think so." He nodded, "don't fret over the livestock. They've been through cold weather before and have plenty of fresh straw. They will be warm enough." He reached a hand out, coaxing her forward. "Come now, let's get you up top and warmed up."

Molly waited in Captain Stein's cabin. Cook had brought in warm broth and ale to warm her and the captain. He had quickly drained his bowl and headed through the hatch, warning her not to leave the cabin. Through the small window behind the desk, she marveled at the dark skies, expecting to see raining pouring down, but instead, seeing soft white flakes filling the air. They landed on the window, sticking thick to it. Curling herself up on the bed with the large fur blanket Leon had gifted her, she opened the book once more but was unable to concentrate. Her thoughts kept going to the men on deck and to the captain. It was biting cold in the cabin, and she could not imagine what the icy winds above deck felt like. Pulling the coat about her shoulders more, she paused, looking down at it. She ran her fingers along the material, realizing she still wore Captain Stein's coat and that he would only have the thin white shirt and vest he often wore to protect him from the elements. Throwing the covers from her legs, she raced to the hatch, tearing the coat from her body. The freezing winds and snow hit her face, stinging it. She tried looking about the deck for the captain, but it was near impossible to see through the thick flakes. A shout came from above her, it was his voice, there was no mistaking his stern and deep tone. She did not pause to hear the reprimand he was surely shouting at her. Gripping the railing, she carefully placed her foot on the first step leading up to the helm. She could feel the slippery ice through her thin shoes.

"Molly, don't take another step!" Captain Stein bellowed. "It's not safe! Get below!" Desperation and anger evident in his voice.

Molly took another step, adjusting the coat in her other arm. She could feel the ship tilting to the side. The wind and snow coming down even harder, the waves causing the ship to pitch with more force than she had imagined possible. Molly felt her foot slip, she tried gripping the railing tighter, but it was no use, the snow and ice had made it far too slippery. She lost her footing as the ship tilted once more. She felt her body go weightless, her eyes meeting the captain's as the waters below engulfed her body. The cold of the sea was sharp, causing her entire body to burn and throb as if she were on fire rather than in icy waters. Molly tried moving her legs and arms, but she could not tell if her body responded to her demands or if the waves were dragging her deeper below. She closed her eyes, willing herself to keep fighting, to push herself above the water. She felt her body going numb, no longer able to feel the burning cold any longer.

26

Alaric placed the boxes in the chest that held his clothes. He did not wish her to discover them before he had a chance to give them to her himself. He had come from the shops to discover the skies growing darker. All had been loaded and repaired on *The Trinity* and they were ready to sail. He did not want to delay, knowing they were so near Thomas, and the storm could last several days. He rather sail through the storm than wait it out and miss Thomas. If he were to leave the colonies, it would only make it that much harder to find the bastard.

"Capt'n, capt'n, you wanna try the blackberry cobbler I made? It's delicious!" Mackay exclaimed, licking a bit of blackberry that was smudged against his lips.

Alaric grinned, "I'll have some with my meal perhaps." He laughed, ruffling the lad's shaggy blonde hair. "Where is Miss Maclean?" He asked, not wanting to interrupt her if she was still with Doc. He had shown Alaric what he had found for the lass and could not wait to give the gifts to her. They had also managed to secure a barrel of seaweed for the animals. He shook his head, *never has the ship's livestock been more spoiled,* he thought.

He walked into the cabin, the smell of the animals and fresh straw assaulted his senses. He paused, seeing the look on Molly's face. He flinched, he did not like that the fear and uncertainty still shown in her eyes when he was around. Catching a glimpse of the book in her hand, he realized he must have interrupted her reading. He did not miss the shiver that passed through her body or the fact he could see the breath from the cow. It was getting colder by the minute. He had felt the ship sway as they set off from the port. They would be heading right into the storm, and he did not want Molly down in the lower cabin where the temperatures would be even lower. At least in his cabin she would be warm in his bed and safe from the weather. Cook and Mackay already had hot broth steaming in the pots, ready to warm the men before having to brave the weather. Of course, most of the men would be below decks, staying safe and manning the pumps and the hull for leaks. He and Lucas had never allowed any of the men but the most experienced to be above decks during a storm. It made it harder with fewer men manning the rigging but at least his crew was safe.

Alaric noted the look of concern that came over Molly's eyes when he asked her to go above to his cabin. If it were up to her, he had the feeling she would rather freeze, making sure the animals were warm and safe during the storm, rather than sitting idle in his cabin, safe. He expected to have to fight her on it but was pleased when she willingly came with him, perhaps the cold was a bit much for her.

Alaric did not bother sipping his broth, as much as he wished he could stay in the cabin with Molly a bit longer, savoring the blackberry cobbler and seeing what she had thought of Charles Town. He had asked her before but only in a brief exchange and was not entirely sure she enjoyed it as much as much as it had seemed, especially after the brawl in McGrady's Tavern. He was needed on deck though. He could feel the waters growing rougher and the chill in the cabin had increased.

"Stay in here. You will be safe and warm." He advised, praying she obeyed his words. A feeling of doubt creeping upon him as he left the cabin, closing the hatch securely behind him. The cold air attacking his face, tearing quickly through his clothes.

"Mind that rigging lads and keep those sails tight." He bellowed over the growing winds. Small flurries of powdery snow beginning to sift down from the grey clouds above, disappearing as soon as they touched the sea below. The deck had grown slippery with slush, a thin layer of ice steadily forming. His hands gripped the helm, welding themselves to the freezing cold wood.

"Eddie, help the others. The steadier we hold her the faster we will pass through this storm." Alaric commanded. The land was no longer in sight and the water below tossed and pitched the ship. The snow was beginning to stick hard to the deck, making it difficult for the men to stay firm on their feet as they scrambled about the deck.

Alaric caught sight of the hatch opening. Molly rushed from it, wearing not but her frayed maid's dress, his coat in her hands. "Molly," he bellowed, trying to make his voice heard above the pounding of the waves. "Get back inside!"

By her reaction, he assumed she heard him yell, though clearly, she did not hear exactly what he had said, or she was choosing to deliberately disobey his commands. He could not let go of the helm and risk the ship being battered and tipped by the raging waters. Waving an arm in the air, he caught the eye of Eddie. He needed him to take control of the helm while he saw to Molly. His hands gripped tighter against the helm, furious she had disobeyed him and risked her life. The ship rocked, he looked over at Molly and saw her struggling with the icy stairs. Cursing under his breath he relinquished his grip on the helm and Eddie made it across the deck with far more ease than Molly. Alaric looked back at Molly as the ship pitched to the side, his heart stopping entirely in that moment as her body fell over the railing. Leaping to the lower deck he yelled for the others to help. Grabbing a rope that lay coiled up, he tied it firmly to his waist. His men securing it to the mast, readying to pull him back up.

Alaric dove into the black waters. Molly's pale skin making her visible in the dark waves. His entire body throbbed from the cold. Pulling against the waves, he felt his hands wrap around Molly's waist. He had seen her arms waving frantically in the waters, but now they floated limply in the currant. Pushing the two of them to the surface, he gasped for air. The wind and snow freezing his face even more than the water had. Tugging hard against the rope, he tried hollering up at the men on the ship, but his voice refused to work.

The crew pulled them up, the rope biting into his ribs as he held Molly firmly against himself. Ethan and Shorty reached over the railing taking Molly from his grasp. He heard her coughing, spilling the contents from her stomach and gasping for air. He struggled over the railing landing unsteadily to the planking of the deck. Pulling her into his arms once more he stood, his legs shaking as he raced to the hatch, calling over his shoulder for one of the men to fetch Doc. She had brought up all the sea water and he could feel her shallow breathes against his own body, but her eyes remained closed, unconscious once again.

He knew little about drowning or illness but remembered once when one of the men had fallen over the edge during a previous storm, many years ago, Doc had ordered the man to be stripped of his wet clothes and placed into dry ones to warm him faster. Clenching his jaw tightly, Alaric threw the heavy, fur blanket over her frozen body. Gripping the worn and stained dress under the blanket, he ripped at the garment, trying to keep her as covered and warm as possible. He could only imagine the look of fury in her eyes if she woke at that moment. No doubt she would finally use her blade on him.

"Aye, well done, lad. You get yourself dry and changed. I'll take matters from here." Doc said, bursting into the cabin. "She will need dry clothes as well." He finished, throwing the wet, torn dress to the floor, careful not remove the blanket from her still body.

Rummaging through the boxes of new gowns and under-garments he had purchased for her earlier that day, he found what he was looking for. The woolen stockings, night shift and shawl. They were not much on their own, but under the thick quilt and heavy fur blanket, the lass would be warm enough. Handing the garments to Doc, he stared down at the women in his bed. Her hair lay about the pillow like an unruly mane. Her pale skin far paler than normal. Even her lips that were typically a soft pink held no color. Aside from the shallow rise and fall of her chest, her body made no move, while his own shivered fiercely.

"Will she make it?" Alaric asked, his voice hoarse.

Doc pulled the covers back over her, tucking them under her shoulders so not an ounce of the chilly cabin air entered the bed. "I suspect so, lad. Though, only time will tell. She may have come from a harsh and cold life in Ireland, but her body is no longer used to that bitter weather. It will have been a shock for her body and no doubt she will come down with a fever. I will stay with her, there is no more you can do for her now, but the crew does need you." He reasoned, guiding Alaric to the hatch.

"Aye," Alaric muttered, staring at the hatch that had closed. The snow and wind had slowed, but the clouds still loomed over for miles. There was no chance of it letting up within the next hour or two. Doc was right, his crew needed him. Heading for the helm he tried keeping his mind off of the lass's pale form, willing her to be stronger than the cold that had consumed her body and wondering why she had risked coming on deck during the storm in the first place. Releasing Eddie from his duties at the helm, he gripped it once more. His hands burning at the touch of the frozen wood. Snow stuck to the clothes of the men on deck, soaking them through. He watched the sailors tend to the rigging and sails, as if the cold did not affect them in the least. They too were not used to the biting cold, much like Molly, but being sailors for so long, their bodies were well adjusted to hardships and injuries. He had little doubt the men would pull through the rest of the storm with very few complications. After most storms, a few of the men would fall ill for a day or two but not with any

240

serious ailments and nothing Doc could not handle. Seeing his crew injured and unwell was never an easy thing, but the feeling of Molly's limp and frozen body against his would forever be etched in his mind. He had never felt so helpless or useless.

Kicking his boots off and changing his soaked clothes once again, Alaric let himself fall into the chair behind his desk. The clumps of snow that had fallen from his boots and clothes quickly melted into puddles on the wooden planks in his cabin. Grabbing for the bottle of whiskey that lay safe in a drawer, he poured himself and Doc each a cup. "How is she? Any change?" He asked, his eyes on Molly.

"Not much, no." Doc replied, coming to the desk. "A bit of color has returned to her, which is a good sign. Her skin is warmer and not yet feverish, but it is still early. We likely won't see changes for another few hours. Until then, it is important she just rests." Doc answered, sitting in the chair opposite Alaric.

"I'll fetch some more broth from Cook and see to the rest of the crew. I'll be back in to check on the lass in a bit. Get some rest." Doc instructed, finishing the last drops in his cup.

Alaric savored the warmth from the whiskey as it traveled down and pooled in his stomach. Letting out a long sigh, he pulled his chair to the edge of the bed, running a hand through his hair. Molly slept peacefully. Alaric's gaze travelled the length of her body that was wrapped warmly in the blankets. Her hair had completely dried, and she did not look at all like a lass that had been thrown from a ship mere hours ago. Alaric shook his head, the woman could have cost herself her own life and his, very easily. Even now, she was still in danger from fever once it struck.

His body ached, his head throbbed, and his legs and hands were only beginning to regain feeling. He sipped the hot broth that Mackay had brought in, feeling the warmth travel through his body once more. Setting the bowl on the desk, he went back to his seat near Molly. His eyes fell upon the woman in his bed, letting out a gruff laugh at the thought. He had not once imagined this is how his voyage would go. He had expected delays, dangers and complications but never believed he would allow a woman aboard his ship.

Alaric heard his name being called, not a shout, more of whisper. A whisper of desperation, a whisper with sadness and terror in the voice. The battle around him continued, guns firing and swords clanging together. Shouts and cries from wounded men filled his ears. He knew he had to find Benjamin before Thomas did. Racing across the deck, he looked around, the fray was too much, he could not focus. Something was wrong. He was failing again. Failing to protect the boy. He caught sight of Benjamin near the edge of the ship, his back against the railing.

"Get down! Benjamin! Move!" He shouted, his own voice ringing in his head like the blasts from the canons did. Shoving men down, trying to reach the boy in time. He stopped, the blood draining from his body. The boy that had stood in front of him a moment ago transformed before him. No longer a tall, scrawny lad with scraggly hair. Instead, a woman with flaming hair that framed her face, eyes fierce and determined, yet full of fear.

"Capt'n," she whispered.

The sound of the flintlock firing, echoed across the deck. The woman fell from the ship and into the waters below.

"Molly!" He shouted. He tried to move but his feet would not allow him to.

Alaric woke with a start, sweat ran down his back and forehead. Groaning, he stood and walked to the water basin. Splashing the cool liquid on his face, trying to rid the imagines from his mind.

"Capt'n," the soft voice filled the air in the cabin.

Alaric looked up from the water basin, his hands on either side of it. "Miss Maclean," he answered, his voice strained. "How are you feeling?" He asked, drying his face with a cloth.

"I'm sorry for disobeying, ye." She replied, moving to sit up.

"Why did you?" He asked, his voice hard and full of confusion. He still did not know what to make of the dream he had awoke from. Relief had filled him when he heard her voice a moment ago, but he could not help feeling the anger at the thought of her disobeying him and risking her life. Walking over to the chair he had slept in, he looked her over. Her face was not as pale, in fact it looked flushed, whether it be from shame or a fever, he could not tell.

"I wished to bring ye, your coat." She confessed, trying to sit up more, but her body was too weak to do so.

Alaric's mouth fell open. He could not be hearing the lass correctly. She had risked her life and his, to bring him his coat? Her words went round in his mind. "Christ, lass. You could have been killed. I have weathered storms before with not but the shirt on my back. I had no need of the coat at the time." He nearly laughed at the absurdity but restrained himself when he saw the look in her eyes. She had only been thinking of his well-being and had not realized the dangers of her actions. Raising his brows, he watched her. Her eyes shown in the light that streamed through the small window at the back of the cabin. "You are rash, stubborn, disobedient and willful," he stated, pausing at the defiant and fiery look in her gaze, "but, I thank you for all you have done. You have saved more than one of the beasts now and therefore saved us from going without milk and cheese and from me having to purchase new livestock. So, I am grateful to you, and I commend you for braving the elements to bring me a coat," his lips twitched, trying to hide his smile. "You must promise me though, not to be so reckless in future."

Nodding, her eyes filled with surprise, "aye, Capt'n." Her voice was weak, and he could see her struggling to remain seated upright.

"I will go and fetch Doc. I think it best if you have a bit of broth." He added, "I'll see if Cook has any left." Alaric said, standing, but hesitant to take his eyes from her. The hair about her brow was wet with perspiration and she did not look as if she had an ounce of strength left in her. "Allow me," he said, approaching the bed once more. Placing a hand on her back, he helped her to lay down again to rest while he fetched Doc and a bowl of broth. He only hoped she would remain awake to eat a bit, she would need the strength.

Molly turned her head on the pillow, her hair and body felt damp. She shivered, unable to control her body from its incessant shaking. She could hear the voices echoing quietly in the cabin, but her eyes would not open to see who spoke. Pulling the blankets tighter against her, she let out a small moan. Her body ached and her head felt like it would break.

"The fever has worsened, Captain." A solemn voice spoke. "She has ate and drank very little in the last couple of days. I have been spooning what little broth I can in her mouth to keep her strong, but I worry it is not enough." Doc explained. "She is likely in a good deal of pain and discomfort, the willow bark tea should help with that."

"What are her chances, Doc?" The captain's voice was un-mistakable. It was deep and commanding, his accent giving away his family heritage.

"If she makes it through the rest of the day and the night to come. I say she has a fairly good chance." Something cool and soothing brushed against her forehead, calming her briefly.

"We have arrived at the next port. Is there anything I can fetch that will aid her in recovery?" The captain asked, his voice clearly strained.

"I was able to get enough in Charles Town. There is not that I need and as for the lass, only time will tell. I am making her as comfortable as I can for now but I'm afraid it is her body and mind that need to do the work." Doc answered, the sound of a chair scraping against the planks. "There is nothing more you can do for her now. You must rest yourself as you have scarcely slept or left her side since the fever struck. Go ashore, take care of the business you need to and try and rid your mind of the cobwebs. You'll feel better and regain your own strength. And when you return, I imagine she will have improved as well. Miss Maclean is strong and a fighter." Doc finished, his tone reassuring.

Molly felt herself drifting off into a restless sleep once more. Visions of a tall, dark-haired captain filled her mind. Confusion, content, terror, and joy filled her all at once. The battles they had been through, the sounds of the wounded men crying out blocked all other sounds. The smell of the ship, the cabin and the animals controlled her senses, giving her a calm that her body desperately needed. She tried rousing herself, taking a deep breath in, the room smelled of wood, the salty sea water that surrounded the ship. A scent of brewed tea steeping, warm broth, and citrus. Since being aboard *The Trinity*, she had quickly realized they ate as much fruit and greens as they could, especially oranges. When the fresh vegetables were unavailable, they relied on the ones Cook had pickled along the voyage. She now found comfort in the scents that filled the ship, in the sounds the waves made as they lapped against the hull. Of the songs the crew sang and even the sound of the captain's commanding voice. In all, she knew she should be afraid, knew she should be finding a way off the ship and to live a new life of her own, but the very truth was she had never felt so safe.

"Here, try taking a small sip." Doc suggested, holding a spoon to her lips. Opening her lips just enough for the warm liquid to spill into her mouth, she relaxed. The broth was delicious and warmed her body through. "I'll give you more of the broth, but I need you to drink a bit of this tea as well. It will help you feel more comfortable." Molly made a small noise in response, unable to make her raspy throat form much else. Taking a sip of the tea that was offered, she winced as she moved to sit up.

"You mustn't move too much. You are still far too weak, and your fever is not yet gone. The tea will help your head." He explained, placing the cool cloth on her head once again, slowly massaging the sides of her head, lessening the ache.

Molly slowly sipped the broth as Doc patiently spooned the warm liquid into her mouth. "Where are we?" She asked, closing her eyes against the pain and chills that wracked her body.

"Bath, in the Carolinas," Doc answered. "And to be quite honest, it is probably best that you are unable to venture out of the cabin. This particular town is not as savory."

"How long have I been asleep?" She whispered, taking another sip of the tea that was offered.

"A few days. We have been in port here most the day.

Captain Stein should be returning to the ship soon. Then we will see if we are to stay here longer or if we are to continue on to the next port." Molly nodded in response, her eyes closing once more.

Rolling over, she sighed. Her body no longer ached, and her hair no longer felt damp with perspiration. Looking about the cabin, she was surprised to see no one in the room. Since she had first fallen ill, in and out of her delirious and restless sleep, she had always felt or heard someone near her. She felt the ship swaying as it moved along the waters. They were no longer in port, she thought. Molly slowly and gingerly began to sit up, cautiously waiting with every movement to see if the pain and chills would return.

A mix between a squeak and a mew sounded beneath the covers. Molly paused, slowly lifting the covers to peer underneath them. A tiny face peered out, white tufts of fur spiked from the little ears, the nose was a tiny, black spot at the tip of the furry face. "And who might you be?" Molly whispered, coaxing the grey kitten from beneath the covers. Little black lines striped the face, long grey fur stuck up at all angles as the kitten crawled out, purring softly and playfully.

"She hasn't left your side," the captain's voice filtered through the cabin. Drawing her attention from the furry creature in her lap. The kitten was no bigger than her hand with small bits of white fur poking between its toes and a tail that appeared longer than the rest of its body.

"Where did she come from?" She asked curiously, tickling the kitten's belly causing her purr louder and playfully attack Molly's hands.

"A woman was giving them away in Bath. She claimed her house was being overrun by cats. I saw that little girl and thought as she grows bigger, she may be the answer to our rat problems as well as a welcome gift for you." He explained, leaning against the wall across from the bed. "What will you name her?"

"Oh, Captain Stein, I cannot thank you enough," she exclaimed, keeping her eyes on the animal so he would not see the tears that were now blurring her vision. "I will have to think on a name. I have never had such a gift before."

"I'm glad you're pleased with her." He grinned, "I brought you more broth with some biscuits. Your fever broke yesterday. You've been abed for nearly a fortnight now." He explained, placing the food on a tray for her so she could eat the meal while still in bed.

Molly sat herself up more, positioning the pillows behind her back, the blankets that kept her so warm had fallen about her waist when she had noticed the kitten. Only now did she realize she was no longer in her tattered maid's dress. She fingered the material of the soft and warm shawl that was snuggly wrapped about her. A white cotton night shift and thick wool stockings made up the rest of her attire. Drawing the blankets back up to her chin she looked up at the captain. She knew the shock, fear, and anger was clear upon her face.

His grin broadened, "not to worry Lass, I didn't peek." Stepping away from the wall, he walked closer to the bed. "Eat up. We are near Williamsburg and Doc says if you feel up to it, you are well enough to go ashore." Grabbing the telescope from his desk he headed for the hatch. "Ah, I nearly forgot, have a look in the chest at the foot of the bed." He said, nodding to the chest he spoke of. Without another word, he left the cabin. Leaving her in silence and confusion.

Looking back down at the kitten that was now gnawing playfully on her hand, she stroked a finger along her back, causing her to squirm in an attempt to grab at her new foe. "What shall I call you, hmm?" She asked, marveling at how soft the kitten's fur was. "How about Aoife?" She whispered, the kitten had curled up next to her, clearly warn out from her wee battle.

Sliding from the bed, she walked over to the chest the captain had mentioned. Opening the lid, timidly she peered in. Several white boxes lay neatly stacked. Molly let out a gasp, lifting the boxes from the chest and setting them on the bed. Opening the first one, she discovered an array of undergarments and another shift. The other boxes remained tied with yellow ribbons. Undoing each box, she laid out the gowns, examining each one. Molly let out a breath, running her fingers along the fabric of a green gown. Her mind unable to focus, she had never been given gowns before and she could not remember the last time she had owned a new one. Lifting a dark red one up, she held it to her, spinning slowly round.

She heard the calls to bring in the sails as the ship slowly turned in the waters, readying to make port. A knock sounded on the hatch, "Miss Maclean, Capt'n sent me to see if you was ready." Ol' Shorty said from behind the hatch.

"I'll be up in just a minute," she called, quickly cleaning the rest of the gowns and garments up, placing them back in the boxes and in the chest once more. The red gown still in her arms, she rushed to change into it. Sliding her hands down the length of her, smoothing the fabric out, she took a deep breath. She had been used to her maids' dress, had felt comfortable in it. Never had she owned such a fine gown as the ones he had purchased for her. Not that they were terribly extravagant, but they were still above her station. Flipping her hair out of her face and over her shoulder, she opened the hatch, glancing back at the bed to see if the kitten remained sleeping. Smiling, she quietly closed the door to the cabin behind her.

"I hope the gowns met with your approval?" Captain Stein asked, stepping up beside her. They were waiting for the plank to the dock to be placed before they could go ashore. Mackay eagerly jumped up and down, peering over the railing best he could.

"Aye, but I'm afraid they're too much. I have no way of repaying you for your kindness, Capt'n." She replied uncertainly. Uncomfortable at his unwavering gaze

"I'm sure we can think of something," he replied. "It suits you," he added, gesturing towards the dress she wore, the shawl wrapped tightly about her, keeping the chilly winds from her.

Keeping her gaze from his, she glanced down at young Mackay. It appeared he was coming ashore with them. *Had Captain Stein learned more about the boy's aunt while he was in Bath?* She wondered as the captain led her down the plank, closely followed by Ethan and Ol' Shorty.

The streets were just as muddy and busy as the ones in

Charles Town had been. Men worked about the docks, loading, and unloading supplies from ships and wagons. Women carried baskets from shop to shop, stopping occasionally to speak with someone they passed. It seemed as much a pleasant town as the previous one she had been in, though there appeared to be far more officers in Williamsburg. She stepped closer to Captain Stein, afraid one of them might know who she was and what she had done. Despite the captain's reassurances on other occasions, she still feared what would happen if she was discovered. In truth, she did not even know if the man had lived or not. It had been some months since that day and she had no reason to believe they would be looking for her, except for the knowledge that if he had lived, he would never allow her to get away with what she had done to him.

"Let's try in here first. We'll ask after *The Amity* and then see if there are any MacDougal's in the area." Captain Stein suggested, leading the group into a tavern that was nestled between a shop that appeared to sell canvases, nets, and more items that sailors may need. The other shop held various goods, such as cloth, sugar, flour, and furs.

Stepping into the tavern, there was no doubt this one was not as savory as the one they had been in, in Charles Town. Looking down at Mackay, his expression nearly made her laugh. His eyes were wider than they had ever been, and his head turned from side to side at a dizzying speed, trying to take in all the sights around him. "It's quite something, don't you agree?" Molly asked the boy, leaning down so he could hear her.

"Aye," he whispered in wonder. "I've no seen anythin' like it, Miss Molly." He said, staring up at a burly man whose hair was shaved off, a tattoo spanning his bare head and face. Large gold rings hanging from his ears. He sneered down at Mackay causing the boy's eyes to grow even wider, retreating between Ethan and Ol' Shorty.

"Excuse me," Captain Stein said, stopping a man that was behind a long wooden counter, filling up jugs of ale. "Are you the owner of this tavern?"

"Aye, what's it to you, sir?" He asked looking the group over curiously, softening slightly at the sight of Molly and Mackay.

"We aren't familiar with the area, and we are looking for a ship that may have docked here recently, *The Amity.*" Captain Stein explained, casually leaning against the counter, watching the man continue his work. Women, came up, collecting cup after cup of ale, handing them out to the men that filled the room.

"I do know all the ships that make port, but I've not heard of that one. What be the Captain's name?" The plump man asked, a small mustache moving up and down as he spoke.

"Thomas Banning," Captain Stein answered, nodding in greeting at a sailor that came up, standing uncomfortably close to Molly.

"No, can't say I know of any sailors by that name." The tavern owner replied, angrily watching a group of sailors that had drawn their flintlocks on one another. Signaling for the man with the tattoos to intervene before the establishment broke out in a brawl.

"Perhaps, it's best we find another place." Ethan advised, nodding towards Mackay who was trying to watch the scene unfold from behind him.

"Aye," Captain Stein agreed, his hand on Molly, guiding her around the crowd as best he could and out the door as a shot fired behind them.

"Let's see if we can't find another tavern or someone who tends the docks." Ethan suggested, looking about for anyone that may contain information about recently docked ships.

"You the salior that be lookin' for Thomas Banning?" A man approached the group cautiously, judging their reactions.

"Who be askin?" Ol' Shorty questioned, eyeing the stranger and stepping forward. Alaric slightly raised his handed, signaling for Shorty to not be too hasty.

"Names Jack," he replied, coming closer to the group. "If it's Banning you seek, I'd be happy to tell you where he last be seen."

"And what's it to you?" Ol' Shorty challenged, clearly not trusting the younger man.

He could not be much older than Molly if he even was older. His blonde hair fell about his head in a disorderly way, streaks of dark brown running through it. "He nearly killed my brother, just a night ago. Them was playin' dice. My brother won, Banning pulled his flintlock and shot 'im. I got word this morning about what happened."

"Was this here, in Williamsburg?" Alaric asked, listening carefully to the young man.

"Nah, it be in Beaufort. Word is, Banning is on his way to Newport. He was recruiting new sailors for a voyage that will take several months." Jack explained, "I ain't no friend of Thomas Banning, Sir. If I could join you in finding him, I would, but I cannot leave my mother and sisters alone."

"I thank you for the information you've givin' us. I hope your brother has a speedy recovery and I'm inclined to agree, I'm sure you'd make a fine sailor, but your place is with your family, especially if you and your brother are the only ones to care for them." He said, placing a few coins in the young man's hands.

A shocked look appeared on Jack's face, "Thank ye, Sir." He said in surprise, pocketing the coins and nodding to the others, before turning and rushing further into the town, most likely wanting to tell his sisters and mother of his good fortune.

"That was kind of you," Molly said, looking up at the captain. "How do you know he can be trusted?" She asked, curiously.

Captain Stein shrugged, "you've got to take that chance," he replied, his eyes locked on hers. "As I recall, you took that same chance on me once, by boarding my ship and stowing away in my cabin, Miss Maclean." He grinned, "it didn't turn out so terrible, did it?" He challenged.

"Aye," she murmured, unsure of what to say. She had not

thought of it in such a way. "I mean, no. It's not so terrible." She stammered, tearing her eyes from his, and focusing on the town around them.

"Weel, if that be it for the questioning, I best see to the ship." Ol' Shorty spoke up, "If I don't see you again, lad, you take care." He said ruffling Mackay's hair. "Mind your auntie and stay out of trouble." He winked at the boy who smiled.

"Aye, Ol' Shorty. You stay out of trouble too." He replied, quickly giving the large man a hug, his arms not even reaching around Shorty's middle.

"Ack, get on with ye," he answered with a sniff. He quickly turned and strode off back down towards the dock.

Molly looked about, watching the folks around her tend to their everyday duties, some having been born in the colonies, others, as new to the area as herself. She noticed Captain Clarke had stepped away from them, now speaking with a group of officers, their coats an intimidating red. Instinctively she moved closer to Captain Stein, cursing her bright hair that stood out. It would not be hard to locate her if a search had been sent for her.

"You needn't fear," the captain whispered in her ear. "I wager Captain Clarke knows those men, nothing more." They watched the exchange between Ethan and the soldiers, clearly a cheerful one as they were smiling and patting each other's shoulders.

"Captain Stein, Miss Maclean, allow me to introduce to you, General Cunningham. We had the pleasure of serving together under Captain Burg.

Molly curtsied, her legs shaking beneath her. "A pleasure to meet you, General Cunningham." She replied, not daring to look up at the man or the officers that now surrounded them.

"The pleasure is mine, Miss Maclean. Tell me, how are you enjoying the colonies?" He asked enthusiastically, while simultaneously greeting Captain Stein.

"It's equally different and inspiring, General Cunningham." She replied glancing at Captain Clarke, who simply nodded his approval of her response, a smile still upon his face at seeing his old comrades.

"Well put, I must say, Miss Maclean." He replied, turning his attention to Captain Stein, "tell me, how long do you plan to stay in Williamsburg?"

"Just for the night. We need to be off first thing in the morning." The captain replied easily.

"That is fortunate. You will accompany me to a dinner party that is to be held at a nearby plantation. Our friend, Captain Burg retired from the Navy some years ago, purchasing a large plantation hereabouts. He'd be pleased if you were to join us tonight." He quickly continued before Captain Stein could refuse the offer, "I insist, and I'm sure you will have plenty of tales to tell us of your travels." He concluded, glancing from Ethan to Captain Stein.

"Aye, we will see you tonight, then." Captain Stein answered, "a good day to you." He said, excusing himself, Molly and Mackay from the rest of the conversation. It was clear young Mackay was getting restless. He was eager to see more of the town and all it had to offer. "Come along, lad." Captain Stein insisted, placing a hand on the boy's shoulder, leaving Ethan to catch up further with his friends.

Walking down the muddy path, Molly peered into each building as they passed. The captain was keeping an eye on their surroundings and Mackay seemed as awestruck by the shops and people around them as Molly was. Mackay suddenly stopped, his mouth falling open at the treasures that sat in the window of a mercantile. Molly could not help but smile at what had caught the boy's eye. "We must catch up to the captain." She urged, looking up to see he had already stopped and was walking back to them, a stern look on his face.

"You two must stay close, it is dangerous to stray." He informed them, looking into the shop's window, seeing what had caused them to stop. "I see," looking from Molly to the boy. "I never did pay you your wages for all the cooking you did in the galley or for tending the animals so well, while Miss Maclean was unwell, did I?"

"No, Capt'n," his face full of excitement and surprise.

"We must remedy that, should we not?" He asked, not bothering to hide his grin as the boy nodded quickly. Digging into his pocket, he pulled out a coin, placing it in Mackay's small hand. "Go on in and pick a couple peppermint sticks or other treat."

"Where will we find his aunt?" Molly asked, sad at the

thought of the young boy no longer being on the ship with them. He had only been aboard *The Trinity* a short time, but she had already grown fond of him. His cheeks were always pink with excitement, and he never once complained about the hardships aboard or the chores that were asked of him.

"She is staying at a friend's house just down the street, or so I've been informed." He answered, watching her carefully. "He's a good lad, and I am thankful we are able to return him to his family."

Molly nodded, her heart feeling as if it would rip from her. There was no doubt he was thinking of sending her to stay with the boy's family as well or find any of her kin in the area. Looking away, she wiped at her face, angry that she had allowed herself to trust and even begin to enjoy the captain's company.

Mackay emerged from the shop, a large peppermint stick in his hand and a pocket full of other treats. "Good choice, lad. Now, it's time to get you to your auntie." He concluded, continuing them on the path between the buildings. A row of small houses lined a street, all of which looked rather similar to the other. "She is staying in the third house down," Captain Stein announced, already heading towards the white house.

Mackay stood back, looking at the home, "what is it?" Molly asked, seeing the boy's hesitancy.

"It's only that, me ma was to be here too." He murmured, no longer licking the candy he still held.

Bending down, Molly placed her hands on his shoulders.

"I understand a bit of how you feel, lad. But you are not alone, you have an auntie and a clan that loves you and has been eagerly awaitin' your arrival. I wager, your folks are proud of all you have learned and how brave you've been. They wouldn't want you being sad on the day you get to finally be with family again." She assured him, drawing him close to her. "Take care of yourself and don't be eatin' all those treats today." She added, wiping a bit of smudged dirt from his face. "I never got to thank you for tending the animals while I was ill. I'm sure you did a fine job. I wouldn't have trusted their care to anyone else."

His eyes lit up briefly, "did ye, name the kitten, Captain Stein got ye?"

"Aye," she said laughing, "Aoife."

"Mackay," a woman came bounding from the house, holding the folds of her dress up. "Oh, Mackay, how worried I've been about ye, laddie." The woman scooped the boy up in a tight embrace. Her dark hair was pulled back in a twisted bun, wispy ringlets falling about her face and sticking up from spots about her head. Her cheeks, rosy with excitement. Setting him down she looked him over, "I'd say, you must be hungry, but giving the treat in your hand, I believe you've been well looked after." She spoke softly, drawing the boy close to her once more.

"I thank ye two for bringing my sweet, dear nephew to me. I trust he was no trouble on the long voyage?" She asked, looking the captain and Molly over.

"None at all, in fact he was a great help and a brave young

man, but I'll let him tell you of his adventures." Captain Stein answered, beaming down at Mackay. The boy ran up to the captain, giving him a quick hug and thanking him.

Molly eyed the captain, holding her breath. She prayed he would not ask the woman to take her in as well. She seemed a kind enough woman, but it was not where Molly wished to be. Aside from going on deck during the storm she had not caused any trouble for the captain that she could think of, but she did not know if he truly wanted her to remain on his ship.

"We best be off, we have further engagements, Miss Mac-Dougal. Take care." Alaric said, winking at young Mackay.

28

Alaric could smell the smoke from the fires that were lit in nearly every building they passed. He enjoyed the cool air and it felt good to stretch his legs. Looking down at Molly, he was glad he had purchased the clothes for her. She would be far warmer in the new gowns and coat than she had been in the tattered maid's dress. He had to admit, he was glad to see the old gown gone and he hoped it would help her move past what had happened on the plantation.

"Captain Clarke didn't say goodbye to Mackay." She suddenly said, concern etched on her face.

"He did, he said his farewells aboard the ship, before we came ashore." Captain Stein assured her.

"What will you do now?" She asked, twisting her hands together.

"I suppose, we should get ready for the dinner party we are expected at tonight." He said, cocking an eyebrow at her. He was not particularly looking forward to the party as he would much rather leave for Newport but knew there was no way of avoiding it, and it might be nice at any rate.

"*We?* Surely not me!" She stammered, looking up at him in surprise.

"The invitation extended to you without a doubt." He returned, looking her over. She seemed completely taken aback by the suggestion.

"But I couldn't go. I'm a maid, a servant. They are esteemed officers, captains, and generals. I couldn't possibly sit about the table with them. What would they think?" Her voice quavered.

"You can and you will, Miss Maclean," he insisted, watching her reaction. "And I will remind you, you are no servant or maid, any longer. You are a guest upon my ship and will be treated as such." His voice was low and deep, he had stepped closer to her without having realizing he had. They now stood mere inches apart. She had regained her color from being unwell and now, despite the cold air around them, appeared flushed. He despised her uncle and Lord Willington for treating her so poorly, making her believe that she was lowly and of no consequence. Clearing his throat, he took a step back. "And as for what the gentlemen there will think," he grinned, "they will be unable to take their eyes from you." Alaric finished, guiding her forward without another word.

Alaric adjusted the stiff coat. He did not care for it much, but he could not very well show up to the dinner party in just his white shirt and vest. He stood on deck, looking out at Williamsburg. The town was quaint with houses that lined the streets further from the docks. The center of town held various shops, inns, and taverns. The sound of a blacksmith working his hammer against iron echoed through the muddy streets. Trees and shrubs dotted the paths and despite the look of the town and how pleasant most of the folks had seemed, he felt uneasy. When he and Molly had been walking back to the ship from depositing Mackay off with his exuberant aunt, he had felt as if someone had been watching them, or perhaps following them. He did not see anyone that looked out of sorts for the area, save for one man but he could not be sure he meant any harm. He had spotted the man just before they came to the docks. He had been leaning against the wall of one of the taverns and looking at Molly, only turning his gaze from her when Alaric spotted him. He could not blame the man for looking at her and had noticed more than one other man look her way but there was something about the older man. His clothes were fine and almost appeared to recognize Molly.

"Might I say, Miss Maclean, you are the picture of perfection." Ethan announced, drawing Alaric from his thoughts. Turning he saw what had caused the crew that had remained on deck to draw silent. Molly stood just outside the hatch to the cabin, her face framed by the mane of hair that fell passed her shoulders. The green gown fitting her form better than he had imagined it would.

"I'm honored to have you on my arm tonight, Miss Maclean." He finally said, walking up to her. "You are lovelier than ever." He smiled, looking her over. Her face flushed once more at his open appraisal.

"Thank you, Capt'n Stein. You don't look such the rogue yourself this evening." She responded, surprising him with her brazen reply.

Holding his arm out for her to take, she hesitantly placed her hand just below the bend of his arm. A carriage was waiting at the docks to take them to the plantation. A man opened the door and took out a box that was used to assist the passengers into the carriage. Guiding Molly into their evenings transport, he did not miss the look of surprise in her eyes. Her hands ran delicately across the seats, smiling to himself, he knew she would have never been in such a carriage. A general, well used, and simple one, yes, but not one such as this.

The ride to the plantation was a simple, yet rather long one. Once passed the edge of the town, they rode under large trees that towered on either side of the path. The sun had already set, and the dark of the night closed in around them, the air colder than it had been earlier that day. Slowing, the carriage turned through large, white gates. The trees now making a tunnel over the road that led up to the plantation house.

"Nearly there now," Ethan announced, smiling down at Molly who sat in the seat next to him. She simply nodded in reply, a slight smile appearing briefly on her lips, quickly replaced by a look of pure nerves. "You will do just fine, Miss Maclean." He assured her, picking up on her uneasiness. His gaze shifting to Alaric as the carriage neared the estate.

The plantation home was a grand one, perhaps as large as, if not larger than Lord Benedict's. Massive white pillars lined the deck that wrapped its way around the home. The carriage came to a slow stop. A man from the house came out, opening the carriage door, allowing the passengers to step out. Alaric tried to hide his smile when Molly immediately grabbed hold of his arm, this time not hesitating. He could not mistake the tremor in her hand. He admired her for putting on a brave form, despite her uneasiness. They were led into a spacious front room, immediately being greeted by General Cunningham.

"I am pleased you could make it. Please, allow me to introduce to you the man of the estate." He announced, guiding the group to a gentleman that was busy discussing the misfortunes he had had at the beginnings of owning such a grand plantation.

"I assure you, Mr. Drakes, it was not an easy venture to take on. The first year our stables were plagued with death and disease. It spread throughout the whole of the area, taking with it many families' livestock and only means of living. The following year, our crops failed us, whether it due to a particularly harsh winter or a failing on our part to spot the problem, I could not say." He explained, pausing in his conversation when he spotted them approaching. His stunned gaze giving away his shock at seeing Ethan.

Captain Burg stood at eye level with Ethan though he was a good few years older than he. His hair marked with grays and whites, a mixture of dark brown breaking it up as if to hold onto the remaining bits of youth. "Captain Clarke," he breathed out. "What a pleasant surprise." He added, greeting his old comrade and friend. "Captain Cunningham had mentioned he had run into an old face but did not give away as to whom."

266

"Aye, we met in the town just today. I had heard you had settled at a plantation around these parts but did not expect to run into you. I'm glad to see you so well." Ethan said, stepping aside, "allow me to introduce to you, Captain Stein and Miss Maclean." He smiled at the pair.

"Captain Clarke has told me much about you and the time he spent under your command." Alaric said. He recalled earlier, after their initial meeting with General Cunningham that day, that Ethan had told him how much he had admired and enjoyed his time aboard Captain Burg's ship. They had shared stories of battles and times when they had both actively served in the Royal Navy as they spoke over many games of chess. They had similar stories. Stories of harder times, trails they would never forget or wish to face again, yet amidst all of it, there were times they had enjoyed more than any other time.

Captain Burg laughed, "we did have some good times. What brings you here to the colonies?" He asked curiously.

"We are in search of a man named, Thomas Banning. He is the captain of the ship, *The Amity*." Ethan explained, grabbing a glass of champagne that was being brought around on trays. Alaric quickly grabbed himself and Molly one before the footman could continue on.

"I see, and what is it that he has done? He does not have information on your sister's attacker, does he?" Captain Burg asked, taking a sip from his own glass. "I was very sorry when I heard about the unfortunate event. I trust you received the letter I sent you?"

"Aye, I did, I was grateful for it. Banning possesses the very bracelet I bestowed upon Helena before I left for the seas again. The same voyage I was on when she was attacked. I had believed Banning to be the very man that had committed the crime, but it is not possible as Banning was off the coast of Africa when the event occurred." Ethan explained, frustration and anger evident in his voice.

"And why not take your own ship to find the man? With your own regiment?" He asked, quickly adding, "no offence, Captain Stein, I am simply trying to get a better scope of the circumstances."

"None taken," Alaric laughed, "I was once an officer in the Royal Navy myself. I enjoyed it greatly, more than I had first imagined I would," pausing he looked from Ethan to the captain. "I think you will find though; under these particular circumstances it is better for Captain Clarke here to act as he has been."

"I can imagine," he said, respectfully. "In pretending to be a mere sailor, our friend here," he continued, gesturing to Ethan, "can get closer to the men that will have been around and possibly even served under this Banning, fellow. Whilst in a Royal Navy uniform, he would likely draw too much attention and pirates would not wish to speak with him." He concluded.

"Aye, that's about the size of it." Ethan nodded, "we are closer to finding him than we have been before."

"That is certainly something to raise a glass to," General Cunningham said cheerfully.

"Aye, aye, it certainly is, my friends." Captain Burg replied, raising his glass with the others. "So, tell me, Captain Stein, how do you come into play? How did you and Ethan meet?

"In truth, I knew Thomas Banning long before I met Captain Clarke. My brother, Captain Lucas Harding was previously the captain of *The Trinity*. Last year, we were sent on a rather unceremonious task by the Governor of Barbados. Along the way we discovered a great deal about a passenger we had managed to procure and the task we were sent on. On the voyage we were set upon by Banning who once had served on our ship but had tried mutinying against my brother. He was cast out onto an island. After which we did not see him for some time until that day along our voyage. During a battle with him, he shot a young sailor, the lad was half his age and had done nothing to make Banning fire at him that day." The memory raising more than one emotion in him.

"I am sorry to hear that. What happened to the lad? Did he recover?" The captain asked taken a bit aback by the story.

"He fell overboard, we never found him." Alaric replied, his voice hard. Letting out a breath and taking a long drink of the champagne, he continued. "But, because Banning managed to capture our captain, we then met, Ethan and during the battle that ensued he was able to procure Banning's logbook which showed him, Banning did not indeed commit the crime and allowed us to have a better idea of where Banning may be headed."

"Quite a fascinating tale," a young woman said, admiring Alaric. During his explanation, several guests had come over to hear the story.

"That's one word for it," Ethan grinned, looking from Alaric to the young woman.

"And I take it you were aboard Banning's ship? That is how you came to meet Captain Stein and his brother?"

"Aye, I had thought to join a pirate crew in order to be able to more easily question them about who may have been in Barbados during the time of the attack and Banning not only fit the vague description but also had the mannerisms of a man that would do just a thing. I signed onto his crew where I ended up being flogged and thrown into the brig. That is actually more specifically where Captain Harding and I met."

The look upon Captain Burg's and General Cunning-ham's faces was enough to cause rolls of laughter in Alaric and Ethan alike, "I think you will find, your old comrade here, is quite changed from his time with scoundrels and rogues." Alaric stated, his eyes feigning shock and intrigue, causing the ladies around them to giggle and whisper to one another. All but one, Molly had been completely silent, taking in every bit of the conversation and guests around them. He had not missed the tensing of her body next to him when he had recounted his previous voyage. He noted her glass was empty and did not blame her, the room was warm, and he knew she was trying to calm her nerves.

"And what of you, Miss Maclean? I believe the name is Scottish, no? How is it you came to be with these fine gentlemen tonight?" The young woman who had spoken up moments ago, asked, looking directly at Molly.

"It is my father who was Scottish and my mother Irish." She confirmed, lifting her chin slightly. "As for how I came to be with Captain Stein and Captain Clarke, I was headed from Ireland to the colonies but unfortunately the ship was bound for the West Indies, and I had not realized. Once there, I met Captain Stein, who kindly agreed to take me to the colonies himself as there were no more passengers ships due in that day and the merchant vessels were not taking on any more passengers, so rather than leave me to fend for myself at the docks, he gallantly accepted to take me along with him." She answered, her gaze unwavering. Alaric stifled his cough, that was not quite how he remembered her gaining passage on his ship, but it was a rather compelling story.

"And now that you have arrived in the colonies, where might you be looking to stay? Do you have friends or family here?" She asked, seemingly unperturbed by the building discomfort in the air.

Alaric watched Molly. He had not thought to come up with a story as to why she remained with his ship. When he was in Bath he had inquired after Mackay's aunt as well as any Macleans that were in the area. Apparently, there were a few, but he had known she was not acquainted with any of them and could not simply deposit her with them and she did not seem particularly eager to leave the vessel, despite its dangers. He himself could not quite answer as to why he did not leave her with Mackay's aunt or another respectable family. It would have been a perfect opportunity for her and for him to not have to worry over her but something inside told him he would still be constantly wondering if she had gotten herself into trouble once again.

As if reading his thoughts, she spoke up. "I am sure there are other Macleans in the area, but I don't know them and would not wish to push myself on their hospitality and unfortunately I have not been able to find my relations and am beginning to believe they are no longer in the colonies."

"And until Miss Maclean sees fit to part from us, she is welcome aboard my ship. She is clever and has talent most ladies lack." Alaric smiled, not sure of which talent he was speaking of, sneaking aboard a privateer ship, her skills with her blade or the work she did with the livestock. All of which he feared would not be received politely by some of the other guests.

"How have you enjoyed your journey thus far? I imagine you have met with more dangers than most ladies would be comfortable with." Captain Burg asked, smiling kindly at her. General Cunningham had scarcely taken his eyes from her.

"Aye, yes," she quickly corrected her speech to match the women around her. "We have met with many dangers, storms and battles alike." She admitted.

"You must have been quite terrified, though I imagine you felt quite safe in the presence of Captain Stein and Captain Clarke." Another lady said, smiling up at the two men in admiration.

"Captain Stein and his crew are skilled fighters and sailors and as I understand it, Captain Clarke helped train the crew and better ready them for future battles. I am sure I was never in grave danger." She replied, taking a sip from the fresh glass of champagne Alaric gave her.

Alaric grimaced, his mind going to the man that had broken into his cabin, to the man that had followed Molly down the companionway. He thought of how he had nearly lost her to the sea and then to the fever. Ethan must have been thinking along the same lines and he looked understandingly at Alaric. In truth, she had been in grave danger more than once, aboard his ship and the thought did not sit well with him.

"Though, I believe Miss Maclean is quite capable of fending for herself, as she has proven on more than one brave occasion. She is not a lady to be trifled with." Ethan spoke up, relieving the tension and grinning at Molly.

"I am sure you are quite right," General Cunningham chuckled, "Ethan, Captain stein, I would like to speak with you a moment." He added, leading them away from the gossiping lips of the guests.

"Of course," Alaric responded, hesitating to leave Molly to her own devices with the other ladies. He had no doubt she would be able to answer any questions they flung at her, but he did not enjoy leaving her to feel more uncomfortable than she already was.

"What is it you would like to speak to us about?" Ethan asked curiously, his brow furrowed.

"I have had word about your voyage. Mainly the battles you have been in of late." He explained, looking at both men. "The source of the rumors that are spreading through the regiments tells me they are nothing but tales to get you in trouble. Not that I would have believed them in the first place but all the same." He began, glancing at Captain Burg who was clearly up to date with these rumors as well.

"What sort of rumors are being said?" Alaric asked, stepping closer and glancing about the room. None of the guests appeared to be listening in. Molly was surrounded by several officers and ladies that were eager to hear of her stories aboard the privateer ship.

"It is said that you have all but lost your senses. You have spent too much time in the company of pirates," General Cunningham apologetically nodded at Alaric. "It is said that you never quite recovered from your sister's tragic accident, that you are now just as bloodthirsty as the pirate captain you seek." He concluded, "of course I needn't add that these rumors reflect badly upon you, as well, Captain Stein and we," he gestured between himself and Captain Burg, "intend to do all we can to remedy any repercussions that may come your way, though you are not the target of these rumors, merely caught in the line of fire."

"This is all nonsense, as you very well know. What does the Admiral say to these rumors?" Ethan asked, furious at the accusations.

"He has asked for your immediate return." Captain Burg said, his tone sympathetic.

"This is outrageous." Ethan said, loud enough to draw the attention of the other guests. "And may I ask who is spreading these rumors?"

"I think we can safely assume who," Alaric scoffed. "Did

you not say that Lieutenant Mason would do just about any-thing to see your rank fall?"

"Aye, though why is his word being credited? Why should the Admiral or any of the others believe his stories? They all know the man he is." Ethan asked, shaking his head, turning from the group briefly.

"More than one man came forward. I cannot say how many and I would wager they were paid to, but they approached the Admiral with witness accounts of the attacks on their ships. They stated that despite their pleads, you laid siege to their vessels, taking what goods you wanted and killing as many as you wished." General Cunningham explained, "now, Captain Burg, and as many others as we can get will testify to your character. We will write to the Admiral and do what we can to put a stop to these rumors, but one thing is certain. If you come home empty handed, without the pirate captain, Thomas Banning, you will lose your rank and more. You may even be tried and hanged for piracy and Captain Stein and his crew along with you." He stated his tone firm.

A bell rang out and the meal was announced. "We should go in." Captain Burg said, "try not to fret, we will see what can be done and buy you as much time as we can." He con-cluded, resting a hand on Ethan's shoulder.

Alaric was raging with the thought of the rumors. He wanted nothing more than to ring the lieutenant's neck for causing such a ruckus not to mention, endangering the lives of more than one man. Of accusing them of piracy. He ran a hand along his jaw, wondering how he could help clear Ethan's name and his own and still revenge Benjamin. He would not be able to kill Banning, they would need to hand him over to the Admiral, alive and kicking.

"How are you faring?" Alaric asked, whispering to Molly who sat next to him.

"It's a grand house and Captain Burg and General Cunningham seem kind enough." She replied, keeping her eyes on the meal in front of her.

"Aye, General Cunningham and several of the officers seem very attentive." He said dryly. "What of the ladies? I trust at least one of them was amiable."

"I couldn't say," she responded, taking a small bite of her meal. "I feel as if they can see right through me. As if no matter how, I change my words or dress, I will never escape my past." Molly whispered, defeat filling her voice.

Alaric sighed, perhaps he had been wrong to bring her along. He had thought she would enjoy herself more. He knew it would not be easy and that she would feel a bit uncomfortable but had not imagined she would be quite so upset. "If you'd like, we can leave after the meal. We mustn't stay longer than you wish." He offered, hoping to ease her fears.

"No," she replied sounding surprised. "I wouldn't want to offend Captain Burg or embarrass Captain Clarke." She shifted her gaze back down to her plate. "In truth, I am rather enjoying myself, despite feeling out of place." She confessed.

It was now Alaric's turn to look shocked. "I'm pleased to hear it." He replied, finishing the sweet pie that had been delicately filled with sliced apples.

"If you all have finished, I suggest we go in together and have a bit of entertainment." Captain Burg suggested, standing, and leading the dinner party to another room. In the corner sat an immaculate piano. The walls were wrapped in a soft, dark red covering. A fire cracked on the other side of the room. Chairs and seats sat about the fire and around a small table, meant for card playing. "Miss Roseburn, Miss Maclean, why don't you give us a song?" He asked, his hand just above the small of Molly's back, guiding her towards the piano.

"Oh, I apologize, I'm afraid I cannot play." Molly murmured, her face flushing.

"Not to worry, not to worry. You sing and Miss Roseburn can play." He said, leaving the two women at the instrument and finding a seat.

Alaric watched as Molly looked about the room, her eyes as wide as a startled animal. He caught her eye, nodding what encouragement he could give her. The words began to flow from her lips, softly and quietly, flowing throughout the room like the flickering light from the fire. The words were of a fair maid and a young man falling in love with the flowers and songs from the birds surrounding them.

Alaric could not look from the sight before him. He had never heard a voice quite like hers. The room around them was silent, completely taken in, mesmerized. On occasion he had caught her singing to the animals on the ship as she tended to them, but she would always stop once she spotted him. The room erupted in an applause when she finished

277

the final verse. Her cheeks were flushed, and she quickly retreated to a quiet place near the fire.

"I dare say, we have none of us heard a song so lovely." General Cunningham announced enthusiastically. "Captain Stein is a blessed man to have you aboard his ship, Miss Maclean."

"I could not say," Molly murmured, her gaze darting to Alaric's for the briefest of moments.

General Cunningham was brazen, and all too obvious in his affections for Molly. Alaric finished the whiskey he had been given. He could tell Molly was uncomfortable by the man's attentions but could not say for certain if she disapproved of them. She had made no obvious motion to send him away nor did she encourage him.

"Do I detect a hint of jealousy?" Ethan asked quietly.

Alaric had not even noticed his approach. He grumbled in reply. "He is far too forward. Any man with eyes can see he is making her discontented and clearly, she is not used to such attentions."

"Aye, and any man with eyes can't help but notice her." He replied, barely managing to hide his smile. "Including you, my friend." Standing in front of Alaric, blocking his view of the pair, he added, "as I said once before, perhaps you have lost your touch. I admit, I doubted it for a moment, the barmaids we've come across and the ladies tonight seem eager for your attention, but perhaps not all of them." Ethan teased, moving off to the table where a game had begun.

Alaric grunted, striding towards Molly and her admirer without further thought. "I should return to the ship and make ready to sail in the morning." He announced. It was true, he did need to return to the ship shortly though he doubted there was much left for him to see to, as his crew would have handled matters already. "Would you like me to accompany you back or would you prefer to remain with Captain Clarke a bit longer?" He knew she would be in safe hands with Ethan though he disliked leaving her to the endless charms of General Cunningham.

"Oh, I am quite tired, I will return with you, if you do not mind." She replied as respectfully as she could manage, quickly standing and bidding the General farewell.

Once they had thoroughly thanked their host, they departed down the long drive once again. The moon was low, making the shadows from the trees above look almost ominous.

"I'm happy you enjoyed the evening. You did splendidly." Alaric said, watching the darkness outside the carriage window pass them by.

"I did," she replied simply. "Thank you."

Alaric looked her over, unsure of how to continue on the conversation or if indeed she wanted too.

"Stop the carriage!" A voice commanded from just outside. "Off," a gruff voice bellowed. A shot fired, followed by the sound of a heavy object hitting the hard ground.

29

"Stay quiet," Alaric whispered, holding his hand up and drawing his flintlock.

Molly's hand flew to her mouth covering it, her eyes wide with alarm. Alaric moved in front of her, his pistol pointing at the carriage door his head turning from the window next to them and back to the door. The sounds of deep, low voices filled the air. Molly dared not breath for fear it would only attract the attention of the highwaymen outside.

"Come on out, Capt'n," the man demanded, his voice sounding as rough as the gravel had been beneath the carriage wheels. "You and your friend, both."

Alaric looked at Molly, he shook his head, telling her to remain where she was. He moved towards the door. Slowly opening it, "very well, if you insist." Alaric responded stepping from the door that he did not allow to open widely, continuing to block Molly from view. "I believe you are mistaken. You must have the wrong carriage, mate. It's only me in there." He said, casually holding his flintlock, gesturing with his head, towards the carriage.

"No, I believe you are mistaken." He said pointedly. "You arrived with a woman and another man." He sneered, "call 'em out, or we will rip 'em from the carriage ourselves."

"I don't think that would be wise." Alaric replied. Molly could hear the anger in his voice. She gasped as the barrel of a gun poked through the window. Without another thought, she reached for the barrel shoving it up towards the top of the carriage. The rifle discharged, causing her ears to ring. She vaguely registered the sound of more shots being fired. She crouched between the two seats, not knowing what to do next. If she remained inside, she risked being shot or dragged from the carriage anyway. If she ran out, she risked being killed as well, but it may save the captain. The highwaymen wanted all the passengers out and may spare him if she came out.

Taking a deep breath, she neared to door, before she could change her mind, she sprang from it. More than one man lay motionless on the muddy ground. The captain now held a blade in his hand. He was fighting a man twice his size, with a much larger knife in his hand. Looking around she spotted a discarded flintlock, laying near another man that was either unconscious or dead, she could not tell. Blood spilled from his mouth and nose. Quickly grabbing the pistol, she pulled the hammer back, knowing it may have already spent it's only shot, but it was all she had.

She knew the captain had seen her come from the carriage, the look on his face, a mixture of relief and frustration. A laugh sounded from behind a tree that stood at the edge of the path. She squinted, unable to make out the figure that slowly came out from the covering of the foliage. Something in the laugh was familiar, it sent a chill down her body. *It*

281

couldn't be, she thought, *there is no way he could have found her.*

The skirmish around them seemed to freeze in time, "You?" Alaric questioned. Shock evident in his voice. Molly looked from one man to the other, confused at how the captain knew Lord Willington. He had told her he had not known him. Had never been acquainted with him.

"You have only one shot in that, Molly, if any at all. Then what?" He asked, coming nearer. Captain Stein stepped closer to her, his eyes on the remaining men around them. There had been at least a dozen. Now several lay upon the ground, the others, their weapons drawn and all pointing at the captain.

"I see I didn't hit ye hard enough the first time, pity." Molly spat out, her mind racing, trying to think of what to do next. They were sure to kill the captain, even if she went willing with Lord Willington, they were unlikely to leave Captain Stein standing and able to alert the authorities or come after them himself.

Molly pulled the trigger. It merely clicked in response, causing a roar of laughter to erupt around them. "Enough of this foolishness. You belong to me, remember? Your own uncle sold you to me." He snickered coming nearer, his own pistol rising. "You will come with me, whether I have to take you by force, or you come willingly," he smiled, his eyes traveling the length of her body.

Alaric suddenly lunged for the man nearest him, digging his blade deep into the man's middle. "Molly, go!" He shouted, immediately grabbing for the next man.

Molly's vision blurred; she knew what Lord Willington was thinking before he fired. She rushed for him, pulling the tiny blade from her corset, and leapt for him, driving the blade against his side, missing her mark, but only just. He bellowed in pain as the blade sliced against him, drawing blood but no more. His pistol fired. Molly whipped around, racing forward towards the captain who had fallen to the ground, unmoving.

A sharp pain emanated across her skull, as Willington yanked her back to him, a fist full of her hair in his hand. Tears streaked down her cheeks, in the dark she could not make out the rise and fall of the captain's chest. She had no knowledge of if he were still alive or not. She did not even know if the shot had hit him or if the other man, he had been fighting had bested him.

"I warned you, I'd take you by force." He growled against her ear. "Come on, we must leave. It won't be long before another carriage comes through." He hissed to the two remaining men.

Molly blinked, shutting her eyes tightly once more against the pain in her head. Reaching up to feel for any damage, she realized her hands were bound. She wracked her brain, the last thing she remembered was looking at Captain Stein's motionless form. She choked back the lump in her throat. He had been trying to protect her, keep her from the vicious and unforgiving hands of Lord Willington. She looked about the room she was in. It was clearly the captain's cabin on a ship, though slightly more luxurious than the one on *The Trinity.* Even before she moved from the bed she had been on, to the large window in the back of the cabin, she knew the ship was not docked. She could feel the steady movements of the waves rolling beneath. She looked about the cabin, for anything she could use as a weapon, though doubted very much Lord Willington would leave such an item within her grasp and she remembered having dropped her knife to the ground when he had pulled her back.

The latch clicked, allowing the cabin door to open. Lord Willington entered, a surprised look on his face. "Ah, you've finally awoken." He shrugged off the heavy coat he wore, tossing it on a nearby chest. "What do you think? A bit of an upgrade from the last ship you were aboard, no?"

"Not at all," she raised her brows. "On the contrary, this one smells of mold and chamber pots." She answered, knowing it would only anger him, but she found she could not stand there remaining silent and meek.

"You will watch your speech! You belong to me. You will do as I command of you or I will have to use force, once again." He growled, striding over to her.

Molly laughed, she could not quite say why she did so, as it was not a humorous situation, but she was at a loss of what else she possibly could do. She had no way off of the ship and they were probably already on their way back to the West Indies. She had no idea of how long she had been unconscious, and no one would be coming to her aid. Her thoughts went to the captain. Even if by some miracle he had lived, would he risk his own life and the life of his crew to save her? And what of the pirate Banning they spoke of. They had said they were close to capturing him, would the captain put all that on hold just to save her from a man that had rightfully purchased her? She doubted it and part of her hoped that if he had lived, he would not come after her. She would not wish to see him risk his life for her again and the crew owed her nothing, there was no need they should risk all they had to come to her aid.

She heard the sound of his meaty hand moving fast through the air before she had even saw what he was about to do. The sting from the impact and the force behind it sent her head throbbing even more than it had been. Flashes of sparks and lights blurred her vision. Blinking, trying to clear her eyes, she stumbled back, afraid of being struck again.

"I did hear that your little scrape caused quite the stir and blotched your spotless reputation." She said, her own hand on the stinging and raw flesh of her face. With her other hand, she pointed to the bright pink scar that began just above his brow, running down the side of his face. "Tis truly a pity I did not pause to make sure I had finished you."

"You can mumble and spit your venom at me, girl, all you want, but I will teach you to obey." He whispered, grabbing hold of her waist, digging his fingers deeply into the fabric. Now more than ever she was thankful for the corset.

A blast sounded outside, followed by the rush of footsteps and shouts. A man burst through the hatch, "Ship's firing at us, my Lord."

"Well, do something about it! Sink it! Don't just stand their gaping at me." He bellowed to the young sailor.

"Aye, my Lord." He stammered, looking from Willington to Molly.

"Wait," he hissed, watching Molly's face carefully. "What does the ship look like? Who's is it?"

"*The Trinity,* my Lord." He bowed, shutting the hatch behind him before Lord Willington could say more.

Molly felt the color drain from her face, her heart pounding harder than ever. If they had come for the ship, was it to avenge the captain or to save her? She could not think straight, if they had come to help her, she could not bear the thought of any of the men losing their lives for her. She had to do something but did not know what. Lord Willington would not spare any of them. He would not hesitate to kill any man that came before him.

Another blast sounded, this one rocking the ship. They had been struck. More shouts sounded from above, a shot from Willington's ship sent it pitching once more. "Aren't you going to captain your ship? Defend it against the enemy? Or are you too much a coward? You prefer to hide away in your cabin, hoping to go unnoticed and let your men do all the fighting for you," she goaded.

"They have no need of me. They are the top sailors and fighters in all the West Indies." He laughed. The sound sending a chill down her spine. "Besides, I have other matters to attend to." He grabbed her waist harder, his grip too strong for her to pull away from.

Molly kicked out, her foot hitting its mark against his leg, causing him to fumble at the sudden shock. Not wasting any time, she grabbed for the flintlock that was strapped to his belt. Pulling it free, she staggered back, pointing it directly at him. Despite all he had done, she was not sure she could simply pull the trigger. When she had killed the man in Captain Stein's cabin, it had been different. Even when she had hit Lord Willington before with the bucket, she had not intended to kill him, though later part of her hoped she had. She strengthened her grip on the pistol.

He chuckled, "you won't kill me, you couldn't. It takes more than simply holding a pistol to kill a man." His smiled waivered slightly, the sounds on deck had changed, no more cannon blasts, instead shouts from wounded men, swords clinking against one another, the occasional shot from a flint-lock, filled the air. They had boarded the ship. She held her breath, hoping the men from *The Trinity* would be alright and wondering if Captain Stein was among them. Her mind went to the image of his still body on the frozen ground. Blinking back the unwanted tears and emotion that filled her.

"Ah, you see, you don't have it in you." He challenged, taking a step closer to her. His eyes dark with anger and want.

The hatch burst open, a dark figure stood in the door, the light from outside shining in, making it hard to tell who stood there. Molly caught the motion from the corner of her eye, Lord Willington had pulled another pistol out, a smaller one. She had not realized he had been carrying another. It was pointing at the figure in the doorway.

"I missed the first time, but won't miss again, Captain. Rest assured; I'll take good care of the girl." He sneered.

A shot fired, echoing in the cabin. Both men looked at each other in surprise, then to Molly. A whisp of smoke streamed up from the end of the flintlock in her grip. Her hands stung from the pressure of the shot being fired. Lord Willington looked down. Crimson blood seeped through his shirt. His body fell to the cabin floor, unmoving. Molly let the pistol fall to the ground, her hands shaking, her eyes not moving from the body.

"Molly, are you harmed?" Captain Stein asked, his voice full of concern. He slowly strode over to her. Looking up, her eyes slowly shifting to the captain. The realization that he was alive and standing before her only stunned her further. "Lass?" He whispered, his hand reaching up, turning her face towards the light that streamed in. "He did this to you?" He asked, his face hard.

"I'm alright," She replied, her voice low. "I thought he had killed you," she finally said.

"It'd take more than a graze to the shoulder to do that." His chest rumbled.

"You should not have come for me. You risked your life at the carriage and now you've risked your life once more and the life of your crew. And for what?" She choked out, beyond thankful yet not believing he really came for her.

"And for what?" He asked in return, disbelief in his eyes. "Did you not think, for one moment that I would come for you? Did you truly believe I would leave you to the grimy hands of that bastard?" He questioned. "And as for the crew, they were just as keen to get you back as I. After all, not one of them would have looked forward to doing the chores with the livestock again," he grinned.

"Come, let's get you back to the right ship." He said, his arm around her to steady her. He guided her on deck and across the plank to The Trinity. Molly could not help but look about the deck. The wounded and dead lying about. She did not recognize any of the fallen, relief flooded her. "Doc needs to look you over, after that, I'll have a small meal brought to the cabin." He explained, leading her through the hatch.

"What of Lord Willington?" She asked, worried that he and his crew would meet with repercussions for attacking and killing a Lord.

"I sent word to General Cunningham before leaving port, letting him know what had transpired. As you saw, though he is retired from the Royal Navy, he still has many connections and will alert those that need to know and inform them of what happened. You have nothing to fear." He assured her, settling her into the bed next to Aoife who woke at the sounds of their voices, ready to play.

"I'll fetch Doc and make sure Cook has a meal prepared." He said, ruffling the kitten's head, causing it to squirm and attack its new foe.

"I really am alright. I could fetch my own meal, capt'n. I don't need such fussin' over." She said, a bit embarrassed and uncomfortable at the attention. She began to stand up to protest further when Doc entered the cabin.

"Ah, Miss Maclean, have a seat, so I can take a look at you." He said gently, coming towards her, placing a salve on the desk. Molly did as he instructed, lifting her head towards the little bit of light that shown from the window so he could see the mark on her face. "The bruising has already begun but will fade soon. The salve will aid the healing." He explained, grabbing the salve from the table, and applying it to the side of her face. Wincing at the cold of it rather than the pain. Doc looked over his shoulder at the captain who frowned and obediently turned, walking a few steps further away to give her some privacy. "Miss Maclean, I must ask to ensure you are well," he paused before continuing. "Did Lord Willington harm you elsewhere?"

"No, he did not force himself on me, not in that way." She answered, her voice hard. "He did not have time, thanks to the captain's timely arrival." She breathed out, looking over at the captain who stood against the opposite wall, his back to them. His hands pressing hard against the wall he stood at, causing the shirt he wore to tighten about his shoulders.

"I'm glad of that." He replied, "and no doubt your own strength and determination kept you from further harm. You are a tough lass, and we are all of us glad to have you back aboard *The Trinity*." He finished saying, examining her once more before standing and heading for the hatch.

Cook brought a tray of various foods, fruits, freshly cooked veggies, potatoes with steam rising from them, a bowl of gravy to coat the foods in and several slices of roast. A large bread was placed in the center of the tray for pulling bits of it off to eat with the rest of the meal. Her stomach grumbled at the sight, her hand flew to her middle, embarrassed at the loud announcement it made.

"Eat up, ye'll need yer feet beneath ye soon enough. I procured a she goat that's due to be birthin' soon and needs your attention." Cook grinned, knowing the news of the new arrivals would have her springing from the bed as soon as she finished the meal. He chuckled at the captain's grumblings about more livestock as he left the cabin.

"Did I not tell you those beasts would be needing you?" He asked, sitting down at the desk in front of the tray.

Molly got up, walking to the table, she pulled a chunk of meat off and gave it to the kitten that meowed impatiently at the bottom of the desk. "And I need them." She smiled down at Aoife.

Captain Stein watched her closely, "Miss Maclean, I must tell you. While in Bath, I discovered there are quite a few Macleans throughout the area. Most are a bit further north but there are a few families here. I know you are not acquainted with any of them, but it is the closest thing you have to being with family. If you choose, I will take you to them once our voyage has ended. We are too close to Banning to turn back now but once my dealings with him are over, if you'd like," he stopped, his brow furrowing. "It is completely your choice, being aboard this ship has nearly cost you your life on more than one occasion and the temptation of being with kin, even those you do not know may be great. I would not want you to think you didn't have a choice or that you are trapped upon this vessel."

Molly tore at the piece of bread she held in her hand, not looking at the captain. She swallowed the feelings creeping into her mind. She dare not speak for fear her voice would give away how she felt. His did no such thing. Molly had not expected him to ask if she would like to stay or leave. For a time, she had thought he would, even thought he would force her off his ship if he must but once they left Williamsburg, she had not thought he would. She believed he enjoyed her company and even wanted her to stay. Afterall, he had risked everything to retrieve her, why do that if he did not wish her to stay. The idea of leaving the ship was unbearable. Living with kin, no matter how she wished to get know her father's people, did not appeal to her. Despite her reservations about them and even bitterness towards them for taking him from her mother and her, she did want to know them and meet them one day, but not leave the ship to live with them. In truth, being aboard the ship could be dangerous to be sure, but no more dangerous than her life would be on land. The man in the tavern, her uncle and Lord Willington had already more than proven that.

"You pull at that bread much more and there will be nothing left." He pointed out, studying her face.

Molly sighed brushing the crumbs she had created, into the palm of her hand, placing mauled bits of bread back on the tray. "Thank you for thinkin' of me. I will give it some thought." She mumbled, unsure of what else to say. She wanted nothing more than to blurt out how much she wanted to stay aboard his ship and ask him why he wished her gone.

"Take the time you need," he agreed, taking a letter from a drawer in his desk. Breaking the seal upon it, he opened it, scanning the parchment. "Not all plantation owners are like Lord Willington. I've told you about my brother and his wife." He began, not quite asking, but rather confirming he had told her about them.

"Aye, you've said as much. You've also failed to mention all the trouble he and you have been in together." She replied simply, glancing over at him from above the rim of her cup.

"Aye, well, I can't say all the stories you've heard are true but nor can I say they are false," he admitted, a slight scowl upon his face. "Who told you such tales?" He asked, his brows pulled together in curiosity.

"Doc," she answered, a smile spreading across her lips.

"Ah, well, in that case, they are likely close enough to the truth." He admitted.

"Cook, Ol' Shorty and Eddie, have told such tales as well." She laughed at the deepening of his frown.

"I wouldn't hold much truth to those ones," he mumbled, focusing on the letter once more.

30

"Amelia," Thomas called out as he entered the house. The dark, front door opening to reveal the entryway. A large cream and dark red runner spread the length of it. A stairway winding its way up to the second landing. His study stood off to the other side of the entryway, striding towards it, he laid his sword and flintlock on his desk, rummaging through letters that lay upon it. He would have to read through them and answer them before he left. Many of them were no doubt unimportant but he did not wish to ignore them and make more enemies for himself when now more than ever he needed the allies. When he was in Beaufort, he had discovered even his fellow pirates were beginning to turn on him. They rather seek the bounty upon his head than fight with him.

"Oh, my dear," Amelia exclaimed, "you are home." Running to him, she wrapped her arms around him. He breathed her in, it had been more than a year since he had been back to see his wife and daughters. Though he had missed them, he never liked staying in town for more than a fortnight or two. Now, it was ever more urgent for him to be on his way. He needed to leave for London as soon as he could.

"Aye, luv," he replied, pulling away from her and looking Amelia over. "You are lovelier than ever." Pulling her to him, he ran his hands along her body, kissing her firmly.

"Papa," a girl came in, squealing in delight at his arrival.

Bending low, he opened his arms, allowing his daughters to leap into his arms. Grinning, he gently pushed them away. Reaching into the inside of his vest, he asked them to close their eyes. Pulling two dolls with hair that matched theirs, he placed the gifts into their outstretched hands. He had picked them up from Charles town before leaving and had been glad to see the look upon the young girls' faces when they opened their eyes to see what he had brought them this time.

"I have something for you as well," he said, standing up and facing his wife. Her eyes filled with want, kissing her again, he pulled a small box from his pocket and handed it to her. Delicately pulling the blue ribbon from it, she opened the box to reveal a silhouette made from the whitest of ivory. A small gasp escaped her lips. "Allow me," he whispered, turning her so he could tie the necklace about her neck.

"Thank you," she breathed out. "I daren't ask how long you'll remain this time, but I'm pleased you've returned for the time you can." Her fingers brushing against the new pendant that lay just above the curve of her dress.

"I'm afraid my stay will be shorter than usual," he admitted. "I've been tasked with a rather important mission. One that will bring us far more riches than any other has." He promised, knowing it would not sooth his wife's heart, but it was all he was willing to offer her. She never understood his want for more riches or the sea. She had tried on more than one occasion to find him high positions in society, but none suited his lust for sailing or all the freedom it offered.

"Oh, papa, why must you leave so soon?" Ava asked, smoothing out the doll's dress. Her bottom lip stuck out, threatening to begin to tremble.

Thomas lifted the girl up, holding her close, "it is not something a young girl is to understand. Do not fret, I will return again, with more gifts, before you know it." Throwing her in the air, making her giggle and scream for another go.

"It is late and time to change for our meal, girls." Amelia smiled, clapping her hands for their daughters to rush from the study and up the stairs. Their laughter and excitement could be heard throughout the house, echoing through the walls.

"I best go change as well, and so should you. You are no longer aboard your ship, Mr. Banning and I am expecting guests," she announced as firmly as she could, giggling herself at the look upon his face.

"We have time before they arrive, and if not, they can wait." He growled, pulling her to him once more, despite her halfhearted protests.

Thomas walked down the steps of his home, sea birds called from above and the sounds of the bustling port nearby calmed his nerves from the previous night's guests. Never had he heard a woman with such a screeching voice, nor had he met men that were such simpletons. He often enjoyed the extravagant dinner parties they took part in. It was a nice change from his life aboard the ship, staring at gruff men, but the guests his wife had invited over had him drowning himself in a bottle of the finest whiskey.

Adjusting his vest, he wore finer clothes while in Newport, he had advanced himself and his wife to the highest of society and did not wish to give any of their acquaintances an excuse to spread rumors. He had business in the town and needed to make sure his ship was ready to sail out within a day or two.

Thomas approached the docks. Grady stood near a group of sailors he did not recognize, handing them a few coins, they turned, leaving his first mate scowling out at the ships that were docked.

"What business did you have with those men?" He asked, anger rising at not knowing his first mate's dealings as well as he thought he had.

"Them just came from another ship, docked 'ere just after we did, capt'n. Them says you best watch yer neck." Grady spat out, shaking his head in disgust. "Them says for a few coin they'd be sayin' more but says no more than a ship is searchin' for you, seekin' revenge upon ye." Grady sniffed, wiping his nose with his sleeve. "I reckon' it's Harding and his brother. You killed the runt of their ship, now they be wantin' ta kill ye." Grady finished, shaking his head and scoffing at the notion.

"I suggest you get that ship ready to sail tonight or it will be you I will be givin' to my enemies." He demanded, grabbing Grady by his shirt.

"But Capt'n, tisn't possible. The damage from the last battle have no been properly repaired and the goods have no been settled. It'll at least be a couple of days til we can sail again." He stammered; his eyes filled with fear.

Thomas dropped him, letting him fall to the wooden planks. Men from the docks, paused their work, watching the scene unfold. "Your business remains elsewhere," he bellowed, kicking a crate, splintering it, and spilling the contents within.

Weaving his way out of the dockyard he found himself at the estate the governor was letting for the time being. He had received a letter just hours after arriving stating he was to report to the governor the next day or else he would be pulling his backing and would no longer support Thomas on his ventures or do his part to protect him from the noose. Knocking on the door, he waited impatiently to be let in.

"You must be Mr. Banning," the butler guessed, looking him over. "If you will please wait in his lordship's study, he will be with you momentarily." He suggested, guiding Thomas to the room down the hall. The home being far larger than his own of course but not much more luxurious. He had made sure to leave Amelia with plenty of money, sending her more when he could and only allowing her to purchase the very best of material and items.

"Ah, Mr. Banning," the governor announced his presence, walking into the study, his butler closing the doors behind him. "I am pleased you headed my warning and came to call. I have a rather delicate and urgent task I need you to do." He began, pouring them each a class of whiskey.

"And what task would that be? I am already to set sail on a voyage that will keep me gone for several months at least. If I am to do this task for you as well, it would cost you a great deal." He replied, eyeing the governor, curious as to what he could possibly want him to do.

"Of course," he acknowledged, hesitating only a brief moment before continuing. "You are to return to the coast of Africa, well, to the waters just off the coast." He said, waiting for Thomas to finish his grumbling before continuing. "A large fleet of French ships are to be there, heading towards the West Indies and then to the colonies."

"And what do you care about a French fleet all the way on the other side of the seas?" Thomas asked, impatient at the governor's ramblings.

"You see, if I send my own fleet of men out to hunt them down, I will be granted the highest of thanks from the Governor, Lords and Plantation owners of the islands, not to mention the gratitude of the colonists. I will soon be Governor of more of the colonies if you succeed, you will be compensated accordingly," he reasoned. Stepping around the desk and leaning over the mantel of the fire. "You will lead a fleet of ships, the other captains are, well, of the same background as you." He concluded, sipping from his glass, watching Thomas's reaction.

"Ah, you mean they are pirates." He said simply, finishing his own glass and standing. "Very well, I will be on my way in a day or two. From here I will head for the coast of Africa. After which I will then attend to the business in London that I have." He said, bowing to the governor and looking about the room. "I look forward to our next meeting," he smirked, letting himself out.

Thomas walked up the steps to his home, opening the door, only to be barraged by Amelia. "I've been hoping you'd return soon. Tonight, we've been asked to attend a dinner at the Smithers's estate. Mrs. Smithers says her husband is most eager to speak with you about your travels." She insisted, pulling him into the house further and closing the door behind them. Curling her arm around his, she added, "I understand you did not enjoy last night's company, but you've always found the Smithers' to be agreeable, have you not?"

"Indeed, love." He answered. In truth, he did enjoy going to the Smithers'. The whiskey was plentiful, and the men typically stayed confined to the gaming tables.

Music could be heard from outside the large estate home before Thomas and his wife even set foot upon the steps. Laughter and jovial speech filtered through the windows. Thomas grinned, the more men that sat about the tables and the more drink they consumed, the more money he would gain that night.

"See, was I not right? You are pleased to be here." Amelia

whispered to him as they made their way into the house. She clung tightly to his arm. "As much as you enjoy your time at sea, you will not fool me, you enjoy your time with me almost as much." She teasingly purred into his ear.

"I will not deny I enjoy my time with you a great deal." He replied, his gaze raking her body.

"Mr. and Mrs. Banning, it is a great pleasure to have you join our party!" Mr. Smithers exclaimed, ushering them into the large room. Folks danced in the middle of the room to the music that was played skillfully by a small group standing in the corner.

"Mrs. Banning, I'm so pleased you are here. I want to introduce you to my niece. She is visiting for a time from London and longs to make more acquaintances while she is with us." A fair woman rushed towards them, quickly taking Amelia from her husband and leading her to a young lady that stood obediently near the outer ring of the dancers. She caught Thomas's eye, blushing, she looked down at her feet, only to boldly smile at him before the two women reached her.

Clearing his throat, Thomas quickly switched his attention to his host. It would not do him or his family any good if he were caught gazing at the newest debutants. He needed to keep his elevated position in order to keep his neck from the noose and had worked hard to reach his new station. He would not have some little chit ruining it for him. "Care for a game?" He asked, gesturing to the card tables.

"Yes, yes, by all means, Mr. Banning. There is a man sitting just there," He pointed at a gentleman who sat at one of the gaming tables, his eyes flickering between the cards in his hands and his opponents. "That is Mr. Farthing, he has been most eager to make your acquaintance and speak to you of your ventures." Mr. Smithers said in a hushed tone. "He's a devil with cards and may even put you to shame." Mr. Smithers laughed loud enough to draw more than one curious eye in their direction. Slapping Thomas on the back, they made their way to the tables.

Thomas sat opposite the man, eyeing him, uncomfortable at the way Mr. Smithers had indicated Mr. Farthing wanted to speak to him of his ventures. He wondered what the man had heard or knew. He kept the details of his voyages as quiet as he could. Thomas knew it would not be long before society knew of his exploits, until then though, he needed to do all he could to ensure his status remained untarnished.

"I hear you are interested in sailing," Thomas spoke up, bringing the man's attention to him.

"I take it you are the famous, Thomas Banning, are you not?" Mr. Farthing picked up the new hand he had been dealt, seemingly unimpressed, whether by Thomas himself or the cards he held, Thomas could not tell.

"Famous? How so? I do no more than any other Privateer or Merchant out there." He replied, casually picking a new card.

"Is that so? Peculiar, that is not how I hear it." He challenged, his gaze growing hard. Placing their cards on the table, Thomas scowled, he was not liking the way the conversation was going, nor did he like the fact that his opponent had just bested him at cards. Thomas had a notorious reputation for being unbeatable at the tables. It was said he had impeccable luck, but the truth remained beneath the folds of his coat.

"Well, I cannot say what you have heard, nor can I say for certain if any of these rumors have truth behind them but if you are interested in investing in my ventures, I suggest we speak elsewhere." Thomas replied pointedly. Glancing towards Amelia, he saw she was cheerfully speaking with a group of women, a few of them he recognized, others must have recently made his wife's acquaintance while he was at sea.

"I take it she is not as pleasing to you as your beloved ship," Mr. Farthing spoke up, breaking up Thomas's thoughts.

He growled in response, "you will do well to keep your eyes from my wife and hold your tongue or you may find you have no more use of it." His voice low so those around him could not hear.

Mr. Farthing merely laughed, "ah, so the fearsome pirate appears finally." He responded, studying the cards in his hand once more. "I must say, you hide him well, Mr. Banning."

Thomas placed the cards face down on the table, "I suggest we talk, elsewhere." He stood, the chair nearly tipping over as he did so. Mr. Farthing laughed once more, slowly rising from his own chair and following Thomas towards Mr. Smithers' study.

"Speak up, who are you? How do you know of me?" Thomas asked, waving a hand in the air, wanting no more than to dispose of the man right at that moment. His insolence and the airs he put on angered Thomas and he disliked that the man knew more of him than he did of Mr. Farthing.

"I don't suppose you remember a merchant ship a few years back. A merchant ship that you attacked, leaving only a few lucky survivors that had lived not on account of you showing mercy but from your men's poor aim." He began, his gaze remaining on the fire below him. His hand upon the wooden mantel.

"There have been many merchant vessels. I can't be expected to remember all of them now, can I?" It was Thomas' turn to goad the man, he had a suspicion he had killed or harmed someone this man cared about, now he was here to ruin Thomas.

Mr. Farthing whipped around, "My wife and myself were aboard that ship. The sailors, did all they could but they were no match for your heartless crew." Undoing his vest and shirt, he lifted it, showing a large, jagged scar that ran across his middle. "I was knocked unconscious only to wake hours later to find myself barely alive and my wife, laying lifeless amongst the rest of the crew and passengers." He stepped closer, "I have vowed to avenge my wife and those that died that day."

Thomas laughed, all this time he had suspected it had been Harding and his brother that had been after him, but instead it was this gentleman. "Very well, a dual," he shrugged, turning towards the door. "Oh, and I don't remember you, but your wife remains clear in my mind." He twisted a small ring that rested on his smallest finger. "Have your second, ready, I

will not remain in town for long and I will not wait for you."
Closing the door to the study, Thomas found Amelia amongst
the guests. He did not know how far this man would go to
avenge his own wife and Thomas had not liked the way Mr.
Farthing had openly eyed Amelia.

"A dance, and then I am afraid we should retire for the
evening." He said, placing Amelia's delicate hand in the
crook of his arm. She beamed up at him, pleased at the offer
to dance.

Alaric watched Molly rush through her meal. Despite all that had happened to her thus far, she remained seemingly unaffected, though he knew somewhere inside her, she would never forget what had happened. He also knew he would never forget the look upon her face when she had realized he was alive and had not been killed when the carriage had been set upon.

Molly's hair fell about her shoulders, she leaned down playfully running her fingers along the kitten's belly. She dropped a bit of the food that was left over on her plate to the floor, offering it to her tiny companion. The small kitten proceeded to silently stalk her prey, pouncing suddenly on it. Molly let out a soft giggle, standing and taking a quick drink from the cup that sat in front of where she had been sitting.

"I'm off to check on the goat," she said, eager to be with the animals once again. Alaric nodded, knowing it was the one place she felt most content and safe, but not ready to have her out of his sight. His mind still reeled from seeing her in the clutches of that man and fearing the worst.

"I'll come with you," he announced, cheerfully smiling at her.

She looked him over in puzzlement. "You wish to check on the animals with me?"

"Aye," he shrugged casually, "I have yet to meet the newest crew member and I will need to approve of her if she is to remain." He winked, leading the way through the hatch, leaving Molly standing in the cabin in bewilderment.

As they neared the large area that held the animals Molly cheerfully greeted each of them as if they were long time friends. She bent down, picking one of the hens up, stroking her feathers gently as the bird nestled deep in her arms. She set the chicken back down in one of the nesting boxes, checking each one for fresh lain eggs.

"Hello, wee lass, you have had quite a day or two, have you not?" Molly carefully approached the new goat. The doe pawed the ground, seemingly pacing the pen, unsure of her new home. Alaric stifled a laugh, the she goat did seem to resemble her new owner with her restless spirit and over cautious countenance.

"As I recall, I tried much the same approach with you when you first came aboard my ship, and you were just as flighty." Alaric commented, earning a scowl from the woman in the pen. "Though, lucky for you she holds no wee dagger."

Molly gained the hesitant trust of the doe, resting a hand on the goat's side, she ran another hand along her back, reassuring the goat of her safety. The doe pawed the ground harder, laying down at Molly's feet, only to stand back up. A small sound emanated from the doe's mouth, sounding very much like a plea. Alaric stepped forward; he had been leaning against the wall but the way the goat was acting did not seem quite right.

"I believe you may have more than one new member of your beasts by the end of the night. She's nearing her time." Alaric pointed towards the doe, slowly walking forward so as not to startle her. "See how she continues to paw the ground and act unsettled?"

"Aye, you no think it's because she is unfamiliar with the ship?" Molly asked, her brow pulled together as she examined the goat further.

Alaric shook his head, "No, lass, have a look at her middle. It should be a bit bigger at this stage and it's not. The babe has moved. You won't have long to wait, now." He concluded, patting the beast. He watched Molly look the doe over, talking to her softly. "Did you see many births at the plantation?"

Molly shrugged, "A few, if I was lucky enough to be hiding away in there when one of them birthed. I saw a foal being born once, the man said the mother and foal would not make it if he did not help her along. He reached right inside her and pulled the wee thing from the mom. He told me to fetch straw and dry the babe off until the mother tended it." Her voice trailed off as her mind retreated into the memory of the moment.

"Aye, when we were lads, the cows on the farms in the village often had troubles with large calves or ones that did not fancy coming into the world proper. Lucas and I often assisted the farmers with them." He patted the cow next to them. Since Molly had begun tending to them, they had never looked healthier. He and Lucas had lost many of the beasts to sicknesses in the past. They had spoken about no longer carrying the animals with them but knew once they did that, they would find themselves starved if the winds died for too long. On more than one occasion the livestock had saved the crews' lives and kept them from starving.

Alaric rubbed his arm, the temperature aboard the ship had dropped. There had been no storm in sight when he had last looked, but now their breath was visible. "Lass, it could still be sometime before the wee babe comes, you should return to the cabin." He was not comfortable with her staying below. Images of her body wracked with fever; her lips paler than he had ever seen. Save for the rise and fall of her chest, he would have thought her gone.

Molly shook her head fiercely, "I couldn't leave her, not now. She is in a new home and is already scared."

Alaric adjusted his stance, her eyes pleading. "Very well," he said, trying to hide his worry and frustration but under-standing why she would not leave the distressed animal. Turning from the hurt and confusion on her face, he headed for his cabin.

Throwing the hatch open, he looked over at the bed, completely empty, save for the heavy blankets and the small ball of fur that had curled up on the pillow. Alaric let out a sigh, grabbing the blankets and kitten with one swoop, he headed back towards the hatch, pausing just before leaving.

Striding back to his desk, he grabbed a bottle of whiskey and left the cabin.

As he neared the large area, he could hear the bleats from the distressed doe. "How's she coming along?"

"Well, so far as I can tell. She is still pawing the ground and occasionally laying down." Molly looked back at him; her eyes widened. "What is it you're doing?"

"If you are to remain down here in this near to freezing pit, I suggest you come wrap up until things move along further." Alaric explained, laying a blanket on the planks, just out of reach of the animals and away from the straw the stuck out from the bottom of the fences. Aoife let out a small mew in protest of being moved from the warmth of the bed. He handed the wee kitten to Molly who proceeded to wrap it in her shawl as she sat on the blanket. Alaric draped another about her shoulders. Before sitting next to her and pulling his own blanket over him.

Keeping a watchful eye over the doe, they passed the bottle of whiskey back and forth, warming their bodies with every sip. "How long do you think she will continue?" Molly asked, not taking her eyes from the goat.

"Hard to say but I reckon it won't be much longer." The doe had begun to push, her body going ridged and arched every few minutes. It had been many years since he had watched any livestock during a birthing. The last time was back on the farm in Ireland. He and Lucas had waited up in the night in case the cow needed assistance. It was the cow's second calf, the first had not made it the previous spring. When it came time for the calf to be born, it once again proved difficult. The calf had been large and had gotten hip locked during the birth. They eventually got the calf out, alive and well, only to have the mother fall ill some hours later and die.

Alaric looked over at Molly, she had sat up straighter, looking closely at the doe. Shifting his gaze, he noticed what she had noticed. A round sack had appeared from the goat. He smiled, pleased with the progress and enjoying Molly's excitement.

Minutes passed, the doe continued to move about her pen, anxious for it to all be over. Her bleats echoed through the cabin. The sack remained intact, and nothing more had appeared. Alaric shifted where he sat, it was growing even later and in truth, the babe should have been born already.

"Perhaps we should fetch Doc," Molly suggested, her face stricken with concern.

"Aye, I'll rouse him." Alaric agreed, hopping up from the blankets and striding towards Doc's surgery.

Doc bent low, slowly approaching the distressed goat. Running a hand along her back as Molly held her firmly, talking to her gently. "The kid is trapped. There are only two hooves coming forward." Doc explained, patting the animal in reassurance. "We will need to bring the head forward ourselves."

Molly nodded in understanding, glancing from the goat to Alaric. "What if it is too late?" She asked, her voice wavering.

"Then at least we can try and save the mother." He replied, nodding to Doc to proceed.

"Hold her firm. She'll not appreciate this much." Doc said, sitting behind the doe. He shook his head, "Nay, I will end up hurting her more, my hands are too large." He explained, looking up at Molly, his brows raised. "You'll have to do it Miss Maclean." He moved aside, taking her spot at the front of the doe.

Molly looked at both men in shock but did not speak up. She did as she was bid and positioned herself behind the goat. "What do I feel for?"

"Slowly reach in. It is alright if the sack breaks. Try and find the head, bring it forward when you feel her push again." Doc instructed. Alaric took a step forward, careful not to startle the goat. Molly had rolled her sleeves up as far as she could. Her breath could still be seen in the cold cabin air.

She did exactly as Doc had instructed, not hesitating even a moment. The sack broke open, spilling the contents upon the straw filled planks and Molly's gown. "I feel the head, it is bent a bit back. I cannot bring it forward." She informed them, sounding as distressed as the she goat looked.

"Steadily push the babe back a bit once she stops pushing. Then with her next one, bring it forward." Doc spoke lowly.

Molly nodded, blowing at a bit of hair that had fallen in her face. Alaric watched the smile spread across her lips "It worked, the nose is out." She exclaimed, removing her hand, and sitting back on her heals to allow the mother to do what she needed.

"Very well done, Miss Maclean." A moment later the wee babe, fell from the mother, landing amongst the straw. Molly quickly grabbed a handful of the golden bedding, rubbing the newborn dry as it made soft sounds. "I'll get some molasses water to give the mother a bit of strength." Doc said, leaving the pen and patting Alaric on the back.

Alaric remained rooted to the spot. He had never seen a lass do what Molly had done. He thought of the women he had spent time with in France and the ones they had recently met at Captain Burg's. Not one of them would have even considered boarding his ship, let alone braving the battles, storms and tending to the animals. Most certainly none of them would have wanted to be present during the birth and absolutely would never had bent down and allowed their gown to be dirtied.

Watching Molly with the mother and her wee babe, he could not peel his gaze from them. She was all but glowing and he'd stake his life on it that the lass had never felt so proud of herself before. "You did remarkably, Miss Maclean." He said, breaking the silence between them.

Molly looked up at him, Aoife in her hands as she stroked the doe who was now licking her babe clean. The kitten had come over during all of the commotion to see what was amiss. Molly's eyes filled, "I've never been trusted to do anything, other than clean my uncle's house and then the plantation after that. And even that I seemed to do poorly at, at least that is what they told me so's they'd have an excuse to whip me."

"That's long since passed, Miss Maclean. You will not be harmed aboard my ship, you have my word. You are more than needed… and wanted here," he told her. He cleared his throat, looking back at the entrance to the cabin, as Doc came back in. A bucket sloshing in his hand.

Placing the bucket in the pen, they retreated back to the blankets, giving the mother a chance to drink. Alaric drew his brow together, the goat lifted her tail, as if she were straining once more.

"There is to be another," Molly exclaimed, unable to contain her excitement.

"Yes, I believe you are right. The molasses water will give her the strength she needs. The second kid tends to come quicker than the first. I expect she will need no assistance with this." Doc assured Molly who was now shivering. Her gown was soaked through, and she was visibly shaking, despite her cheerful smile. Alaric only hoped Doc was correct, and the second wee goat would come quickly. He did not like the idea of Molly remaining in the wet clothes much longer. Doc laughed, shaking his head, more than pleased about the outcome of the night. He retreated back to his surgery, leaving Molly and Alaric alone once more.

Molly squealed in surprise as the mother goat pushed once more, the kid dropping to the flooring next to its sibling who was beginning to try and stand on its wobbling and weak legs. Turning to Alaric, she suddenly wrapped her arms around his neck. His hand moving quickly to her waist. Their lips met. Molly froze, realizing what she had done. Pulling away, she avoided his eyes, feeling her face flushing, her entire body equally numb from the cold as well as from the embrace.

Alaric cleared his throat, he stood frozen in place. His mind reeling, he had not expected her excitement in that moment to get the best of her. He had not been able to take his eyes from her all evening and had been more than impressed with her and had even thought of kissing her but had refrained as Doc was still in the cabin. When he felt her arms circle around his neck though, he had been unable to stop himself. "We need to get you back to the cabin. Your dress is completely wet, and you are too cold to stay down here. The goats will be alright now." He assured her; afraid she would refuse to come with him once more.

"Aye," she laughed looking down at her gown. "It'll need a fair scrubbing to be sure." Keeping hold of the squirming kitten, she gathered the blankets as best she could, being careful not to get the filth from the dress on the blankets.

Alaric kept his eyes on the ground, his back to Molly as she quickly changed into a new gown. He had to admit, he truly admired her for all she had done that day and for her strength at braving Lord Willington. "Are you decent now?" He asked, his voice low. He waited, no response. Hesitantly turning around, he saw that Molly was already in the bed, the covers tucked under her chin, her eyes shut tight. He smiled, Aoife was curled up next to Molly, seemingly just as exhausted.

32

Alaric signaled for the crew to bring in the sails and prepare to dock. Newport was far busier than any of the other ports they had been in recently. Ships were lining the docks, more were coming in and leaving, causing all of them to blend together. *The Trinity* swayed as it anchored at the dock, the crew scrambled about the deck, readying the planks to go ashore.

Alaric turned, catching sight of Molly as she came on deck. She had woken early to check on the mother goat and her babies, only coming up to the galley to have a quick bite of food. She returned to the animals, promising she would be on deck in time to go ashore. "How are your patients?"

"Doing well," she beamed. The little ones are full of vigor and were bouncing about the pen." She replied, nodding to the city in front of them, "It is quite big."

"Aye, and that may make it much harder to find our man." Alaric murmured; not happy about the slim chance they would have at finding Thomas there. He held his arm out, indicating she could walk down the planking towards the docks.

"Stay close, in large ports like this, there are pickpockets on every street." He advised, placing his hand just inches from her back. Ethan following next to them. Alaric had advised Ol' Shorty to remain with the crew, he did not wish to attract more attention than they likely already would.

"Let's try the nearest tavern and go from there," Ethan suggested, nodding to one that sat a few buildings down. A sign hung above the door that read, *Red Sky Inn.*

A man stood at the back of the tavern. A white apron around his waist. He nodded to the newcomers, continuing to wipe down the counter. Men sat at the tables, talking, playing dice, cards and other games they would bet all their earnings on.

"Can I help you gentlemen? Miss," he asked, dropping the cloth in a bucket behind the counter.

"Aye, we were told a ship called *The Amity* is or was in port recently. I believe the captain's name in Thomas Banning." Alaric asked, dropping a couple coins on the counter.

The tavern owner pocketed them, pouring each of them an ale. "Can't say that the captain you seek was at my tavern, but I have heard tell *The Amity* is in port. I can't say when they set sail again. Causes quite the stir each time it lands here. They brings goods of the best quality from around the world." He chuckled, "this tavern ain't for the likes of the captain. I'd 'spect. Try takin' a carriage to one of the more, *reputable* establishments." He offered, moving off to deal with another sailor.

Ethan exchanged looks with Alaric, "surely we cannot be talking of the same man." He exclaimed.

"I suppose we will find out soon enough," Alaric shrugged, still pondering what the man had said. He wondered how and why Thomas had bothered to keep his reputation clean in this particular town. The only conclusion he could draw from what they had learned is that he managed to have a friend higher in society, one that could keep him safe from being locked up and branded the pirate he is.

They did not bother with a carriage as suggested. He rather be able to observe their surroundings better and more than did not trust the enclosed boxes since their last encounter. As they moved further from the docks, the building began to slowly change. The houses and various businesses came into view. Women stood outside speaking of the latest fashions, of the balls and dinner parties they had attended the night before. Men moved about their business, tipping their hats at those they knew as they passed them. Alaric led the group down another street, grabbing Molly closer to him as a carriage rounded the corner, nearly running the group over. He heard Ethan mumble curses but could not quite make out his exact words but would wager he was thinking along the same words as his friend.

"How about there?" Molly suddenly stopped, pointing up to an elegantly ornate building. Women walked in, their arms interlocked, whispering closely to one another. "It is no tavern or gambling room but from what I've gathered about your *friend* he may be acquainted with more than one of the women in there." She suggested, watching groups of women enter and exit the tearoom.

"What do we have to lose? I see no other tavern and Miss Maclean does have a point." Ethan reasoned, shrugging.

"Aye, but perhaps you should ask the questions in here?" He told Molly, looking through the window. He saw only a handful of men in there and they looked to be more than preoccupied by swooning over the ladies next to them and as about as delicate as the swirls that encircled the letters on the sign that rested above the door.

When they entered the room, more than one lady looked up, eyeing the group. Alaric could not blame them. They did look far out of place. He cleared his throat uncomfortably. "Excuse me," Molly said to a group of women standing near the entrance. "I wonder if you ladies could help us. We recently arrived in Newport and were told to ask after a Mr. Banning. You wouldn't happen to know of him, would you?" She asked as politely as she could. Alaric blinked at her, stifling his urge to burst into laughter. Never had he heard her speak in such a manner, in fact, when she had thought no one was around, he had even caught her cursing like the rest of his crew did.

"It is a Mr. Thomas Banning you seek?" A woman stepped forward in the group, smiling politely. "I most definitely can point you in the right direction." She curtsied, "I am Amelia Banning, Thomas's wife."

Alaric shuffled his feet, looking at the woman in pure shock. He felt Ethan stiffen next to him. It had never occurred to him that Thomas was married. His mind whirled with the images of the horrors this woman's husband had committed. "I apologize, we are a bit taken aback. We had expected it would be rather difficult to locate a single man in such a town. We also were not aware he had a wife so you can understand our shock."

"Of course, I am pleased you found me so that I am able to help. I take it you would like to speak with him about his shipments." She said it in not so much as a question but rather as a set statement as if that was the only reason folks like them would be seeking her husband. Alaric did not miss the fondest in her voice or the proud way she held herself when she spoke of him.

"Yes, indeed we are. We are making a new life here in the colonies and are in need of a great deal of items." Molly replied confidently, so much so that Alaric nearly believed it himself.

"I think that is splendid," Amelia encouraged, glancing at the women around her for conformation. Her eyes shifted to Alaric who stood directly behind Molly. "And you must be this lady's…?" She asked, letting her sentence fall so he could fill in what he was to Molly.

Alaric wracked his brain, what was he to say? He could not very well say she was part of his crew, "her brother." He finally replied simply. He felt Ethan turn to him, he ignored his friend as best he could, not wishing to see the look upon his face and grateful he could not see Molly's reaction.

"Ahh, I see. Well, might I invite you all to dine with me tonight?" She asked politely. "Unfortunately, my husband will not be accompanying us, but it will still be a pleasant evening."

"I am afraid we are already spoken for, Mrs. Banning. Might I ask where your husband may be?" Ethan responded, stepping forward.

"Oh, I suppose you would like to know since you have business with him, of course you would. He had business to attend to early this more and then he is to sail for London this day. In fact, he may have already departed." Her gaze back on Molly, "It is rather lonely at times, having a husband as such a highly admired Merchant, you see. He is gone most of the time and only returns for short times." Her friends all nodded in sympathy, one handing her a steaming cup of tea to calm her.

"I'm sure it is. It was a great pleasure making your acquaintance, Mrs. Banning." Molly finished, curtsying to her and the ladies surrounding them.

"Of course, my friend." She reached out, giving Molly's hand a gentle squeeze. They walked from the tearoom, heading back the way they had come.

Ethan grabbed Alaric's arm, causing him to halt his steps and look at his friend in surprise. "What is it?" Alaric asked.

"Brother? What…" Ethan looked at him incredulously. Alaric glared at him and continued to walk forward, wanting to catch up to Molly who was now waiting at the edge of a shop a couple buildings down.

"What would you have had me say?" He challenged, irritated at himself for his own response and for giving Ethan a change to enjoy himself in that moment.

Ethan grinned, "I can think of a few other labels that would have better suited, mate." They continued their steps. He laughed, unable to contain himself any longer. "Brother!" He repeated, shaking his head. Alaric mumbled in reply as they reached Molly, shooting Ethan a stern look.

"Once we reach *The Trinity,* I'll send Eddie to scour the docks for *The Amity.* He won't be recognized by Thomas or his first mate if they are still in port. Once he returns with news, we will decide what to do from there." Alaric explained as they neared the busy docks once more. The smell of the sea, ships and the men filled their noses. The sounds of the footsteps on the wooden planks and the thundering noise of crates being drug across them made it near impossible to hear one another. Voices mingled, men from all over spoke in rich accents commanding their crew about, shouting orders to those that did not move quick enough.

Alaric watched Molly safely retreat below decks, knowing she was eager to check on the animals. "Eddie, you go see what you can find out. See if *The Amity* is still anchored here. Ol' Shorty, how close are we to being able to sail?" He asked, knowing they had needed to stalk up on supplies and have plenty of extra materials in case their ship needed more repairs than he anticipated.

"Couple hours, no more, Capt'n." He replied, taking over the logbook, marking the materials that came onboard. Normally it was not a duty that he performed but with Eddie busy, he took it over.

"Very good," Alaric replied, his hands resting on the railing. Looking over the dock he eyed each sailor, each ship he could see, waiting to see Thomas, or at least Eddie. He did not know what he preferred, if Thomas was still in Newport, he could easily challenge him, but judging by his wife's appearance Alaric wagered Banning had many friends in society in this particular town at least. It would save his ship and crew from a fight and Molly would be safer, but it would not be guaranteed he would follow through with an honorable duel. Thomas may turn him and his crew over to the authorities, claiming they did the very things that he himself had done. If Thomas had already left, then a battle was sure to happen and that would put Molly and his entire crew at risk, though in truth, his men seemed as eager to take Banning down as he did.

33

Thomas threw back the covers, sitting up in bed. He felt Amelia stir next to him. Leaning over he placed a kiss on her lips, "go back to sleep. It's still early, luv." He whispered. "I'll see you in a few months' time." Grabbing his pants from the table near the bed, he pulled his pants and boots on, his shirt hanging open. Glancing back at Amelia, he was relieved she had fallen back asleep, he did not wish to make excuses for where he was bound.

Thomas strapped his flintlocks and sword to his waist. He breathed a sigh. He had been missing the feel and weight of the weapons. Closing the door to his study, he headed for the door. A carriage sat at the bottom of the stairs to his estate. He had requested Grady meet him in the hired carriage just before first light. They needed to reach the outer parts of the city, where the cliffs were steep, leading down to rocky beaches that no one ventured. Thomas had sent a letter the day before to ensure he and Mr. Farthing met at the same area. Thomas had changed the location from the park, not wanting to risk them being seen by early risers. Opening the door to the carriage and taking his spot on the rough seats.

"Remember what I told you?" He asked Grady gruffly, adjusting the flintlocks at his hips. They dug uncomfortably into his sides when he sat in the small space.

"Aye, Cap. Kill the bastard if he bests you." He replied, scrunching his face.

"And his second. Do not leave any of them alive." He commanded him, "not that it will be necessary for you to handle that. I very much doubt he is a competent shot."

"What of the note ye sent? Will they no trace it back to ye?" He asked, squirming in his seat uncomfortably.

"No, I paid the young cabin boy to send the note and had one of the wenches at the docks write it for me. Neither will speak." Thomas replied confidently, his words rumbling as the carriage hit the rough roads as they headed from the town. Pulling a flintlock from the strap, he checked it over. He had thoroughly cleaned them the night before and sharpened his sword.

The carriage came to a jagged halt at the edge of a steep cliff. The waves crashed loudly over the rocks, echoing in a small cave that sat hidden below. A narrow path led to a pebbly beach just down from the cliffs. Another carriage sat empty, save for the driver who patiently waited on his seat. They began their descent. Two figures could be seen at the bottom, standing at the edge of the water, just out of reach of the foamy waves.

"Mr. Farthing, I half expected you not to show." Thomas shouted over the waves. "I wouldn't have blamed you of course. It is rather foolish of you to partake in this duel with me. Of course, if death is in fact what you wish." He paused, judging his opponent's emotions. "Perhaps you'd like to be reunited with your lovely wife, once more?" He asked, enjoying the anger rise steadily in Farthing's gaze.

"Believe what you will, Banning. I am ready to settle this once and for all." He spat, nodding towards his second.

The two men stepped forward, their bodies nearly touching. Thomas laughed in surprise. Mr. Farthing showed no fear nor eagerness to die. He simply turned, stepping as the other man counted. For a brief moment all that could be heard was the crashing and rumbling of the waves. The wind blew, whipping a sliver of hair across Thomas's face. Ignoring the few strands, he turned, his hand moving steadily to his side. Sliding his fingers around the wood, he slipped the flintlock from its strap. Thomas raised the pistol, feeling his finger pulled hard against the trigger. The blasts sounded at once, neither man moved. Thomas looked down at his own body, he felt no pain, except for a dull ache in his left arm. A small stream of blood began to soak his torn sleeve. The ball had merely grazed his arm. Grinning, he raised his eyes, Farthing staggered back, his eyes erased of all emotion. Thomas switched his gaze to Mr. Farthing's second. He did not know his name or even recognize him. Pulling his second flintlock, he pointed it directly at the man who continued to stare at his fallen friend in shock as Thomas pulled the trigger.

"Let's go." Thomas shouted, not bothering to look back at the two men who lay lifeless on the beach. With any luck, the tide would rise and take the bodies before any unsuspecting travelers spotted them.

34

Molly stepped through the hatch, the brisk air piercing her lungs as she took a deep breath in. The sun was just beginning to rise, causing the ocean to look nearly black and the sky bright yellows, pinks and oranges. She smiled and waved to Ol' Shorty before heading down to the galley for her morning meal. Alaric was usually up before the morning light broke through the window in the back of the cabin. Molly often went to fetch her own meal during the morning so Cook or one of the younger sailors did not have to bring her food to her. It suited her just fine, rather than sitting alone in the cabin she either sat on deck and ate or took it to the surgery to eat with Doc and look over his medical books on livestock.

Walking into the narrow galley, she greeted Cook, scrapping her portion of eggs, bits of meat and a hotcake onto her plate. She looked about the small galley, looking into the pots and at the sticky ball of batter that sat about it. They had just restocked their supplies, so it was not unlike Cook to make an extravagant meal or two but even for Cook this was a lot more food than he normally made. Setting her plate down, she picked up a large spoon, slowly stirring the contents in one of the large pots. "What is this?" She asked curiously.

"That be the fresh corn an' potato chowder. I have a cousin in the colonies. She sends me new recipes to try. "And that there," he pointed to the sticky, brown batter, "is goin' to be molasses cakes. "ave a smell an' tell me what ye think." He suggested, gesturing to the mass.

Molly leaned over, trying to separate the smell of the batter from the steaming broth, chowder and freshly cooked eggs. Taking a deep breath in she could smell the sweet, almost smokey scent. "It smells wonderful, but why all the food?"

"There is going to be a rough battle ahead and them men out there will need plenty of food to keep their strength up." He explained, focusing on the broth.

"Oh," she murmured simply. She had not thought of what was to come when they reached Thomas's ship. Eddie had run back to *The Trinity*, not long after he had left to scout the docks for *The Amity*, saying Thomas had left like Mrs. Banning had assumed he had. They were only an hour or two behind them. A part of her had known there would be a battle but it had not seemed real until that moment. Stepping back on deck and sitting on the steps that sat on either side of Alaric's cabin, she silently ate her meal, watching the men move about the deck. A lump began to form in her throat. The men were quieter than normal. They seemed determined and focused. A group of the youngest sailors on the ship stood before Captain Clarke. They were listening intently as he instructed them on form and precision with the sword. Each of the lads raised their own in mock display, repeating Captain Clarke's movements. Slapping one of the lad's legs with the side of his sword, he informed the sailor his leg was wide open and was not positioned to withstand the force behind a blow. That if he were to enter a fight with a larger sailor, he would be unbalanced and would be an easy target.

Molly was fascinated. She had never watched such instruction before. The men eagerly clung to every word Captain Clarke called out. She put the last bite in her mouth, chewing it slowly as she continued to watch, setting the plate on the planks at the base of the stairs. Standing, she slowly walked over to Captain Clarke.

"Could you teach me as well?" She asked, standing a bit straighter. The lads that were taking their instruction from Captain Clarke stood silently, awaiting his answer.

"Aye, I see no harm in it, though I will wager, Captain Stein will not be too pleased at the idea of you having to use a sword. He's instructed that you are to stay below with Doc and one or two of these men." He said, pointing his sword at the group in front of them. Looking about the deck for said captain. He breathed out a sigh. "Alright, Miss Maclean, take a sword," he commanded, gesturing to the pile below the railing they stood near. "Let's start again with stance," he suggested. "Show me how you plant your feet and hold your body." He bellowed out, pacing slowly in front of the group, looking carefully at each man. He came to Molly, she swallowed, suddenly afraid he would discipline her if she made a wrong move. "Very good form, Miss Maclean," he grinned.

"Remember, the men you fight will not always attack from the front. You must be prepared to block your body as a whole at all times. They will not be afraid to attack from the side or even from the back, especially these men we will be going against," he began. Demonstrating the correct stance. "Key, step forward if you please."

Molly watched carefully, desperate not to miss a moment of the instruction. Key bravely walked up to Captain Clarke. He was currently the youngest member of the crew at just fifteen. She had been surprised when she learned his age, and even more surprised when she learned that on most ships, even Royal Navy ships, they had crews with mere children on board doing work. Children no older than Mackay. Ol' Shorty had told her that Captain Harding and Captain Stein were always very cautious about taking younger lads aboard, always ensuring they had no other options and tried their best to keep them safe during battles and storms. Molly had learned that Key was recently made an orphan and had longed to be aboard a privateer ship since he was little. When he caught sight of Captain Stein at one of the islands, just before Molly herself had boarded the ship, he had eagerly joined the crew.

"Turn, face your back to me, lad." Captain Clarke commanded. "Good, now, show me what you can do." He said, coming at the sailor in a mock attack. Key turned as fast as he could, keeping his sword raised in front of him protecting his front as he began to face his foe. Captain Stein brought his sword down, smacking it lightly against Key's arm. "You failed to protect yourself, now your arm is gravely wounded, and you will be unable to survive the rest of the battle, unless you are lucky enough to make it to Doc in time for him to patch you up." Captain Clarke explained, his face sober. "Try again, this time I want you to kneel as you turn to me, raising your sword higher." They began again, taking their positions. Key did as he was told, successfully blocking the blow. He rose up, his sword locked with Captain Clarke's. "Now, quickly push your blade down and to the side, that will unlock the swords and allow you to properly face your opponent." Captain Stein clapped Key on his shoulder, "Well done, mate." He said, Key returned to his spot with the rest of the lads. "Pair up and practice," he ordered, coming directly in front of Molly.

Molly could not contain her nerves or excitement. She was eager to learn and wanted to prove to herself she was capable. They began to spar, Captain Clarke making comments all the while. "Remember, Miss Maclean, I am not bringing my blade down with much force, but if you end up having to defend yourself, they will not be so gentle. The force that will be brought upon your blade can be shattering. I have seen young lad's arms snap against the blows. You must be ready for it. Your hands will burn and ache with every hit, weakening your grip. Your strength is no match against even the younger of the lads. You must use your size to your advantage. You are quick and must stay one step ahead of the man you go up against," Captain Clarke explained.

The sounds of the blades clanking together began to lessen. Molly remained focused on Captain Clarke, ignoring whatever had caused the others to stay their hands.

"May I ask what is going on here?" Captain Stein's voice rumbled across the deck. Molly lowered her sword but did not put it down entirely.

"I saw Captain Clarke teaching the lads to fight. I asked if I could join them in learnin'." She explained, waiting for the sharp words that were sure to come.

"You will have no need of this," he responded, waving his hand at the sword in her grip. "You will remain below, guarded and safe from the battle."

"Captain Stein, I agree. It is best that she remains below, safe out of harm's way," he paused stepping closer to Alaric so only the three of them could hear. "I am sure she will be safe, but men have broken through our defenses before. Miss Maclean was lucky enough to defend herself and you were able to reach her in time, but she may not be so lucky next time and having more than her dagger and a one shot flintlock will give her an even greater chance, especially if she learns a little of how to wield it," he reasoned.

Molly watched the pained and concerned look on Captain Stein's face. His gaze flicked between the two of them. He ran a hand over his face, clearly not happy with the thought of her having to defend herself once more.

"Miss Maclean has proven herself on more than one occasion," Captain Clarke began.

"She shouldn't have had to," Captain Stein's voice was hard.

"Alaric, if I had taught my sister to defend herself and given her a dagger like Miss Maclean's instead of a useless bracelet, perhaps that night would have ended differently." He said softly, his voice filled with emotion

Captain Stein finally nodded, "alright, but don't think this means you will be leaving the surgery." He said sternly, backing against the railing. His eyes remaining fixed on Molly.

Sticking her chin up, she was determined to prove to herself and Captain Stein that she was brave enough and could handle what came if she needed to. His words from the other night echoed in her mind. She feared if she was injured or caused Captain Stein to doubt her strength in any way that he would give her no choice. That he would take her back to the colonies and deposit her with the Macleans he had discovered there.

Bracing herself against every charge and blow from Captain Clarke, she spun and dodged when she could. He had not lied, her arms and hands ached just from the gentle force he used against her now. She hated to imagine what it would be like to feel the angry force behind an enemy's charge. She planned to do as Captain Stein had ordered. She had no doubt it would be better for her if she stayed below. She intended to help Doc where she could, though she knew she would not be nearly as competent as Mrs. Harding. She had heard grand tales of her ability and hoped that in time she might be as well trained with healing animals as Mrs. Harding was with healing people. But with all that, she knew anything could happen, if the enemy managed to make their way through the ship and to the surgery, she did not want to be helpless, she wanted to help protect the wounded and Doc who would need to focus all his attention on his patients.

"Switch rivals!" Captain Clarke yelled out, smiling, and nodding to Molly as he changed sparring partners.

She caught movement out of the corner of her eye. Captain Stein had pushed off the railing and now faced her with a sword in his hand. "I'm not as slow as your last opponent," he winked, raising a brow in challenge, and laughing at the incredulous look Captain Clarke shot him.

"And I'm not as weak as I look, Captain." She countered, remembering the correct stance she had been taught moments ago.

Captain Stein tapped her blade with his, stepping closer. Pushing her blade closer to her body, making it harder for her to block his next move. Swinging his sword down, he slapped it against her leg. Chuckling at the angered look in her eyes. Shaking the hair from her face, she regained her original stance, as did he.

Molly swung out, their swords meeting once more. This time with a bit more vigor. Molly knew all the men on deck had ceased what they had been doing to watch her and their captain. She successfully blocked each blow, stepping to the side occasionally or ducking down. The captain cocked his head to the side, smiling, his swings coming at her a bit quicker, pushing her back as she tried to gain control once again. She felt her back press against the main mast. A ripple of chuckles spread across the ship. Molly brought her sword straight down, only to have it meet the captain's. His blade did not yield, even in the slightest. Her arms began to tremble. She felt her sword moving up. A smile began to spread across the captain's lips as he pinned her sword above her head with his blade.

"You are impressive, lass," he began. Molly brought her foot up, kicking him as hard as she might, causing him to recoil in pain and surprise. A roar of laughter erupted from the crew. It was her turn to grin at him.

"I'd say we are fairly evenly matched, Capt'n." She said, glancing over at Captain Clarke who had not quite recovered from his laughter.

Captain Stein composed himself and stepped closer to Molly. "Looks like I finally met a worthy opponent," he admitted.

"Capt'n! Capt'n!" A shout sounded from above. Molly shielded her eyes against the bright sun, trying to see the man that had yelled down at them. "Capt'n, sails ahead!" He announced, making his way down the rigging.

Captain Stein nodded, his gaze moving back to Molly. She swallowed; the sparring had taken her mind off of the impending battle. "Best go see to your animals, Lass. Once we get nearer *The Amity,* you will not be able to see to them until I fetch you."

Molly nodded in response, wanting to say something, anything, but not knowing what. She stepped around him and headed for the hatch. She heard Alaric's orders for Joseph and Key to remain in the surgery and help to guard Doc and her if men got passed the rest of the crew.

35

Alaric strapped his flintlocks to his waist, making sure they had been cleaned and loaded. He grabbed one more, shoving it against his back and into his belt. He had an extra one readied for Molly. His stomach about dropped when he saw her wielding the sword. He knew Ethan was right, she needed to know how to use the sword but the thought of her having to use it made his heart clench. He hated himself for allowing her to be put into so much danger. He had failed to keep her from Lord Willington and had failed to keep one of the sailors from entering his cabin. If he failed to keep her safe this time, it could be the last.

Ruffling Aoife's head, he placed her on the bed, tucking her against the blankets. "You stay in here." He whispered, adjusting the weapons at his side, then heading out the hatch before the kitten could follow him.

Stepping onboard the deck, he looked over at the white sails in the distance. He ran a hand through his hair. All this time, all these months hunting Thomas down, he was finally within his grasp. It made imagines of Benjamin flood his mind. From the moment he saw him dying on the stone streets, to every time Alaric would return to Barbados and Benjamin was waiting for him. His eyes filled with excitement and amazement at Alaric and Lucas's stories and wonder at the ship. Then to the final moment, the moment Catherine's scream pierced his ears. He had not realized at the time why she had done it. He remembered staring into the water, desperately wishing Benjamin would appear.

"Ready the guns!" He bellowed. The sharp shooters were already in place. All was set.

He strode down the steps, heading for Molly. It was time for her to take her place with Doc. "Miss Maclean," he hollered down the companionway.

"I'm ready," he heard her call back. "I gave them extra straw and they are fed." She explained, bending low and kissing each of the baby goats. "I'm worried the cannons will scare them." She admitted, looking up at him as he entered the room.

"They are tougher and braver than one would think." He answered, offering his hand to help her from the pen. "Much like someone else I know."

Her face flushed, "are we very near the ship now?"

"Aye, I've come to take you to Doc." He motioned for her to lead the way back through the companionway.

The surgery was fully prepped. Tables and hammocks lined the room. Tools sat at the ready. The strong smell of vinegar penetrated his nose, flooding his senses, making his stomach turn. It meant wounded men, his friends and crew lying in pain or dead. The scent of blood would be mixing with it in less than a couple hours. "Miss Maclean, you have your wee dagger?" He asked, noting the sword she had placed on the table.

"Aye, Capt'n," she confirmed.

"Take this as well. Keep it close." He handed her the flintlock. He nodded, not knowing what more to say.

"Alaric, keep safe." She whispered, making him pause his steps.

Turning back, he stepped closer to her once more. He pulled her close to his body. Her form pressing firmly against his. Leaning down, he met her lips with his. This time neither of them pulled away. He deepened the kiss. He had thought of little else since their last kiss, if it could have even been called that. He could not tell if the room and the noises about the ship had indeed grown silent or if his mind had shut everything else out. All he could hear was the sound of his heart thundering in his chest and the feel Molly pressed up against him.

A rush of footsteps thundered into the room, pulling them back to the ship and from their thoughts.

"Capt'n, another ship has been spotted and it's begun firing at *The Amity*." Ian exclaimed, ducking back up the stairs.

Alaric pulled his brows together, processing the turn of

events. He turned his attention back to Molly, placing a hand on her arm. He winked, reassuring her of his safety.

Running back on deck, he pulled the spyglass from his belt. "Do you recognize the vessel?" He murmured to Ethan.

"No, but we might as well give the poor souls a hand." He replied, snapping his own spyglass closed and grinning at Alaric. They had both been waiting for this moment for many months and it appeared they now gained a few extra, unexpected men.

"Half sail," Alaric shouted. "Turn her and ready to fire." Alaric held tight to the railing, watching the battle in front of him. Shaking his head, he could not believe their luck. He felt *The Trinity* sway beneath his feet, turning in the already anxious waters. Debris fell into the foamy sea with every blast from the two ships in front of them. "Fire!" Alaric commanded. He rocked with the ship as the cannons sounded, sending the vessel rocking. The shots splintered through the middle of *The Amity,* sending wood flying into the air. Shouts from the other ships reached his ears. As they neared, he scanned the deck of the other vessel, looking for familiar faces, but seeing none.

A shot from *The Amity* struck their ship, rocking it slightly. A deafening cracking sound echoed across the deck. Alaric turned, "get down!" He shouted, the main mast gave way, sending bits of wood flying as the mast crashed into the side of the ship, slipping mostly into the waters below. He cursed, looking around, for any wounded crew. He spotted one of the lads laying on the ground, clutching his arm. A large shard of wood jutting out from it. "Get him below," Alaric ordered.

The ships were getting too close to continue firing and if he and the other vessels blasted anymore into The Amity, it would be sure to sink. "Prepare to board!" Alaric took his sword from its strap, scanning the deck for Thomas. Ethan stood at the ready next to him, doing the same. Wood scraped; the planks fell across the railings of both ships. Alaric leading his crew across. He leapt, his sword digging deep into one of the men facing the charge. Pulling his blade out, he swung for his next opponent. Moving forward, away from the railing and towards the center of the ship. All the while keeping an eye out for Banning and another on the planks leading to his vessel. With both ships on either side of The Amity it would not allow Thomas to make the same escape he had done last time.

Alaric's sword met with another, ducking low, the enemy's blade missed his scalp by mere inches. Standing, he knocked the hilt of his sword into the side of the man's head. Blood flowed from the fresh wound. Stepping over the fallen sailor he checked behind him. He saw Ethan shoved another sailor back, swinging his blade across his chest. Alaric looked wildly around, being sure none of his crew needed assistance. His gaze faltered on a young man standing before him.

His breath caught, "Benjamin?"